I0557603

Serum

Paul Baldwin

DJ Baldwin Books

Contents

*To my wife and soulmate, Michelle. I love you so much.
And to my niece, Brianna Salo, who left us too soon from spinal
muscular atrophy. A portion of royalties goes to Cure SMA.*

And what do you benefit if you gain the whole world but lose your soul? Is anything worth more than your soul?

Matthew 16:26

Prologue

Mia

M ia sat beside her twin sister and weighed the merits of parricide.

They were on their way to her parents' favorite activity: watching Unity in another series of athletic endeavors. Today it was a karate tournament, tomorrow a shooting competition—a two-day lovefest devoted to their darling gem. It would make for a dreadful weekend, and Mia offered a silent prayer to the universe for a blowout tire, a sudden illness, or an act of God to intervene.

"Are you nervous?" their father asked, glancing in the rearview mirror.

Unity sat perfectly still, wearing her white gi, her blonde hair pulled back in a ponytail with a red scrunchie. "I don't know. I seem to have plateaued."

"You're the best in your dojo," their mother said. "All the parents say so."

The bullshit never ended.

Mia loved her sister more than oxygen, but God bless her soul, Unity was only a red belt at sixteen. Mia had even taken Unity down on the mat a few times when her sister needed a sparring partner, though she never bragged about it. It wouldn't have mattered if she did.

Her parents were the type of people who wore business stiff-collars until bedtime, even on weekends. Perhaps they wanted to flaunt their status as well-known scientists or give the impression that they were wealthy—as if the GMC Hummer wasn't already proof of that. They ruled over Unity's clubs like North Korean generals: strict adherence to the mission, or else. They also insisted on a certain formality—it was Dr. Jeff and Dr. Theresa, thank you very much.

"I got an A on my advanced biology test," Mia said.

The self-praise was Mia's budding dark humor. She liked to lob grenades into the front seat just to check another box on the "We Love U" scoresheet. Mia sometimes called Unity "U." One syllable was easier than three, and the letter's irony symbolized her state of mind. In this car and at home, it was always all about U.

"You've never had a B in your life. Why is this news?" her mom asked. She adjusted the climate control. "But good job, of course. We've always... expected you to succeed in scie—"

"Great job, Mia," her father interrupted. He glanced at their mom and shook his head.

The air in the car grew heavy, the kind of silence that usually preceded a lecture or a cover-up. Mia figured it was their perfectionism bubbling over, or perhaps a glitch in their parental programming.

Her mom flipped the sun visor down and applied a layer of dung-shaded lipstick. "We heard someone from the University of Virginia was coming to watch you today."

"Sensei mentioned it yesterday," Unity said. "It's a club, not a scholarship thing."

"Well, your mother and I are proud of you."

Unity glanced at Mia and mouthed, *Sorry.*

Mia smiled and squeezed her sister's hand. She would never blame Unity for the discrepancy in their affection. Unity had challenged the favoritism when they were younger, but their parents had looked at her with blank stares, as if their brains had crashed and couldn't compute the logic. After that, the twins did their best to ignore it.

Why her parents adored one sibling and merely tolerated the other remained a mystery. The sisters were practically the same person. The sole physical difference between them was a tiny circular birthmark on Mia's left forearm. A dot, really. Easily mistaken as a freckle, except for its nearly perfect circumference. Aside from that, they were mirror images, yet at fifteen, their paths had diverged.

Mia had fallen for the quiet logic of science, hoping to find cures for humanity's worst diseases. Unity had chosen the roar of the crowd. Unfortunately for Mia, "Dr. Jeff" and "Dr. Theresa" preferred the crowd.

Mia withdrew into her "wall." Over the last few years, she had built the psychological barrier brick by brick to deflect the friendly fire coming from the front seat. First, it was leaving the room. Then, it was tuning out conversations. Today, the wall was music.

She unzipped her purse, dug out her noise-canceling Pixel Buds, and shoved them into her ears. She cranked the volume until the bass seemed to thump in her chest, staring out the window at the blur of the passing Virginia landscape.

She didn't hear the horn.

A flash of chrome filled her vision. The world tilted sideways before her brain could even register the impact.

The Hummer, manufactured to withstand an apocalypse, crumpled like aluminum foil. Metal screamed, a high-pitched shriek that cut through her noise-canceling buds as the frame buckled under the force of the commercial truck barreling through the intersection.

The vehicle rolled. Sky. Asphalt. Sky. Asphalt.

Mia slammed against her seatbelt, the fabric biting into

her collarbone as the air left her lungs. The cabin filled with the acrid taste of airbag dust and the deafening crunch of shattering glass.

When the world finally stopped spinning, the silence was heavy, broken only by the hiss of a ruptured radiator. Mia turned her head through the haze. Unity was slumped forward. Her body looked broken—mangled in a way that bodies weren't supposed to bend.

"Unity!"

The scream came from the front seat.

"Unity, baby, answer me!"

Mia's vision blurred, silver vignettes creeping in from the corners of her eyes. She tried to speak, to tell them she was hurt too, but the darkness was heavy and demanding. As she slipped away, the last thing she heard wasn't a siren. It was her parents screaming her sister's name, and never once calling out for her.

Twenty Years Later

Mia

M ia caressed the stock of her rifle, waiting for the wind to tell her its secrets.

High above the Blue Ridge Mountains, the sun glared off white cirrus clouds, casting a haze over the valley. It was picturesque for the spectators bundled in beanies and thick coats, but down on the plain, it was a battlefield of variable physics. The wind gusted, pushing the tan grass back and forth in a mocking rhythm.

At thirty-six, Mia was entering her eighteenth season. She was also losing.

The rival two lanes down was younger, precise, and hungry—a reminder that biology didn't negotiate. Mia knew this better than anyone. After taking over her parents' lab a decade ago, she had dedicated her life to maximizing human physiology. She called it her *reason*, a scientific crusade to rewrite the limits of the body. This sport was just one of her field tests. Before she could improve the human vessel, she had to push her own to the breaking point.

"Mia Peers," the announcer called.

She bobbed her head. No wind coaches today. In these individual events, she computed the variables herself.

Depending on her own skill had always been the only safety net she trusted.

She adjusted her reverb earmuffs and left the prep area. Mia lowered herself onto the mat, the familiar smell of gun oil and dry grass filling her nose. She took her time settling into the prone position, jamming the rifle butt into her shoulder until it found the bruised pocket of muscle.

She exhaled. She tried to zero in.

But the mental image she used to steady her heart rate—a visualization technique she'd perfected over years—fractured. The target blurred. The wind shifted. Mia blinked, trying to force the focus, and squeezed the trigger anyway.

The shot broke the silence.

The crowd gasped, then cheered. But the world went sharp and cold for Mia because the applause wasn't for her. A girl half her age had just knocked her off the podium.

As the noise subsided, a pocket of loyal fans chanted her name. Mia stood, tipped the bill of her hat, and offered a practiced curtsy. She felt like a retired Katniss Everdeen—still going through the motions long after the credits had rolled. Except Katniss usually hit the target.

She disassembled her gun with mechanical precision, securing it in its case. It might be years before she took the weapon out again.

"Congratulations," Mia said, approaching the winner behind the media line.

Susan's eyes went wide. "Thank you. I'm... in shock. I've followed your entire career. How did you stay at the top for so long?"

"I don't know, girl." Mia forced a smile. "But you're the future of stationary target shooting now. I'm proud of you."

"Thank you!" Susan squealed and ran back to her family.

"Mia! Can I—"

"Get an autograph?" Mia laughed, turning toward the voice.

"Tom, you'll never change."

She ambled toward her number-one fan and his two shadows. Tom was twenty-nine, a six-foot-two frame of molten muscle wrapped in a plaid shirt and tight jeans. He looked less like a shooting enthusiast and more like he'd walked off a Country Music Awards red carpet.

"What am I supposed to write on?" Mia asked. "Last time, it was your undershirt."

"I have a few ideas," Tom said.

"Keep it clean. Impressionable children are listening."

"They can't hear us." He glanced at the kids swarming Susan.

"I'm talking about these two morons." Mia jokingly shoved Tom's lackeys, Jim and Andrew.

Tom flashed the sexy grin that had attracted her after her second divorce. They were pros at this dynamic—a game Mia found almost as enjoyable as the sex itself.

"You free tonight?" he asked.

"Perhaps."

Mia offered a sly smile, masking the introvert's dread curling in her stomach. She didn't want to make plans, not with the sting of the loss still fresh. "Don't wait for me, though."

His eyes sparkled. "You're keeping me on the hook in case you don't get a better offer."

"At least you know it. It's not like you're any different."

She gave him a hug and a quick kiss, then retreated to the sanctuary of her vehicle.

The silence of the truck was immediate. She cranked the air conditioning, letting the cold air soothe the headache throbbing behind her eyes. She sank into the leather, exhaling the tension of the day.

Her phone buzzed against the center console.

It was Sophia—Mia's recent hire from Italy. The woman insisted on working weekends, a level of dedication Mia hadn't asked for but couldn't bring herself to stop.

The text was two lines.

They all died.

I'm sorry.

Mia stared at the screen. The white letters seemed to float, detached from reality. A second-place finish in the tournament was one thing; a total wipeout in the lab was another.

I'll see you tomorrow. I'll tweak the formula like always, Mia replied, her thumbs moving on autopilot.

Sophia fired back instantly: **Have you considered my idea?**

Mia tossed the phone onto the passenger seat. First the podium, now the serum. She didn't have the bandwidth to manage Sophia's nagging about the delivery method. This was why Mia preferred working alone—when she had the luxury.

She grabbed the phone. **Yes, I need more time to test the current method.**

She put the Highlander in gear. The heavy feeling in her chest wasn't just disappointment anymore; it was a suffocating cocktail of professional failure and scientific dead ends. She needed to numb it. The brewery on the edge of town hadn't failed her yet, and unlike her serum, at least the alcohol there did exactly what it was supposed to do.

New York

Bianca

Bianca smoothed the lapels of her leather jacket and navigated the tables of the dimly lit Italian restaurant. She kept her chin high, forcing a confident sway in her hips that she didn't feel. To the casual observer, she was just another patron in jeans and a black tee. To the five people waiting at the back table, she was the new recruit.

She had to play this cool.

The smell of garlic and slow-simmered tomato sauce usually calmed her—her mother's family had roots in Italy after all—but tonight, the aroma only churned her stomach. She spotted the crew. Lucas was there, of course. He caught her eye, his expression unreadable in front of the others, but his presence anchored her. They had been together for two years, ever since she and her mother had fled to New York after the funeral. He had been the one to pull her out of the darkness following her father's death.

Now, he was pulling her into his world.

Dylan, the crew's captain, gestured toward the empty seat.

"You're late, so we ordered for you," Dylan said. "Lucas said anything on the menu was fine."

"Sorry. The traffic..." Bianca let the excuse trail off.

"Walk next time," Lucas said. His grin was sharp, a private sarcasm she knew well.

She sat, acutely aware of the hierarchy at the table. Dylan was in his late thirties, a man who radiated the kind of strict authority that reminded her of the military officers her father used to complain about. Beside him sat Sandra, the only other woman. Lucas had described her as a "mother hen," but the way Sandra surveyed the restaurant suggested she was checking for exits, not fussing over napkins.

"Now that you're here, we can get started," Dylan said.

"It's safe to... talk here?" Bianca asked.

"We more or less own this joint," Sandra said, her voice raspy. "We meet here all the time."

Bianca nodded, trying to look like she belonged. If her mother knew where she was right now, the poor woman would drop dead. As far as Mom knew, she was currently settling into a dorm room overseas for an exchange program. Lying was a necessary evil; her mother had already lost a husband to the Army Rangers and the botched withdrawal from Afghanistan. She wouldn't survive losing a daughter to the underworld.

"Okay," Dylan said, leaning in. "Here's the short of it. A pharmaceutical client wants her hands on an experimental drug being developed by a Dr. Mia Peers. She didn't say why, and we didn't ask. Our job is to make contact, talk this Mia chick into sharing her formula under the table, and if she says no... well, you know how these things go."

Bianca suppressed a shudder. She knew exactly how these things go. That was why she was here. The system had chewed her father up and spit him out; she was done playing by its rules.

"Lucas, you, Bianca, and Sandra will play tail and backup," Dylan continued. "Sandra, stay in your lane this time. Everything comes through me before acting."

"Fine," Sandra said, rolling her eyes.

"Ethan, we need your tech magic to get in the building if things go bad, so you'll stay with me and Mason. Bianca, we'll pull you for tech if Ethan is needed elsewhere."

Bianca glanced at Ethan. He looked like a college professor who hadn't slept in a week, but Lucas swore the guy was a genius. Bianca wasn't intimidated, though. She had no formal degree, but grief was a powerful motivator. After her dad died, she had poured her rage into understanding the machines that ran the world. She'd spent thousands of hours tearing apart hardware and learning code on the dark web. She could hold her own.

"Not likely," Ethan grumbled. "I've already got blueprints. The lab is secure, but small. We shouldn't have problems."

"Don't jinx us," Dylan warned. "Going in unannounced is the backup plan. This client wants to minimize violence and see if a partnership is possible first."

"Yeah, right," a deep voice rumbled.

Mason. The man was a mountain of muscle with a round head and tattoos creeping up his neck like ivy. He looked like he could snap a pool cue with two fingers.

"When has that ever worked?" Mason asked.

"The family agreed to this approach, so watch what you say," Lucas snapped, his protective streak flaring up. "We're safe here, but people talk."

"Let them." Mason stared him down. "I don't give a rat's ass."

The air at the table stiffened. Bianca watched the interaction, realizing that her boyfriend's team wasn't exactly a cohesive family unit.

"Okay, enough." Dylan tapped the table, commanding attention. "Do as I say, and we'll be back in a few weeks with a heavy payday. Got it?"

The group nodded as the servers arrived with steaming plates of pasta.

"Good. Bianca, now's the time to ask questions. The floor is yours."

Bianca accepted her plate. She glanced at Lucas, who gave her a subtle nod of encouragement. She glanced at the scars on Mason's knuckles and the cold calculation in Dylan's eyes. She was really doing this. She was crossing the line.

She stared back at Dylan, her voice steady.

"Okay. When do I get a gun?"

Two Silos

Mia

A gentle evening breeze drifted over Northern Virginia, carrying the scent of hops and humidity through the open-air layout of Two Silos Brewing. The expansive property, with its stage, restaurant, and thatched-roof bars, was usually a place for celebration. For Mia, it was a conveniently located trauma center.

It was close enough to her lab to be dangerous, but far enough to pretend her problems didn't exist.

Mia signaled for her seventh shot. Alcohol had become her religion since the second divorce—or maybe it started during the first. She'd lost count. Husband One, the brilliant Harvard lawyer, had turned out to prefer men. Husband Two, the "Rebound Musician," had preferred *every* woman plus Mia.

Both had left her with a ring-sized void and a deep-seated belief that she was better off alone. Tragedy was supposedly the soul of great art, but so far, it was just giving her a hangover.

She downed the shot. The burn was familiar, but the buzz was elusive.

"Ted, hit me again."

"Hey, Mia." Ted leaned his forearms on the bar, his expression shifting from bartender to concerned friend. "You're not leaving yet, are ya?"

"I was planning on it." She pushed off the stool. The ground tilted slightly, and she stumbled over a piece of gravel, correcting her balance with a heavy hand on the counter.

"It was a big rock," she lied. "It's dark."

"Look, why don't you hang with me until you can drive?"

"I can drive. What's the saying? Mind over matter?" She gestured at herself, a sloppy presentation of a prize nobody had won. "See? Voilà."

"I don't know how safe or legal that is."

Mia paused. The fog in her brain cleared just enough to let the logic in. He was right. She was a professional athlete, a respected scientist, and currently, a woman on the verge of a DUI that would scare off every investor she had left.

"Fine," she said. "I'll tell you what. How about *you* come to my place tonight? You drive. Problem solved."

Ted opened his mouth to answer, but a scream cut through the warm air like jagged glass.

Mia spun around. Behind the shack, the crowd parted. A man in a wife-beater tank top had a woman on the ground, his hand raised for a second strike.

"I saw you kissing him!" the man roared, his voice slurring.

The patrons and staff froze, that paralyzed bystander effect taking hold. Mia didn't think; she just moved. She shoved through the gap in the crowd, the alcohol in her system momentarily forgotten, replaced by a surge of cold adrenaline.

She shoved the man's shoulder. "Back off."

He stumbled in the gravel but recovered instantly, turning on her like a bull seeing red. Veins bulged in his tattooed arms. "Stay the hell out of this! What's it to you?"

Mia glanced at the woman scrambling backward in the dust. No ring. Not that it mattered.

"I think you better go home," Mia said, settling into a stance that felt natural despite the whiskey swimming in her blood.

The brute swung. It was a clumsy, haymaker punch, telegraphed from a mile away.

Mia didn't need to be sober to handle this; she just needed muscle memory. She slipped the punch, the wind of his fist brushing her ear. As he overcommitted, she shifted her weight and snapped a sidekick into his groin.

The air left him in a rush. He doubled over, clutching himself.

Mia didn't wait for him to recover. She stepped in, delivering a sharp uppercut that connected with a sickening *crack* of teeth snapping together.

He folded, hitting the dirt with a heavy thud.

The silence that followed was broken by scattered applause. The paralysis of the crowd broke, and two men rushed forward to pin the groaning attacker until security arrived. An off-duty cop eventually arrived and gave Mia a nod, signaling he'd need a statement in a minute.

Mia shook out her aching hand. Her knuckles were already swelling. She turned back to the bar, where Ted was staring at her with wide eyes.

"That was insane," he said. "You box, too? How do you have time to be a scientist and a pro athlete?"

"Karate. And if I had a dollar for every time I heard that question, I wouldn't need venture capital."

"You need some ice?"

"Yes, please."

Mia leaned against the bar, the adrenaline fading, leaving behind the heavy dread she'd been trying to outrun all evening. The fight was a distraction, a momentary victory. But the rats were still dead. The serum was still poison. And she was still alone.

She flicked her eyes at Ted. He was safe. He was uncomplicated.

"I need something else, too," she said, her voice dropping. "Offer still stands. My place. You drive. I don't want to be alone tonight."

Mirror Mirror

Mia

The mirror spanning the length of the gym wall reflected a row of runners, but Mia was the only one punishing the machine.

She pounded the tread, her feet striking the belt with a rhythm that drowned out the terrible techno playlist pumping through the overhead speakers. She was hustling. She'd been hustling for an hour. Cardio wasn't her favorite form of torture, but today she needed the endorphins more than she needed oxygen.

Mia jabbed the console, increasing the speed and incline.

This luxury fitness center, built conveniently close to her lab, offered every amenity a wealthy sadist could want: Olympic-sized pool, full-time trainers, and a massage parlor where Nick, her favorite masseur, usually kneaded the tension out of her joints. But today, she didn't deserve comfort. She deserved the burn.

She stared at the glossy white wall ahead. A motivational poster stared back—a blown-up photograph of Mia holding a martial arts trophy from three years ago. The gym management had asked to feature "local talent" in exchange for a free membership. At the time, she'd been desperate for any discount.

Now, the image mocked her.

The woman in the frame was young, sharp, and still on top. The woman on the treadmill was a thirty-six-year-old hangover victim trying to outrun a metabolic decline. She was sliding down the backside of her prime, and she didn't know what waited at the bottom.

Boredom began to creep in, so Mia upped the speed again.

Her old cross-country coach used to say, *"If you can speak a full sentence, you're going too slow."*

Mia spoke three words. "Fuck, this hurts." She doubted her old coach, God rest his soul, would be happy.

The physical pain was a welcome distraction from the mental replay of the previous twenty-four hours: the second-place finish, the dead rats in the lab, and the embarrassing memory of begging the bartender for sex. Ted had said no. Even hot Tom hadn't replied to her late-night texts.

Rejection was a bitter pill, especially when swallowed with stale tequila.

Her lungs burned. *Good.* This was the only way to keep the pact she'd made with herself and Unity. If she couldn't fix her own biology with science, she'd force it into submission with sheer will. Her "reason"—the obsession with human advancement—required a vessel capable of enduring the testing.

A notification chimed, cutting through the thumping bass in her ears.

Mia considered ignoring it. She wanted to run until her legs gave out, but the vibration against the cup holder was persistent. She glanced down.

Brian Carter: *I have something for you when you come in.*

Cryptic. That was Brian's brand. Her young assistant.

Mia slapped the red emergency stop button. The motor whined down, a high-pitched sound of relief that matched the screaming in her shins. She stood there for a moment, hands on her hips, sweat dripping from her nose like rain from a storm cloud.

She grabbed a towel and wiped her face. The run hadn't fixed her problems, but it had numbed them.

Fifteen minutes later, showered and dressed in a sharp blazer that hid her soreness, Mia stopped at the café counter. She grabbed her pre-ordered vegan smoothie from the to-go shelf.

"Hey, Ms. Peers," the teenage employee chirped. "I saw you on TV yesterday. You were incredible."

Mia winced behind her sunglasses. "Thank you. Second place isn't exactly incredible, though."

"You'll get 'em next year."

"Sure."

Mia pushed through the glass doors and into the cool breeze of the parking lot. *Next year.* She had no plans for shooting competitions next year. There may not even be a next year for her. She was all in at the lab, needed her stay-awake pill, *Moratusom*, to get FDA approval for the funding. Otherwise, she'd go broke. But mostly, she wanted her main research effort, the physical enhancement serum, to stop killing her test subjects. If she could fix the formula, maybe she wouldn't sell it right away. She could...

She scanned the lot for her car.

Her heart skipped a beat. A black Cadillac Escalade was double-parked directly in front of her sangria-shaded Porsche Taycan, boxing her in.

A man in a dark, tailored suit stood on the sidewalk between the vehicles. He wasn't on his phone. He wasn't looking for keys. He was staring directly at her.

Mia slowed her pace, her hand instinctively drifting toward the pepper spray on her keychain. She nodded to the guy, a silent challenge, and unlocked her Porsche. The chirp of the alarm seemed to break the spell.

The man didn't say a word. He simply turned, climbed into the passenger side of the Escalade, and the massive SUV peeled away, disappearing into the morning traffic.

Mia climbed into her car and locked the doors instantly. She checked the rearview mirror, her pulse hammering harder than it had on the treadmill. The road behind her was empty, but the skin on the back of her neck prickled.

Celebrity status drew weirdos; she knew that. But that man hadn't looked like a fan. He looked like a professional. And he hadn't been looking at her like she was a star—he'd been looking at her like she was a target.

Zombie Rat

Mia

The vase of red roses on the corner of Mia's desk was a nice gesture, but the scent was cloying, masking the sterile tang of ozone and rodent feed that defined her life.

Brian had left them there earlier with a card reading *To My First-Place Boss*. He was brilliant with medical tech—a savant, really—but socially, he was operating on a different frequency. He didn't understand that red roses meant passion, or that while Mia liked younger men, she didn't date employees who wore bell-bottoms and butterfly collars unironically.

She pushed the vase aside, removing her glasses to rub the bridge of her nose. Her eyes burned. At thirty-six, her vision was becoming a liability. She needed a procedure, but she couldn't justify the downtime or the expense until the new formula worked.

And right now, the formula was a disaster.

Mia leaned back into the microscope, fighting to focus on the slide. The lab hummed around her—a symphony of whirring centrifuges and the low drone of computer fans straining like tiny jet engines.

It had been six months of Groundhog Day.

A year ago, she had been the darling of the scientific world.

Her sleep-delay drug, *Moratusom*, had the Department of Defense drooling. Space Force wanted it for Mars; the Air Force wanted it for pilots. She had secured the bag, the fame, and the investors. But *Moratusom* was just the appetizer. Her "reason"—the obsession with advanced tissue regeneration and physiology—was the main course.

But the main course was killing the patrons.

Under the lens, the cells were a chaotic, necrotic mess. Today's batch of rats had lasted six hours post-injection before crashing. It was baffling. None of the ingredients were poisonous, yet the specimens died with a consistency that mocked her expertise.

It felt too much like her parents' failure with Unity. They had spent decades trying to solve a genetic mystery, only to hit a wall. Now, Mia was hitting hers.

"Time of death recorded for the final cluster," Sophia said from the station behind her.

Mia spun her chair around. Sophia tossed a clipboard onto a desk with a sharp *clack*. Standing less than five feet tall, the Italian virologist was a bundle of kinetic energy and lean muscle. Mia had hired her for her credentials, but also because she respected the discipline it took to maintain that kind of physique.

"It's late," Sophia said, grabbing her gym bag. "We can begin a new trial in the morning. You should get some rest, Mia. You look..."

"Like I've been staring at dead cells for nine hours?"

"I was going to say 'dedicated,' but sure."

Mia sighed. "Go. Hit the gym for me."

"Mia," a flat voice interrupted.

Brian stood in the doorway of the storage room, wiping his hands on a rag. He was pale, his eyes darting between the two women. "Sorry to interrupt. There's something you should see."

"Not now, Brian," Sophia said, slinging her bag over her shoulder.

"But there's something—"

"What is it?" Mia snapped, her patience fraying.

Brian motioned for them to follow. He led them past the rows of empty cages to the quarantine closet in the back. The room was silent, save for the hum of the ventilation.

"One's alive," he said.

Mia stopped. "One what is alive?"

"A rat. From the current batch. Number 77."

Mia exchanged a look with Sophia. "That's impossible. We cleared the room an hour ago."

"Did you follow protocol?" Sophia asked, stepping forward.

"Checklist was completed," Brian said, his voice trembling slightly. "We examined them. No heartbeat. No respiration. Cold to the touch. They were dead, Sophia. Rigor had already set in on the limbs."

"Maybe we missed one," Sophia said, though she sounded unconvinced.

"We didn't miss it," Brian whispered. "Maybe... maybe he's a zombie."

Mia opened her mouth to scold him, but the sound stopped her.

Click. Click. Click.

It was the sound of the metal ball in a water bottle spout being manipulated.

Mia pushed past Brian and peered into the cage.

Rat 77 was not just alive; it was frantic. It gripped the water spout with a ferocity Mia had never seen in a lab animal, drinking as if it were dehydrated by days, not hours. Its movements were jerky, mechanical, but undeniably powerful.

"We confirmed death," Sophia said softly, staring through the wire mesh. "I felt the body myself. It was stiff."

"I know," Brian said. He held out his arms, letting his hands hang limp like a corpse. "Rigor mortis. You can't fake that."

Mia stared at the creature. A chill that had nothing to do with the lab's air conditioning skittered down her spine. *Rats don't reanimate.* Biology didn't work like that. Unless... unless the serum didn't prevent death.

Unless it reversed it.

A surge of possessiveness roared through her. This wasn't just a survivor. This was a miracle. And if it was a miracle, she needed to understand it before anyone else touched it. She needed to be alone with it.

"Okay," Mia said, forcing a smile she didn't feel. She turned to them, her voice firm. "You two get out of here. Seriously. Go home. I'll run the pretrial vitals and verify the data."

"Don't you need us to prep him?" Brian asked.

"No," Mia said, remaining between them and the cage, blocking their view. "I've got it. I want to run the initial workup myself. Go. I'll see you tomorrow."

Sophia hesitated, eyeing the cage one last time, but eventually nodded. She grabbed Brian's arm and steered him out.

Mia waited until the heavy door of the lab clicked shut, engaging the magnetic lock.

She turned back to the cage. The rat had stopped drinking. It was standing on its hind legs, gripping the wire mesh with tiny, pink claws. It wasn't looking for food. It was staring directly at her, its black eyes unblinking, waiting for what came next.

The Choice

Mia

M ia sat in her car in the parking lot of Virginia Comfort Care, staring at the brick façade that looked more like a minimum-security prison than a medical facility.

She popped two Tylenol into her mouth, crunching down on the dry pills and grinding them into powder between her molars. The bitter taste coated her tongue—a habit she'd started in high school to spite her mother's insistence on swallowing pills with water. Now, it was just a ritual. A small spike of bitterness to prepare her for the bigger one waiting inside.

She bypassed the gym to come here. The adrenaline from the lab—the rat, the movement, the impossible resurrection—was still humming in her blood, and it had drawn her here like a magnet.

Inside, the air was stifling. The petite woman at the welcome desk smiled and pushed a clipboard toward her. Mia signed in with a practiced scrawl. Electronic records were standard everywhere else, but this place seemed determined to stay two decades in the past.

Mia moved through the hallways, a ghost passing through a graveyard of the living. Open doorways revealed glimpses of motionless shapes under white sheets, accompanied by the rhythmic *whoosh-hiss* of ventilators.

She paused at the door to her personal hell.

The smell hit her first. It wasn't dirty—the staff was excellent—but it was the heavy, sweet scent of antiseptic trying to mask the underlying odor of slow atrophy. It smelled like a body that had forgotten how to live but refused to die.

Mia stepped inside.

Unity lay in the bed, a pale statue carved from bone.

Mia inspected her sister's face. The deterioration had accelerated in the last year. Her cheeks were sunken caves, her skin translucent enough to show the roadmap of blue veins beneath.

A sheet covered the rest, hiding the body that had once been strong enough to throw a grown man to the mat.

Mia grabbed the cushioned chair—the vinyl still warm from a previous visitor—and dragged it to the bedside.

"Hey, U," she whispered. "I know it's been a while."

The life support machine hummed its monotone response.

Mia leaned her elbows on her knees, rubbing the bridge of her nose. "I've been busy. Work. Sports. The usual attempts to outrun genetics." She gazed at her sister's closed eyes. "I lost the tournament, by the way. Came in second. Some kid half my age wiped the floor with me."

She waited for a retort. A laugh. A challenge.

Nothing.

"Tough crowd today," Mia muttered.

She stood and paced the small room, her energy too high for the stillness of the space. "But the lab... the lab is interesting. You remember the no-sleep drug? *Moratusom*? Well, the FDA is still sitting on it, probably playing politics. But the new formula... the enhancement serum..."

She stopped at the foot of the bed. She shouldn't say it out loud. It sounded insane.

The rat came back.

"It's complicated," she said instead. "But I think I found something. Something that changes the rules."

Movement in the hallway caught her peripheral vision.

Mia froze. A man and a woman in dark, tailored suits walked past the open door. They didn't look like family members. They looked like corporate sharks circling a reef.

Mia's heart hammered against her ribs, flashing back to the Escalade in the gym parking lot. She stepped to the doorway and peered out, but the hallway was empty. Just nurses and carts.

Paranoia, she told herself. *You're losing it, Mia.*

She turned toward her sister, muttering, "Why am I even here?" when a dark figure approached her from a corner of Unity's room.

"Hope—and because you love your sister."

The deep voice nearly made her jump out of her skin.

Jon, the second-shift nurse, must have entered from the adjoining room. His white uniform seemed to glow in the dim light, and he smelled of expensive French cologne—a jarring contrast to the scent of the room.

Mia exhaled, forcing her shoulders to drop. "Jesus, Jon. You scared me."

"Apologies." He offered a warm smile. "I didn't mean to sneak up on you."

"How is she?"

"Stable. Unchanged." Jon moved to the bedside, checking the monitors with gentle efficiency. "And how are you, Dr. Peers?"

"Fine. Tired."

"We're expecting, you know," Jon said, his voice brightening. "My wife and I. In a few months."

"A baby?" Mia blinked, shifting gears. "That's... that's amazing, Jon. Congratulations. How come I'm only hearing about this now?"

"We waited to tell people," he said, tucking the sheet around Unity's wasted legs. "You and I haven't bumped into each other in a while, so I couldn't share the news."

The guilt pricked her. It was a polite way of saying, *You haven't visited your dying sister in months.*

"I'll do better," Mia said, more to herself than to him.

"She knows you're here," Jon said softly. "I believe that." He winked, finished his check, and slipped out of the room, leaving Mia alone with the silence.

Mia turned back to the bed. She brushed a wisp of brittle blonde hair from Unity's forehead.

"God, has it been *twenty* years?" Mia whispered. "Mom and Dad... they broke after you left. They spent every dime they had trying to fix this. Trying to fix you."

She scanned her sister's hand. It was curled into a permanent claw, the muscles atrophied.

Mia thought of the rat in the cage. Number 77. It had been dead. Stiff. Cold. And then, it had been drinking water, gripping the metal mesh with a strength it shouldn't have had.

Rigor mortis reversed. Function restored.

If the serum could jumpstart a dead rat, what could it do to a damaged human?

It wasn't meant for someone with a brain injury, though.

And besides, Mia had already...

The voice from the dormant section of her brain—the one she called the wall—whispered: *The choice.*

Mia slid her phone from her pocket. She usually played music for Unity and to drown out the sound of the ventilator, to say goodbye before she ran back to her life. But not today.

She glanced at the screen, then at Unity.

"I told you I was working on a cure for diseases," Mia whispered, her voice trembling with a sudden, terrifying clarity. "But maybe I've been aiming too low."

She put the phone away without playing a note. She didn't

need music. She needed to get back to the lab.

The Call

Mia

I ce chimed against the glass as Mia drained the last of the bourbon. It was 7:58 AM.

The burn coated her throat, a chemical blanket against the morning chill of the office, but it did little to settle the tremor in her hands. She set the glass down on a coaster, staring at the amber residue. She knew the rule: *No drinking before noon.* She also knew that rules were for people who weren't facing financial extinction.

Mia swiveled her chair toward the window. Outside, Northern Virginia was waking up—traffic clogging the arteries of the DC metro area, money flowing like blood through the veins of the defense contractors and lobbyists. She was stuck here. Moving the lab was impossible; the equipment alone cost more than her organs were worth on the black market.

She glimpsed the framed photo on her desk. It was from a puff piece from a local magazine: *The Scientist Warrior.* In the photo, Mia stood in her white gi, holding a trophy, looking like the reincarnation of Unity. Strong. Unbreakable.

The woman in the chair felt like she was made of cracked porcelain.

Yesterday's visit to the care facility still clung to her—the smell of atrophy, the sight of Unity's wasted limbs, but her mind raced back to the "zombie rat" in the lab. The pieces were all there, floating in the ether, but she couldn't fit them together fast enough to build a shield against what was coming.

Her phone buzzed at 8:00 AM sharp.

Mia closed her eyes, exhaled the whiskey fumes away from the receiver, and answered.

"Hello, Dr. Kasudia."

"Good morning, Mia. And please, call me Arjun."

Arjun had been a mentor since grad school, the kind of friend who supported her career when everyone else thought she was riding her parents' coattails. But today, his voice lacked its usual warmth. It was tight. Professional.

"How are things going?" he asked.

"Oh, you know," Mia said, forcing a lightness she didn't feel. "The joy of coming to work and finding the specimens dearly departed."

"I can imagine. It must be frustrating." He paused. A beat of silence that stretched too long. "Mia, you know why I'm calling. I'll get right to it. The investors are ready to bolt. It's been six months. You're burning cash, and the rats are dying."

"We had a breakthrough yesterday," Mia said quickly.

"A breakthrough? Or an anomaly?"

"A survivor," Mia corrected, choosing her words carefully. She couldn't tell him the rat had died and *come back*. He would commit her. She had to sell the results, not the miracle. "The data shows muscle repair at speeds we haven't seen before. Cognitive function is intact."

"Mia, listen to me," Arjun said, cutting her off. "One rat isn't a trial. It's a fluke. Telita Johnson is leading the board, and she's looking at overseas options. There's a lab in Singapore claiming they're already moving to primate trials. They're further along."

Mia gripped the empty glass until her hand hurt. "They're

lying. You know they are. Nobody is as far as I am."

"It doesn't matter if they're lying. It matters that they're promising results *now*. You have two weeks, Mia. If you don't have a viable, repeatable dataset by the next board meeting, they're pulling the plug."

"Two weeks? You told me I had a year."

"I told you what I hoped for. Telita wants results." Arjun's voice softened. "I'm sorry, Mia. I really am. I've bought you as much time as I can. Present your findings in fourteen days, or... well, prepare an exit strategy."

The line went dead.

Mia lowered the phone. She didn't throw it. She didn't scream. She felt a cold, heavy silence settle over her chest.

Two weeks.

She couldn't replicate the long-term study in two weeks. She couldn't figure out *why* Rat 77 had resurrected in two weeks—not with standard protocols.

She stood up and shoved everything off her desk. The laptop clattered to the floor; the picture frame shattered.

"Damn it!"

She leaned over the empty desk, breathing hard. There was alternative money—but that would involve *the choice*. No. Not yet.

She eyed the shattered glass of the picture frame.

In sports, when you were losing, you didn't stick to the game plan. You took a risk. You pulled the goalie. You threw the Hail Mary.

The investors wanted results. They wanted to see that the serum worked on complex biology. They didn't care about rats. They cared about the product. *Wait.* That wasn't all. They cared about the competition!

Mia's pulse quickened. The idea didn't come to her like a blessing; it came like a fever.

Standard FDA trials took years. Animal testing took months.

But if she ignored her non-disclosure agreement—she could put the pressure back on Arjun. There was no way they could ignore Rat 77, nor Mia's original one-year agreement.

She didn't need to figure out Rat 77 yet. She didn't need approval. She needed a former lover to say yes just one more time.

She snatched her phone.

Interview with a Rat

Mia

The production lights mounted on tripods were hot enough to simulate a tropical noon, baking the alcohol sweat right out of Mia's pores.

She checked her reflection in her compact mirror. The makeup artist had done miracles burying the dark circles under her eyes, but she couldn't hide the manic gleam in them. She felt like a wire pulled to its breaking point, vibrating with a dangerous mix of exhaustion, desperation, and caffeine.

"Thanks for doing this, Trevor," Mia said, snapping the compact shut.

Trevor, a reporter with a jawline sharp enough to cut glass, adjusted his earpiece. "Don't take this the wrong way, Dr. Peers, but it's a slow news day. But, the boss said if your demonstration is as eye-catching as you claim, the network might pick it up for the evening slot. If not, well... there's always the local weather."

"It'll be eye-catching," Mia said. "I know lab rats aren't sexy, but your viewers won't change the channel."

"They'll stay for you," Trevor said with a practiced smile. "The Olympic darling turned mad scientist? It's a good hook."

"I'll take what I can get."

Mia did a final lap around the setup. Brian and Sophia stood by the far wall, looking like terrified parents at a recital. In the center of the room sat The Maze—a monstrosity of plexiglass, water tanks, and reinforced barriers that Mia and her team had constructed in a fever fugue over the last six hours before sunrise.

"Remember," Trevor said, stepping into the light. "Ninth-grade vocabulary. Keep the answers to fifteen seconds. The public scares easily."

"I've had media training, Trevor."

"Great. Let's make the evening news."

Trevor nodded to the camera operator. "In three, two..."

He turned on the charm instantly. "We're here today with Dr. Mia Peers, leading neuroscientist and three-time Olympic medalist. Dr. Peers, thank you for inviting us into your sanctum."

"Thanks for coming, Trevor." Mia forced her posture to relax, channeling the cool confidence of her athletic days.

"Now, before we get to the main event, update us on *Moratusom*, the sleep drug currently with the FDA. Is that still your main focus?"

"It's part of the portfolio," Mia said, sticking to the script. "But today isn't about sleep. It's about potential. We're working on physical enhancement at a genetic level."

"Enhancement," Trevor repeated, raising an eyebrow at the camera. "Are we talking Captain America?"

"I'm talking about the next phase of evolution." Mia gestured to the covered cage on the table. "And this is the prototype."

She pulled the cover off.

Inside, Lazarus—formerly Rat 77—sat on his haunches. He didn't look like a monster. He looked like a common lab rat, perhaps a bit more muscular around the shoulders, his black eyes scanning the room with an unsettling intelligence.

"This is Lazarus," Mia said.

"He looks... cute," Trevor said, sounding underwhelmed.

"Don't let the size fool you. Lazarus possesses physical capabilities that shouldn't be biologically possible for his species."

"Show, don't tell," Trevor said. "Let's see what he can do."

Mia picked up the cage. "We've designed a course that is impossible for a normal specimen. Barriers of grease, underwater tunnels, and heavy obstacles. A regular rat would give up or drown."

She carried Lazarus to the entrance of the maze. The camera boom swooped overhead for a bird's-eye view.

"Brian," Mia said. "Timer?"

"Ready," Brian squeaked.

Mia opened the cage door. She scooped Lazarus out. His body felt dense, like a coiled spring made of iron. There was a heat radiating from him that penetrated her gloves.

"Don't disappoint me, little buddy," she whispered.

She placed him at the start line.

Lazarus didn't sniff around. He didn't hesitate. He locked eyes with the camera lens for a split second, and then—

Boom.

He didn't run; he exploded.

"Whoa!" Trevor jerked back as the rat became a blur of white fur.

Lazarus hit the first obstacle—a five-foot vertical wall coated in industrial grease. An ordinary rat would slide off. Lazarus dug his claws into the slick surface, ascending with the speed of a spider, vaulting the top in under two seconds.

"Is he... is he flying?" the cameraman muttered.

Lazarus dove into the water tank. He didn't paddle. He torpedoed through the winding clear tubes, holding his breath for a solid minute, navigating the twists without slowing down.

He burst from the water, shaking himself dry in a single violent motion, and sprinted toward the finale.

"The final barrier," Mia narrated, her voice rising over the hum of the equipment. "A reinforced concrete slab. Five inches thick. There is no way around it. He has to—"

She didn't finish the sentence.

Lazarus hit the concrete. He didn't use his head; he spun, delivering a dual-legged kick with his hind legs that generated a force entirely disproportionate to his mass.

CRACK.

The sound was like a gunshot in the enclosed space.

Dust plumed. The concrete shattered outward, chunks of debris flying across the room. Lazarus shot through the hole he'd created and landed on the finish platform, chest heaving, eyes wild.

Silence descended on the lab.

Trevor's mouth hung open. The cameraman had flinched, shaking the frame. Brian was staring at the shattered concrete, his face pale. Sophia whispered, "*Cazzo!*"

"That," Trevor said, forgetting his microphone, "was not ninth-grade vocabulary."

Four hours later, Mia sat alone in her office, swiveling slowly in her chair.

On the monitor in front of her, the clip was playing on a loop on the network's home page. The headline screamed: **THE HULK IS REAL, AND HE'S A RAT.**

It had already been shared two million times. The memes were instantaneous. Lazarus breaking the wall. Lazarus as a superhero. Lazarus running for president.

Mia spun faster, the room blurring around her. It was the same game she and Unity used to play in their father's den—spin until you couldn't stand, spin until the world stopped making sense.

She stopped the chair, letting the dizziness wash over her.

She grabbed the framed photo of herself on the desk—the one she had smashed earlier. She ran a thumb over the cracked glass.

"We did it," she whispered to the empty room. "I can't wait to tell Dad."

The barrier—her wall—felt thin for the moment. The victory was too big to keep inside. She had saved the funding. The investors would be calling within the hour, begging to keep their money in the pot.

But as the adrenaline faded, the cold reality crept back in.

She fixated on the screen again. Slow-motion footage of Lazarus shattering the concrete.

She had proven the serum worked. She had proven it granted incredible strength and aggression. But she had skipped the part where it had killed him first. Killed all the other rats before him.

The investors didn't want a super-rat. They wanted a super-soldier. They wanted a *human*.

Mia opened her desk drawer and pulled out a fresh syringe kit. She set it on the blotter, next to the vial of pasty white serum. The media stunt was a bandage. The real test—the one that would save the lab, and change the world—couldn't be performed on a rodent.

She rolled up her sleeve... then bolted to her feet, chair falling over, eyes wide with shock about what she had almost done.

Mia panted in disbelief at herself, then barreled toward the bar cart.

First Contact

Mia

T he video of Lazarus shattering the concrete wall hit twenty million views by noon the following day.

Mia spent hours fielding calls from the BBC, CNN, and Al Jazeera. The world was mesmerized. The internet was ablaze with theories about super-rats and genetic mutation. But the one phone call that mattered—the one connected to Arjun and the investors—remained silent.

The silence was louder than the media frenzy.

By evening, Mia couldn't take the quiet anymore. She fled to the gym, running until her lungs burned and her legs felt like lead, desperate to outrun the fear that she had played her ace card and nobody at the table had blinked.

She left the gym late.

Outside, the unseasonably warm Virginia humidity had turned into a thick, suffocating fog. The parking lot lights created halos in the mist, obscuring the rows of cars. Mia scanned the area, her senses dull from exhaustion.

She spotted the black Escalade idling three rows down.

Two men in suits stood by the doors. They weren't on their phones. They weren't smoking. They were waiting.

Mia tightened her grip on her gym bag. She kept her head

down, aiming for her Porsche, calculating the distance. *Twenty feet. Ten.*

As she passed the bumper of a sedan, a hand clamped onto her elbow.

It wasn't a polite touch; it was a vice grip.

Mia didn't have time to scream. Another man rushed toward them, clapping a heavy hand over her mouth. They moved with coordinated precision—one controlling her arm, the other sweeping her legs. They lifted her off the asphalt and shoved her into the open back door of the Escalade like a sack of laundry.

Mia's head slammed against the roof liner as she tumbled onto the leather seats. The door slammed shut, sealing out the world.

Locks engaged with a heavy *thud.*

Mia scrambled upright, adrenaline clearing the fog in her brain. She was sandwiched. To her left, a mountain of a man took up half the bench seat. In the front passenger seat, a sharp-featured man twisted around to look at her. The driver kept his eyes on the rearview mirror.

"What do you assholes want?" Mia demanded, her voice steady despite the hammering of her heart.

"Language, Dr. Peers," the man in the passenger seat said. His accent was New York, his tone dangerously calm. "Let's be civil."

"Civil?" Mia shifted her weight, testing the space. It was tight. "You just kidnapped me. Which pharmaceutical do you work for?"

"We're independent contractors," the New Yorker said. "And we know everything about you. The lab. The sister. The serum."

Mia's blood ran cold. "You want the formula."

"Smart. We have a customer who prefers not to wait for the FDA. We saw the rat video. Very impressive. But submitting that kind of power to the government isn't wise. Our client wants to protect it."

"Let me guess," Mia said, coiling her muscles. "Out of the goodness of his heart?"

"Her." The man beside her rumbled.

"Shut up, Mason," the New Yorker snapped. He glared at Mia. "You're stalling."

"I'm processing the stupidity," Mia said. "If the drug was ready, I'd have given it to the FDA already. It kills everything it touches. Lazarus is a fluke. You three must have flunked out of henchman school."

The New Yorker's jaw tightened. He signaled to Mason. "Quiet her down."

Mason reached for her.

Mia didn't wait. She wasn't a scientist in that moment; she was a fighter in a cage match.

As Mason reached, Mia lunged *toward* him, reducing the space. She drove her elbow into his solar plexus, doubling him over. The New Yorker in the front seat lunged over the center console to grab her. Mia used the door frame for leverage and snapped a backfist into his nose.

Crunch.

Blood sprayed the dashboard.

"Dammit!" the driver shouted, fumbling for something in his jacket. A gun.

Mia saw the glint of metal. She grabbed the New Yorker by his tie and yanked him down, using his head as a shield. The driver hesitated.

Mia didn't. She chopped the driver's forearm.

BANG.

The gun discharged through the roof, the sound deafening in the enclosed space. The driver screamed, clutching his ringing ears. Mia twisted his wrist, digging her thumb into the nerve cluster. His fingers went slack.

The gun dropped onto the center console.

Mia snatched it.

She scrambled back against the door, leveling the barrel at the New Yorker's bleeding face.

"Nobody move," she hissed. Her ears were ringing, but her hand was rock steady.

The silence in the SUV was heavy, broken only by Mason's wheezing.

"Impressive, Dr. Peers," the New Yorker said, pulling a handkerchief from his pocket to dab his nose. "You're even better in person."

"Open the locks," Mia ordered.

"Take it easy."

"Unlock the doors, or the next shot doesn't go through the roof."

The locks clicked.

"You three are missing a few bolts," Mia said.

The New Yorker laughed, a wet, gurgling sound. "Check your left."

Mia kept the gun trained on them but flicked her gaze out the window. A black BMW had pulled up silently alongside the Escalade. A window rolled down. A man and two women sat inside, staring at her. They weren't panicking. They were smiling. And they all had weapons aimed at her.

Backup.

Mia calculated the odds. Six targets. One gun. She was fast, but not bulletproof.

"This is how it ends," Mia said, her voice low. "I'm leaving. You're letting me leave because you need me alive. If I die, the formula dies."

"Go," the New Yorker said. "If you run, we'll find you. We're everywhere, lady. The investor meeting is in two weeks. We know the schedule. Give my boss what she wants, or we pay a visit to Virginia Comfort Care."

The threat to Unity hit Mia like a physical blow.

"What's your name?" Mia asked. "Since we're being *civil*."

The New Yorker wiped his nose again and grinned. "Look, our client wants an amicable relationship with you. But it's not as if I'd give you our real names. But you can call me Dylan. Call him... Ethan. The big guy you winded is Mason. My sharpshooters outside are... I don't know, just making this up as I go... Lucas, Sandra and Bianca. How do those work for you, Dr. Mia Peers, sister of Unity Peers, daughter of the famous Jeff and Theresa Peers? Go ahead, tell the cops. See if names matter. We own them. We own *you*."

"We'll see about that."

Mia opened the door, keeping the gun trained on Dylan until her feet hit the pavement. She backed away, swinging the weapon toward the BMW. The occupants didn't flinch. They just watched her, predators studying prey.

Mia turned and sprinted to her Porsche. She didn't look back until she was on the highway, doing ninety, weaving through traffic toward the police station.

———

The fluorescent lights of the precinct hummed with a soul-crushing monotony.

Mia stood at the front desk, her blazer torn, her knuckles bruised. She slammed the stolen gun onto the counter.

"I want to report a kidnapping attempt," she said.

Officer Brown, a man who looked like he was two days away from a pension he didn't deserve, glanced up from his computer. He eyed the gun, then Mia.

"You have a permit for that?"

"It's not mine," Mia snapped. "I took it from the man who tried to abduct me ten minutes ago."

Brown slowly reached for a rag and pulled the gun toward him. "You took a gun. From a kidnapper."

"There were three of them. Three more in a backup car. They knew my schedule. They threatened my family."

"Names?"

"Right. Like they'd tell me their real names. But one was definitely a Mason. Big, with tattoos. The leader had a New York accent. Driving a black Escalade and a black BMW."

Brown sighed, sliding a clipboard across the riser. "Your Mason matches a thousand felons. Fill this out."

"Did you hear me? They are armed and dangerous professionals."

"Ma'am, without physical evidence or witnesses, it's your word against a ghost. You say you disarmed three men?" He peered at her, smirking. "You don't look like The Black Widow."

"I'm an Olympic medalist in the biathlon and a black belt," Mia said, her voice rising. "Run the serial number on the gun."

"I will. But I'm guessing it's filed off or stolen." Brown leaned back. "Look, Dr. Peers, go home. Lock your doors. We'll file the report."

"That's it? 'File a report'?"

"Unless you have a body or a video, that's all I can do right now."

Mia stared at him. Dylan's voice echoed in her head: *We own them.* Maybe they didn't literally own Officer Brown, but they relied on exactly this—the apathy of a system too tired to care.

She turned and walked out.

Safe inside her Porsche, the adrenaline finally crashed. Mia locked the doors and slumped over the steering wheel. The tears came hot and fast, a release of the terror she had bottled up in the SUV. She cried for the fear in the parking lot, for the threat to Unity, and for the absolute isolation of knowing no one was coming to save her.

Ten minutes later, the tears stopped.

Mia wiped her face. She inspected her bruised hands. They had held a gun. They had broken a nose.

They wanted a fight? Fine.

She keyed the ignition. The engine roared to life. She wasn't going to hide. She was a scientist, and she had just field-tested her own capability for real violence.

She had the formula. She had the rats. And now, she had a target.

Bare Necessities

Mia

M ia swept the neighborhood in her Porsche, doing a
tactical loop of the block. The streetlights hummed over
empty asphalt. No black Escalades. No BMWs whatsoever.

Just silence.

She triggered the garage door opener and slid the car inside,
waiting until the heavy door rattled shut and the lock engaged
before she exhaled.

The garage was cold, smelling of oil and concrete. Mia didn't
go inside the house immediately. She unlocked her gun safe
by the workbench and pulled out her competition rifle. It was
a precision instrument designed for paper targets at three
hundred yards, not close-quarters combat in a hallway, but it
was the only option she had.

She loaded a magazine, the metallic *clack* echoing off the
drywall.

Mia pressed her ear against the interior door. Aside from
the high-pitched whine of tinnitus and the jackhammer of her
own heart, the house was silent. She entered low, slicing the
pie at every corner, clearing the kitchen, the living room, the
bedrooms.

Clear.

She moved to the windows, peering through the blinds. Darkness pressed against the glass.

The adrenaline that had sustained her through the fight and the police station refused to return, leaving behind a crater of exhaustion. Mia lowered the rifle. She couldn't stay here. Her address was on public record. If Dylan and his crew knew about her gym schedule, they knew where she slept.

This house wasn't a fortress; it was a trap.

There was only one place secure enough to hold off a siege: The lab. It had industrial locks and reinforced doors. Sophia and Brian would think she'd lost her mind moving in, but she didn't care.

Mia moved fast.

She dragged a suitcase from the closet, bypassing the outfits she would normally wear and grabbing necessities: tactical pants, black hoodies, running gear, extra ammunition, and her cleaning kits. She packed like she was deploying, not vacationing.

Twenty minutes later, the bags were by the door, Mia's forehead against it.

Her body was demanding sleep, but sleep was a liability.

She hurried to the spare room, where her old university equipment collected dust. She bypassed the cabinets and went straight to the bookshelf. She pulled down her copy of *Cognitive Neuroscience* and shook it.

An envelope slid out, followed by a blister pack.

Mia popped two *Moratusom* pills. She dry-swallowed them, waiting for the familiar electric hum to kickstart her nervous system.

She bent down to pick up the items that had fallen with the pills. Two photographs. Her parents, sitting in the front row at her first karate tournament. It was the only competition they had ever attended. In the photo, they seemed tired, their smiles failing to reach their eyes. They had been hollowed out by the crash, by the guilt, by the endless quest to save Unity.

Mia shoved the photos into her pocket. She wasn't going to let the same thing happen to her. She wasn't going to just *survive* her work; she was going to finish it.

She pulled her phone out. It was a risk, but she needed the lab sterile.

Mia: *Be extra careful at the lab. No visitors. No exceptions.*

She sent the text to Sophia and Brian, then powered the phone down completely.

One last item.

Mia returned to the kitchen. She opened the refrigerator, bypassing the empty shelves and the expired almond milk. She pulled out the crisper drawer completely, revealing the false bottom she had taped underneath.

There it was.

The vial was small, no larger than a lipstick tube. The blue liquid inside shimmered in the fridge light, viscous and heavy, as if it contained suspended glitter.

The Secret Serum. Not FDA approved. Her soul-crushing *choice*.

Mia tucked the vial into the coin pocket of her jeans.

The police had made it clear they wouldn't help until there was a body bag to zip up. Mia wasn't planning on being the one inside it. She grabbed her rifle case and the suitcase, taking one last look at her empty, vulnerable house.

She killed the lights, plunging the room into darkness. If the "professionals" came for her tonight, they would find nothing but dust. By the time they realized she was gone, she'd be entrenched in the lab, and God help anyone who tried to breach that door.

Wellness Check

Mia

The *Moratusom* hit her bloodstream twenty minutes onto the Beltway.

It wasn't a buzz; it was a lens adjustment. The fog of exhaustion vanished, replaced by a high-definition clarity that made the world look like it was rendered in 4K. The taillights of the cars ahead didn't just streak; they formed precise vectors. The hum of the Porsche's engine wasn't a noise; it was a diagnostic report.

Mia drove for four hours, not because she was lost, but because she was running counter-surveillance. She took Route 66 west, doubled back on the 495, and executed random exits to ensure the fan club—the Escalade and the BMW—wasn't tracking her.

She checked her mirrors every eight seconds. No tails.

At sunrise, she pulled into the arched driveway of The Kensington.

The facility cost six thousand dollars a month—money she was currently bleeding dry—and it looked every cent of it. The foyer smelled of lilies and aggressive bleach. A brass chandelier hung over a red carpet that was plush enough to silence footsteps, or perhaps just thick enough to cushion the inevitable falls of the clientele.

It was a pre-coffin. A luxury waiting room for the pearly gates, complete with a concierge.

Mia approached the desk. Her movement felt fluid, frictionless.

"Sign in for Peers," she said, her voice clipped.

The young woman behind the desk tapped an earbud, looking annoyed at the interruption. "Room 135. Down the hall, past the fountain, left."

"Thanks."

Mia moved through the corridors. The walls were lined with generic impressionist art, innocuous and calming. She reached Room 135 and knocked.

"Come in," a baritone voice answered. It was scratchy, weakened by age, but unmistakably her father's.

Mia pushed the door open.

Jeff and Theresa Peers were frozen in a tableau of decline. Jeff sat in a recliner, a blanket over his legs. Theresa was in the hospital bed, her eyes fixed on a muted television until Mia strolled in.

They gasped in unison.

Jeff struggled to stand, the effort visible in the trembling of his triceps. He appeared thinner than the last time Mia had seen him. The skin hung loose on his arms, translucent enough to show the dark, precarious map of his veins, similar to Unity.

"Mia?" he asked.

"Hi, Dad."

He didn't hug her immediately. He studied her, as if verifying her identity against a mental checklist. Finally, he patted her shoulder—a gesture more appropriate for a colleague than a daughter.

"This is a surprise," he said, settling back into his chair. "We thought you'd abandoned us."

The guilt trip. Right on schedule.

"I've been working," Mia said, walking to her mother's bedside. Theresa was frail, her muscle tone nonexistent. The dementia had hollowed her out, leaving only a shell. "Hi, Mom. It's me."

Theresa stared at her, hands hovering over her mouth. "Is it really you?"

"It's me." Mia sat on the edge of the bed, patting her mother's leg through the blanket. It felt like holding a bundle of dry sticks.

"So," Jeff said, clearing his throat. "What brings you here? Did you lose your job?"

"No, Dad. Actually, the opposite. I made a breakthrough."

Jeff's eyes narrowed. The scientist in him flickered to life, displacing the father. "What kind of breakthrough?"

"I have a drug with the FDA called *Moratusom*. It extends wakefulness and cognitive function without side effects. It's... it's going to be huge. The military is interested. Space Force is interested."

Jeff tilted his head, his expression souring. "A stimulant? We have coffee, Mia. Why is that useful? Sleep is necessary for synaptic pruning."

"It allows the brain to perform those functions while awake," Mia explained, trying to keep the edge out of her voice. "We spend a third of our lives unconscious. This changes that."

"But does it repair tissue?" Jeff asked, cutting her off. "Does it regenerate neurons?"

"No, but—"

"Then why aren't you working on that?" He sighed, a sound of profound disappointment. "You have the lab. You have the education. Why are you wasting time on caffeine pills when you could be solving... the real problem?"

He glanced at Theresa, then at the empty space in the room where Unity should have been.

Mia felt a spike of heat in her chest, but the *Moratusom*

clamped down on it, turning the anger into cold logic. He didn't want her to succeed. He wanted her to be him. He wanted her to fix the mistakes he made twenty years ago.

"I needed funding, Dad," Mia said tightly. "This drug should pay the bills. So I can do the other research later."

"Unity would have done it by now," her father whispered.

The room went dead silent.

Mia turned slowly to her mother. Theresa was beaming, her eyes wet with tears.

"I knew it was you," Theresa said, reaching out a trembling hand to touch Mia's face. "Unity. You came back. You're walking."

Mia froze.

"Mom," she said softly. "It's Mia."

Theresa frowned, pulling her hand back as if burned. She squinted at Jeff, confused. "She looks just like Unity."

"She has dementia, Mia," Jeff said, waving a hand dismissively. "Don't take it personally. We did our best with you, you know. But you can't expect us to... well, it's hard on us."

Mia stood up. The chair scraped against the floor.

She reached into her pocket, her fingers brushing the cold glass of the vial.

"I made another drug, Dad," Mia said, her voice steady. "One that brings the dead back to life."

Jeff examined her, his eyes glazing over with disinterest. "Sure you did. That's nice, Mia. Listen, are you dating anyone? You look tired. You should find a nice man to take care of you."

Mia stared at him. The chasm between them wasn't just wide; it was infinite. She could cure cancer, stop aging, and conquer death, and to him, she would just be the daughter who wasn't Unity.

"No, Dad. I'm not dating anyone."

She headed to the door.

"Leaving so soon?" Jeff asked.

"I have work to do."

"Well, visit more often. Your mother misses you."

"Goodbye, Dad."

Mia left the room and went down the hall. She didn't look back. She didn't cry. The tears threatened to come, but the chemicals in her blood burned them away before they reached her eyes.

She hurried past the fountain, past the reception desk, and out into the cool morning air.

She climbed into the Porsche and pressed the ignition. The engine roared, a beast waking up.

She was done seeking approval. She was done playing the dutiful daughter.

Mia touched the pocket where *the choice* rested against her hip.

She checked the GPS. Destination: Work.

It was time to fortify the castle.

Moving Day

Mia

The *Moratusom* crash hit Mia the moment she parked the Porsche in the lab's lot.

The high-definition clarity of the last four hours dissolved into a sandy static of exhaustion. Her limbs felt heavy, her brain sluggish. The drug shouldn't have worn off this fast.

Maybe the emotional toll of the nursing home visit had burned through the chemicals faster than her metabolism could handle.

She slapped her own cheek, hard.

Focus.

She exiled the image of her parents' faces and the sound of her mother calling her Unity. She had to secure the perimeter.

Mia dragged her bags to the entrance, scanning the tree line for movement. Nothing.

She swiped her badge and slipped inside. The lab was cool and sterile, the hum of the air filtration system a welcome white noise. This was her fortress. If Dylan and his crew wanted in, they'd have to breach a castle.

She hauled the luggage to her office, dumping the duffels on the floor. The rifle case she slid behind the desk, out of sight.

"Can we chat?"

Mia spun around. Sophia stood in the doorway, holding a clipboard. She looked impeccable as always, her gym-toned arms crossed over her chest.

"Sure," Mia said, forcing a smile.

"I'll have Brian put Laz in the maze," Sophia said. "I can finish the data collection afterward. What's with the bags? Are you moving in?"

Mia leaned against her desk, blocking the view of the rifle case. She hadn't prepared a cover story, but the truth was close enough.

"I'm sleeping here for a while. We're close to the presentation, and I get my best work done at 3:00 AM. It's easier if I don't have to commute."

Sophia surveyed the pile of luggage—enough gear for a small war—and frowned. "That's a lot of clothes for a few late nights, Mia."

"I like options."

Sophia stepped into the room, her expression softening. She opened her arms. "Come here."

Mia hesitated, then accepted the hug. Sophia smelled of lavender and optimism. She was maternal, solid, the kind of woman who brought casseroles to funerals. But as Mia pulled away, the paranoia from the kidnapping crept back in.

We know your schedule.

"I need to ask you something," Mia said, keeping her voice casual. "Did you mention the investor meeting to anyone? Maybe you and Brian were overheard chatting at Starbucks?"

Sophia blinked. "Of course not. Why?"

"I got an inquiry from Dr. Kasudia. Someone on the outside knew the exact date. He asked if we had a leak."

Sophia bit her thumbnail, a nervous habit Mia had noticed before. "Who would know? We would never talk about work outside these walls. You know that."

"I know," Mia said, watching her closely. "But the leak had to come from somewhere."

"It wasn't us," Sophia said firmly. "Brian is... eccentric, but he's not stupid. He knows we're sitting on a billion-dollar product. He wouldn't risk his job."

"A billion dollars," Mia repeated.

"Easily." Sophia's eyes drifted to the luggage again. "You know, Mia... if the pressure is getting to you, I could still reach out to my contacts in Europe. For the primates."

Mia stiffened. This was the dozenth time Sophia had pushed for illegal testing. Before, it seemed like enthusiasm. Now, with the kidnapping attempt fresh in her mind, it felt like... desperation? Or a test?

"No primates," Mia said coldly. "We do this by the book. If we get caught trafficking animals, we lose the lab."

"Just a thought," Sophia said, holding up her hands in surrender. "I'll go check on Brian."

"Send him in here when you're done."

Sophia left, closing the door with a soft click.

Mia waited a beat, then grabbed the picture frame from her desk—the one she had smashed earlier—and threw it into the trash can. She didn't trust anyone. Not even the woman who hugged her.

"Hey, boss."

Brian poked his head in. He was wearing a tie-dye lab coat today, looking like a scientific hippie. "You gotta see this."

"Not now, Brian. I need to unpack."

"No, seriously. Laz is doing something... weird. Wicked weird."

Mia sighed. She rubbed her temples, trying to stave off the headache blooming behind her eyes. "Fine. Show me."

She followed him to the main lab. Lazarus was in his cage, pacing. He seemed bigger today—his fur sleek and thick. When he saw Mia, he stopped pacing and stood on his hind legs, gripping the bars.

"Okay," Mia said, crossing her arms. "What am I looking at?"

Brian opened the cage door.

Instead of running, Lazarus hopped onto Brian's palm. Brian lifted him to eye level.

"Hey there, little guy," Brian cooed. "Who am I?"

Mia rolled her eyes. "Brian, rats don't recognize faces the way we—"

Lazarus twitched his nose. He stared directly at Brian.

Then, a sound came from the rat's throat. It wasn't a squeak. It was a guttural, raspy vocalization, shaped by vocal cords that shouldn't have been capable of speech.

"Bri... an."

Mia froze. The air left the room.

"Did you hear that?" Brian beamed, looking like a proud father.

Mia stepped closer, her heart hammering against her ribs. "Do it again."

Brian nodded at the rat. "Who is she?"

Lazarus turned his black, intelligent eyes toward Mia. He sniffed the air.

"Mi... a."

Mia grabbed the edge of the table to steady herself.

Cognitive enhancement. That wasn't possible. Rapid muscle growth. Okay. Resurrection. Also not possible. And now... mimicry? Or actual speech?

"This isn't—" she whispered.

"I know!" Brian said. "It's awesome, right? Imagine what he'll say tomorrow."

Mia stared at the creature. She wasn't thinking about tomorrow. She was thinking about the investors. She was thinking about the hitmen who wanted this serum.

And she was thinking about her sister.

If the serum did this to a rat... what would it do to a human? But first, why had Lazarus survived at all?

Family

Sophia

Sophia unlocked the door to her penthouse apartment, the silence of the hallway pressing against her ears.

She paused on the threshold. The air inside felt different—displaced. A subtle shift in pressure that only someone raised in her particular household would notice.

She didn't reach for a weapon—she didn't carry one, that wasn't her role this time—but she tightened her grip on her keys, ready to use the serrated edges as a makeshift claw.

She stepped inside.

A lamp in the corner clicked on.

"You're late," a voice said.

Alessia sat in the wingback chair, legs crossed, looking as if she'd been waiting there for years rather than hours.

"Oh my goodness," Sophia exhaled, dropping the defensive posture but keeping her tone sharp. "What are you doing here? I told... Mother I didn't need help. How did you get past the doorman?"

Alessia stood up. She was younger, sharper, wearing a leather jacket that cost more than most people's cars. "The doorman was... accommodating. And you know Mother doesn't take 'no' for an answer."

Sophia strode over and hugged her sister, though the embrace was stiff. "You shouldn't be here, Alessia. Things are complicated."

"We know," a male voice said from the shadows of the kitchen.

Sophia flinched. She hadn't cleared the room.

A young man stepped into the circle of light. He was dressed in a fitted brown jacket and black trousers, his dark hair manicured to precision. He moved with a predatory grace that made him seem older than his twenty years.

"Gabriele, if I'm not mistaken?" Sophia asked, squinting.

"Well done. Yes. Gabriele. Hello, sister."

"I haven't seen you since you were... twelve," Sophia said, shaking her head. "Mother sent the baby?"

"The baby is the best shot in the family," Alessia corrected. "And we took the jet. We landed two hours ago."

Sophia went to the kitchen island and poured herself a glass of wine. Her hand shook slightly—not from fear, but from the sheer complication of this development. Her family was influential in Italy, a "business" empire built on silence and leverage. If the Matriarch had sent Gabriele, it meant she viewed the op in Virginia as nearing failure.

"I told her everything was under control," Sophia said, taking a long sip of the Barolo.

"You lied," Gabriele said smoothly. "Mia Peers has barricaded herself in a lab. She's armed. And she's being hunted."

Sophia froze. "How do you know that?"

"We contacted the cousins upstate," Alessia said, leaning against the counter. "Intel travels fast. There's a crew operating out of New York. Low-level. Sloppy. A guy named Dylan is running point."

"The *so called* Mafia?" Sophia asked.

"Wannabes," Gabriele scoffed. "Hired guns. But they're dangerous because they're desperate. They want the serum,

Sophia. And they know Mia's the weak link to get to it."

Sophia set the glass down hard. The crack of the stem against the marble echoed. "She is *not* the weak link. I am the one keeping Mia and this project alive."

"We're here to ensure that continues," Alessia said. "Let us handle the New York crew. Gabriele can remove them from the board tonight. Six targets. Easy work."

Sophia leered at her brother. He was watching her with cold, dead eyes—the eyes of a soldier waiting for a command.

She thought about Mia. Mia, who was currently locked in a bunker with a talking rat and a rifle. Mia, who was teetering on the edge of a breakdown. If six bodies turned up dead in Virginia with ties to the New York underworld, the FBI would descend on the lab. The scrutiny could destroy everything. Then again, Mia *had* gone and televised Lazarus and a serum meant exclusively for *the family* to the entire planet.

"No," Sophia said firmly.

"No?" Gabriele raised an eyebrow.

"Mia is paranoid. If she sees you, she'll shoot first and ask questions later. And if you kill Dylan's crew, it brings heat we don't need. We are days away from the presentation. I need silence, not a turf war."

"So we just watch?" Alessia asked, clearly disappointed.

"You watch," Sophia ordered. "You stay in the shadows. If Dylan makes a move on the lab, you stop him. But do it quietly. No bodies. No police reports."

"That's a restrictive rule of engagement," Gabriele muttered.

"Those are the rules," Sophia said, channeling her mother's voice. "I am the lead on this operation. You are support. Do you understand?"

The siblings exchanged a glance, a silent communication of shared lethal capability, before nodding.

"Understood," Alessia said.

"Good." Sophia picked up her wine again. "Now, go to the

guest room. Unpack your gear. And stay out of sight. I have to figure out how to keep a billion-dollar project from exploding in my face."

She watched them leave the room. *The family* had arrived. Sophia just hoped she could control them before they turned Virginia into a slaughterhouse.

A plan

Bianca

The mood inside the surveillance car was heavier than the out-of-season thick air clinging to the Virginia trees.

It had been three days since the botched encounter. Dylan had a broken nose, Ethan had lost his gun to a biochemist, and worst of all, Mia Peers could put faces to names. *Fucking Dylan and his "We own the cops" mobster bullshit.* Perhaps in New York City. Not in Northern Virginia.

The element of surprise was gone. They were no longer predators; they were liabilities.

Bianca sat in the back seat of a new rental sedan, her laptop glowing in the dim light. In the front, Sandra and Lucas watched the rear exit of the lab through binoculars.

"She's still in there," Sandra muttered, adjusting the focus. "Three days. The bitch hasn't even cracked a window."

"She's scared," Lucas said, tapping a cigarette against the dashboard but not lighting it. "She's bunkered down."

"Or she's making more of that juice," Sandra said. "And every hour we sit here, the price goes up."

Bianca ignored them, her fingers flying across the keyboard. The waiting was agonizing, but Dylan had ordered a hold. He wanted to find a soft entry point before they tried a hard breach.

And Bianca had found one.

His name was Brian Carter.

"He's online," Bianca said, checking the dating app on her screen.

She had found Mia's assistant the night before. It hadn't been hard; guys like Brian—socially awkward, hyper-intelligent, isolated—often turned to apps for connection. His profile was a tragedy of bad selfies and niche interests: medical technology, craft beer, and a desperate desire for someone who understood "the singularity."

Bianca had tailored her fake profile to be his dream girl. *Tech enthusiast. Python coder. Loves IPAs.* At least the first two entries were true.

The deal breaker would be whether Mia had shared their botched meeting in the gym parking lot, *and their identities*, with her assistants. Bianca and the crew were doubtful. Mia's file told a story of self reliance and being a loner.

"He hasn't canceled?" Sandra asked, glancing over her shoulder.

"No. We're still on for tonight."

"You're gonna ride him," Sandra said flatly.

"God, no." Bianca shot a look at the back of Lucas's head. "It's a first date. I'm just getting information. Codes, schedules, security protocols."

"Getting a guy like that to talk is easy," Sandra said with a smirk. "Getting him to shut up afterwards is the hard part. A little skin goes a long way, honey."

Lucas shifted in the front seat, the leather creaking. He didn't look back, but Bianca saw his jaw tighten.

"I can handle Brian without sleeping with him," Bianca said, her voice firm. "He's lonely. I just have to be nice to him."

"Nice doesn't open locked lab doors," Sandra countered. "If he has a keycard, you get it. Whatever it takes."

Lucas opened the car door abruptly. "I need air."

He stepped out into the damp night.

Bianca watched him go. They had been a couple for two years, but this job was testing them. Lucas didn't like her playing the honey pot. He knew it was part of the business, but knowing it and watching her prep for a date were two different things.

Sandra's phone buzzed on the center console. She put it on speaker.

"Yeah?"

"Mason's taking a walk," Dylan's voice crackled over the line. He sounded stuffed up, his broken nose clearly still an issue. "He's checking the perimeter fence."

"Bianca's bored," Sandra said. "Want her to go with?"

Bianca kicked the back of Sandra's seat. "Shut up."

"Welcome to the grind, girl," Dylan said. "This isn't *The Godfather*. It's mostly sitting in cars smelling each other's farts."

"I know," Bianca said, leaning forward. "I just want to help."

"You help by nailing that date tonight. Brian is the weak link. If you can turn him, we don't have to burn the village."

"I'll turn him," Bianca promised.

"Good. Dylan out."

The line went dead.

"See?" Sandra said, picking at a loose thread on her jeans. "Even the boss knows what you have to do. Just don't fall in love with the nerd."

"He's actually kind of cute," Bianca teased, trying to lighten the mood. "In a 'I fix microscopes' kind of way."

Sandra snorted. "Boring equals safe. Safe keeps you alive."

Bianca opened her door. "I'm going to talk to Lucas."

She stepped out into the night. The air smelled of pine needles and impending rain. Lucas was leaning against the hood of the car, the unlit cigarette finally glowing at the tip.

Bianca inched up beside him, wrapping her arms around her waist to steady her nerves.

"You okay?" she asked.

Lucas exhaled a stream of smoke. He didn't look at her. "You're really going to do this?"

"It's the job, Lucas. We need the serum. If I can get access from Brian over a glass of wine, nobody gets hurt. Isn't that better than a shootout?"

Lucas sneered at her then. His eyes were dark, unreadable. "Just make sure you remember who you're coming home to."

"I always do."

He flicked the cigarette onto the asphalt and crushed it with his boot. "You better get ready. You don't want to keep the geek waiting."

Bianca watched the ember die. She felt a twinge of guilt, but she pushed it down. She was good at tech. She was good at lies. Tonight, she just had to be good at being the girl of Brian Carter's dreams.

And if that required crossing a line... well, they were already criminals. What was one more sin?

The Alley

Alessia

Alessia parked the tiny rented Yaris in the shadow of a dilapidated manufacturing plant, two hundred meters from the lab's perimeter fence.

She hated the car. It was automatic, soulless, and smelled of "new car" spray. She shifted into park, her left foot twitching for a clutch that wasn't there.

"Relax," Gabriele said from the passenger seat, wiping a coffee stain from his jeans. "What's gotten into you? You're typically a mindfulness master."

"I hate sitting still," Alessia muttered. She adjusted her leggings. They were tactical black, chosen for movement, but right now they felt like a straightjacket. "Outnumbered six to two. Splitting up is suicide. Waiting is worse."

Through the windshield, they watched the black Cadillac Escalade idling by the main gate.

A large man exited the vehicle.

"That's Mason," Gabriele said, checking the dossier on his phone. "The muscle."

Mason didn't go to the gate. He veered off, walking in a wide arc toward the alley between two brick warehouses. He moved with the lumbering confidence of a man who knew he was the biggest predator in the ecosystem.

"He's isolating himself," Alessia said, her pulse quickening. "Going for a leak or a smoke."

"We're under orders to observe only," Gabriele reminded her.

"Mother wants the serum protected. If we take out the heavy hitter, their offensive capability drops by thirty percent. We can interrogate him. Find out when they plan to breach."

Gabriele ejected the magazine from his pistol, checked the load, and slammed it back in. *Click-clack.*

"Mia is inside that lab with a rifle," he said. "If we start a war outside, she might shoot anything that moves."

"We do it quiet," Alessia said, opening her door. "The wallet trick. We bag him, drag him, and vanish before his friends finish their cigarettes."

Gabriele smirked. "Fine. But if he kills you, I'm telling Sophia it was your idea."

They moved fast, keeping to the shadows. Mason had turned into the narrow alley, his back to them.

Alessia hung back near the mouth of the alley, crouching behind a dumpster. Gabriele jogged ahead, pitching his voice to a perfect American mid-Atlantic accent.

"Hey, buddy! You dropped your wallet!"

Mason stopped. He turned slowly.

He patted his jacket, then his pants. He didn't look confused. He looked amused. He smiled, a wide, terrifying expression that didn't reach his eyes, and started walking toward Gabriele.

Alessia's stomach dropped. *He knows.*

Mason's hand drifted behind his back.

"Gun!" Alessia screamed.

She launched herself from cover just as Mason drew a heavy revolver.

Gabriele lunged, batting Mason's arm upward. The gun discharged—a deafening boom that echoed off the brick walls.

Mason didn't flinch. He laughed, a wet, guttural sound, and

drove a fist into Gabriele's face. Gabriele crumpled like a paper cup.

Alessia hit Mason at full speed. She didn't try to grapple; he was a monolith. She went for the knees, driving her shoulder into his joint.

He barely stumbled.

He reached down, grabbed Alessia by her tactical vest, and hurled her against the brick wall.

The impact knocked the wind out of her. She slid down, gasping, tasting copper.

Mason turned back to Gabriele, who was scrambling for his dropped gun. Mason kicked him in the ribs, flipping him over.

"You two are dead," Mason lisped, grinning. "My turn."

Alessia forced herself up. Her vision swam. This wasn't a sloppy American thug. This was a tank.

She drew her knife. "Hey!"

Mason turned.

Alessia feinted left, then slashed right, aiming for his hamstring. The blade connected, sinking deep.

Mason roared. He backhanded her, a blow that felt like a sledgehammer. Alessia flew backward, hitting the pavement hard. Her head bounced. Darkness crowded the edges of her vision.

She gaped at him. Mason was limping toward her, blood soaking his pant leg, raising the revolver.

"Goodbye, sweetheart."

Alessia scrabbled for her holster, but her fingers were numb. *Too slow.* She squeezed her eyes shut.

Bang.

She waited for the pain.

It didn't come.

A heavy weight collapsed on top of her, pinning her to the asphalt.

Alessia shoved the mass aside, gasping for air. Mason lay face down, a neat hole in his shoulder.

She surveyed the alley.

Gabriele was leaning against the wall, his face a mask of blood, his gun trembling in his hand.

"Help me," he wheezed. "We have to move him."

"Is he dead?" Alessia asked, her voice trembling.

"I hope not. Get the car."

Alessia scrambled to her feet. Her ribs screamed in protest. She limped to the Yaris and reversed it into the alley, popping the trunk.

"We can't leave him here," Gabriele said, grabbing Mason's arms. "They'll find him and storm the lab."

"He weighs three hundred pounds!"

"More. Lift!"

Together, fueled by panic and adrenaline, they heaved the giant into the small trunk.

"Drive," Gabriele commanded, falling into the passenger seat.

Alessia floored it. She was suddenly grateful the car was an automatic; something was wrong with her left foot. The Yaris squealed out of the alley, the suspension groaning under the weight in the back.

She checked the rearview mirror. The alley was empty. But the gunshot had been loud.

"We screwed up," Alessia whispered, wiping blood from her eyes. "We just started a war."

Blood

Bianca

The sun was setting, casting long, jagged shadows across the alleyway, but it couldn't hide the stain on the asphalt. It was a pool of crimson, thick and starting to congeal, reflecting the dying light like black oil.

Bianca stood near the bumper of the parked car, her hands tucked into her jacket pockets to hide their shaking. She had expected a fistfight. Maybe a broken nose. But this? This was a slaughter.

"He didn't walk away from this," Lucas said. He was crouching near the center of the blood pool, his voice devoid of emotion.

Bianca forced herself to look. Drag marks smeared the pavement, leading away from the blood and vanishing onto the main road. Tire tracks cut through the gore.

"Maybe he won," Bianca whispered, though she didn't believe it. "Maybe that's the other guy's blood."

"Mason is an NFL lineman," Lucas said, standing up. "And look at the drag marks. Two distinct sets of footprints. Two people carried him."

"Mia?"

"Mia Peers is locked inside her lab," Lucas said, scanning the rooftops. "We've had eyes on the exits for three days. She hasn't moved."

"Then who did this?"

Lucas didn't answer. He headed to where a glint of brass caught the light. He picked up a shell casing with a handkerchief. "High caliber. Mason fired. But there's no body."

A chill that had nothing to do with the evening temperature settled over Bianca.

She had moved to Hollywood once, convinced her pretty face and ability to cry on cue would make her a star. She had failed there, but the skills were saving her now. She locked the panic behind a mental wall, smoothing her expression into a mask of professional detachment.

"If it wasn't Mia," Bianca said, "then there's a third player on the board."

"And they just took our heavy hitter off the field." Lucas pocketed the casing. "We need to go. Now. Before the actual cops show up."

They hurried back to their car. The silence between them was heavy, loaded with the realization that they were no longer the hunters. They were being hunted.

Inside the car, Lucas gripped the steering wheel until his knuckles buldged.

"Dylan is going to lose his mind," Bianca said softly.

"Screw Dylan," Lucas snapped. He turned to her, his eyes wild. "We are blind, Bianca. We don't know who took Mason. We don't know what to expect if we enter the lab. We are exposed."

He scrutinized her outfit—a sleek black blouse she had chosen for her date with Brian.

"The date," Lucas said. "It's the only lead we have."

"I know. I'm going."

"You need to get that badge," Lucas said, his voice hard. "I don't care what you have to do. Flirt, drug him, sleep with him.

I don't care. Get us inside that lab."

Bianca recoiled. She had expected jealousy. She had expected him to tell her to be careful. Instead, he was pimping her out because he was terrified.

"I thought you had a problem with me crossing that line," she said coldly.

"That was before Mason got snatched off the street," Lucas said, starting the engine. "Survival first. Morals second."

Bianca scowled and stared out the window as they pulled away from the curb. The bloodstain was already disappearing into the twilight, a dark secret on a dirty street.

She checked her reflection in the vanity mirror. She applied a fresh coat of lip gloss, masking the fear in her eyes.

"Fine," she said to her reflection. "Survival first."

She pulled up Brian's profile on her phone.

Time to go to work.

Red, Red Wine

Bianca

The winery was bathed in the warm, golden glow of Edison bulbs, a stark contrast to the cold dread sitting in Bianca's stomach.

She sat at a corner table, nursing a glass of Cabernet, watching the entrance. Her phone buzzed on the table—Lucas checking in—but she ignored it. She checked her reflection in the dark windowpane. Black blouse, top two buttons undone. Silver earrings catching the light. Just enough edge to intrigue a guy like Brian, but not enough to intimidate him.

Brian Carter trod in.

He was wearing a Hawaiian shirt with yellow flowers and brown cargo pants. On his feet were red Crocs.

Bianca suppressed a wince. This was going to be harder than she thought. Or easier.

He scanned the room, his eyes locking onto her with laser precision. He marched over, his gait stiff, like he was manually operating his own limbs.

"Hi," he said, offering a hand. "I'm Brian. Sorry I'm late. I got out of work as soon as I could."

Bianca bypassed the hand and pulled him into a quick, friendly hug. He went rigid, smelling of lemony cologne and nervous sweat.

"I'm Bianca," she said, pulling back with a smile that hopefully reached her eyes. "Nice shoes."

"Thanks. They're breathable."

"I ordered us a red. I hope that's okay."

"I wouldn't know. I usually drink beer."

She poured him a glass. "Well, you're in for a treat. This is a Cabernet. It's bold."

Brian picked up the glass and tipped it back like a shot of tequila.

"Whoa, slow down, haole," Bianca laughed, reaching out to touch his wrist. "You're supposed to savor it."

"How do I savor it if I don't drink it?"

"Here. Let me teach you. The Six S's of Wine Tasting."

Brian blinked. "Is there a quiz?"

"Only if you want a prize." Bianca leaned forward, letting her earrings dangle. "See. Swirl. Smell. Sip. Swish. Savor."

"That's a lot of work for a drink."

"It's about the experience, Brian. Like coding. You don't just type; you build."

He fixated on her then, really *looked* at her, and for a second, the social awkwardness vanished. "You're too pretty to be interested in technology."

Bianca's smile faltered for a fraction of a second. "Too pretty to be a geek? Ouch."

"I didn't mean it like that. I meant... you look like you belong in movies. Not behind a monitor."

"I tried the actress thing in LA," she admitted smoothly. "Didn't work out. I prefer systems that make sense. People are messy. Code is clean."

Brian nodded, relaxing slightly. "That's exactly it. Code doesn't lie."

He took another drink—slower this time. Bianca kept the bottle moving, refilling his glass before he hit the bottom. She needed him loose. She needed him talking.

"So, tell me about work," she said casually. "You mentioned you were busy."

"Consuming me," he corrected. "But I'm thinking of quitting."

"Quitting? Why?"

"Funding issues. And... weirdness. We had a breakthrough, but the boss is locked in her office. Paranoia level ten."

"Paranoia?" Bianca swirled her glass. "Does she think someone is stealing her secrets?"

Brian chuckled, a dry, humorless sound. "Maybe. She sent a text at O dark hundred telling us not to let anyone in. It's intense. All the subjects were dying, and then one... didn't."

"Is something wrong with the rats?" Bianca asked.

Brian froze. His glass stopped halfway to his mouth.

"I didn't say rats," he said.

Bianca's heart skipped a beat. *Sloppy.*

"You're a medical lab," she said quickly, covering the slip with a dismissive wave. "Isn't it always rats? Unless you're testing on monkeys?"

Brian stared at her for a beat too long. Then he shrugged. "Yeah. Rats. But this one... he's smart. Crazy smart. I think he said my name."

"A talking rat?" Bianca laughed, leaning in to touch his hand. "Okay, mister. Code may not lie, but wine tells some tall tales. No pun intended."

She checked his glass. Empty. Poured him more. After twenty minutes, the second bottle was dry too.

"Give me your keys," she said. "Let's go sit in your car for a bit. I shouldn't drive yet either."

Outside, the air was unusually cool. Brian stumbled slightly on the gravel, and Bianca caught him, wrapping an arm around his waist. She felt the hard rectangle of a lanyard card in his cargo pocket.

They got into his sedan. It smelled of fast-food wrappers and loneliness.

Brian leaned his head back. "Did I ruin it?"

"Ruin what?"

"The date. I'm not good at this."

"You're doing fine," Bianca whispered. She turned in her seat, cupping his cheek. "You're sweet."

She kissed him.

He froze again, then melted, his hands coming up to awkwardly touch her waist. Bianca deepened the kiss, moving her hand to his leg, walking her fingers up his thigh.

"Whoa," Brian breathed, pulling back. "First date."

"I know," she murmured, leaning her forehead against his. "I just really like smart guys."

She kissed him again, harder this time, distracting him. Her hand slid into his cargo pocket. She hoped he was too focused on her lips, on the feel of a woman actually touching him, to notice the slight weight leaving his pants.

She palmed the keycard and slid it into her sleeve.

"I should go," she said, pulling away abruptly after five minutes. "My friends are waiting."

"Oh. Okay." Brian looked dazed. "Can I... see you again?"

"Count on it," Bianca said.

She climbed out of the car, blew him a kiss, and strolled toward the parking lot exit. She didn't look back until she was sliding into the backseat of the rental car.

Lucas turned around. "What took so long? Did you have fun steaming up the windows?"

"I did what I had to do," Bianca said, wiping her mouth with the back of her hand.

"Did you get the prize?" Sandra asked from the front seat. "Or did you just get a hickey?"

Bianca reached into her sleeve and tossed the plastic keycard onto the center console. It landed with a satisfying *clack*.

"Access granted," Bianca said. "Now let's go rob a lab."

Genetic Revolution

Mia

The coffee in the carafe had turned to sludge hours ago, but Mia poured another cup anyway.

She sat at the head of the conference table, surrounded by stacks of paper—Lazarus's scans, the autopsy reports of the dead rats, and the endless, mocking data from the failed trials.

"You honestly think he can talk?" Sophia asked, not looking up from her laptop.

"I know what I heard," Mia said, rubbing her temples. "Brian heard it too. He said our names."

"Parrots say names. It doesn't mean they understand them."

"Lazarus isn't a parrot. He's a Rattus norvegicus. His vocal cords shouldn't be able to form consonants. His brain shouldn't be able to process language." Mia shoved a scan across the table. "Look at the hippocampus. The density is off the charts."

Sophia picked up the scan. "We know the serum accelerates cell regeneration. Maybe it accelerated... everything?"

"Macroevolution takes millions of years," Mia muttered. "We did it in a week. That's not evolution. That's mutation."

"Or overflow," Sophia said softly.

Mia eyed Sophia. "What?"

"Overflow," Sophia repeated. She set the paper down. "Think

about it. The serum forces rapid cell growth. In the other rats, the body couldn't handle the energy demands. The heart fails, the organs shut down. But Lazarus... maybe his physiology was different enough to handle the surge. Instead of burning out his organs, the energy overflowed... somewhere. Maybe to the... brain. It forced new neural pathways to open. Or... somewhere externally."

Mia stared at her, not fully understanding. It was a wild theory.

"But why him?" Mia asked. "We used the same batch on loads of rats. Why did all the others die and one turn into Einstein?"

"Maybe it's not just the serum," Sophia said, leaning forward. "Maybe it's the host. Maybe Lazarus had a genetic anomaly we missed. Or maybe..." She hesitated. "Maybe the rat model is flawed. Their brains are too small to handle the expansion. That's why I keep mentioning primates. A larger brain might—"

"Stop," Mia said, holding up a hand. "No primates."

"We're running out of time, Mia. The investors are silent. If we don't figure out why Lazarus survived, we lose everything."

Mia stood up and wandered to the window. The blinds were drawn tight.

Sophia was right. They were dead in the water without data. And they couldn't get data without risking another species—or risking something else.

"Run the next batch with the exact formula we gave Lazarus," Mia said. "Double the glucose drip. If it's an energy issue, maybe we can feed your so-called overflow."

"On it," Sophia said. She stood up, collected her papers, and left the room.

Mia waited until the door clicked shut.

She locked it.

She turned back to the room. Her reflection in the darkened

window looked ghostly—pale, tired, desperate.

She checked her phone. Still no call from Arjun. The silence from the investors was a death sentence. They had seen the video, and they had decided it wasn't enough. Or worse, they had decided it was too dangerous. Plus, the Mafia was at her doorstep. Seemed *someone* knew its value more than the investors did. Laughable.

Mia strode to her desk.

She opened the safe. The biometric lock beeped, a cheerful sound in the quiet room. Inside, next to the blue Secret Serum sat the spare vial of Laz's white serum. Both formulas whispered such seductive, sweet lies to Mia's desperate ears.

Trust thyself. The words she had inscribed on her mental wall echoed in her head.

She couldn't wait for the FDA. She couldn't wait for primates. She couldn't wait for the Mafia to break down the door.

If the "overflow" theory was correct—or if the serum required a host strong enough to handle the energy surge—then a rat was the wrong vessel. A human, however... a human who had spent twenty years pushing her body to the absolute limit of physical endurance...

Mia picked up the vial.

She rolled up her left sleeve. The tiny, circular birthmark on her forearm—the only thing that distinguished her from Unity—stared up at her like a target.

"For science," she whispered.

She drew the liquid into the syringe. She tapped the barrel to clear the air bubbles.

But she hesitated, leaned back in her chair, and closed her eyes.

Before she knew it, her office was dark. She eyed the clock. 3 AM.

Grabbing the syringe, she decided she couldn't afford to think about the dozens of dead rats. She had to think about the one that lived.

Mia pressed the needle into her arm. She depressed the plunger.

The sensation was immediate. It wasn't pain; it was cold. A glacial chill swept up her arm, into her shoulder, and slammed into her chest.

Then, the world tilted.

Mia gasped, gripping the edge of the desk. Her vision blurred, the colors of the lab smearing into a Van Gogh painting of swirling grays and blues.

The floor rushed up to meet her.

But she didn't hit the carpet.

Instead, she was in a bed.

The room was dark, smelling of Murphy floor cleaner and lilies. Her legs felt heavy, immovable, buried under a wool blanket. A machine hummed rhythmically to her left—*whoosh-hiss, whoosh-hiss.*

She tried to move her head, but her neck was stiff, locked in place.

In the corner of her vision, a figure sat in a chair. A man. He was a blur of shadow, but she could feel waves of emotion radiating from him—grief, exhaustion, love.

Dad?

Mia tried to speak, but her mouth wouldn't open. Her lips felt glued shut. Panic flared in her chest, a hot, bright terror. She was trapped in her own body.

Get up, she screamed internally. *Get up!*

She pushed against the paralysis with everything she had. She felt a connection—a thin, silver wire stretching from her mind into the darkness.

She focused on her hand. Just one finger. Move one finger.

In the chair, the shadow man glowered.

Mia pushed. The strain was immense, a physical weight crushing her skull.

Move.

Her left pinky twitched.

The shadow man gasped.

Then, the connection snapped. The darkness imploded.

Mia crashed back into her own body, hitting the floor of her office with a bone-jarring thud.

Bad Idea, Right?

Mia

T he pounding wasn't coming from the door. It was coming from the tectonic plates shifting inside Mia's skull.

She gasped, sucking in air that tasted of rodent droppings and ozone. Her body felt heavy, like she was surfacing from the bottom of the Mariana Trench.

Thud. Thud. Thud.

No. The sound was external.

Mia peeled her face off the floor. Her vision was a kaleidoscope of fractured light. The sun streaming through the window wasn't just bright; it was aggressive, a white-hot laser burning through her retinas.

She tried to push herself up, but her muscles seized.

Laz. The formula. The injection.

She patted her chest, checking for a heartbeat. It was there—slow, powerful, rhythmic like a war drum. She was alive.

She rolled onto her back and blinked the world into focus.

Her office looked like a bomb had detonated inside a filing cabinet. The blinds were torn from the window, twisted into aluminum pretzels. The sofa cushions were scattered. Papers blanketed the floor like snow.

Mia stared at the wreckage. *I did this.* She hadn't just slept; she had thrashed. She had convulsed.

The serum had tried to tear her apart.

"Mia! Dr. Peers!"

Brian's voice was muffled by the heavy oak door, but the panic in it was clear.

"Mia, I'm calling 911 if you don't answer!"

Mia stumbled to her feet. The room spun, then snapped into hyper-focus. She lurched to the door, unlocked it, and swung it open just as Brian raised his fist to hammer it again.

"Stop," she rasped. Her voice sounded like she'd swallowed sharp rocks.

Brian froze. He gawked at her—hair matted, clothes rumpled—then peered past her at the devastation of the office. His jaw unhinged.

"Holy..." He stepped back. "Are you okay? It looks like... did someone break in?"

"No," Mia said, leaning against the doorframe. "I'm fine. I just... had a rough night."

"Rough night? Mia, the blinds are ripped off."

"What day is it?"

Brian blinked. "What?"

"The day, Brian. What day is it?" Mia glanced at the clock.

"It's Wednesday."

Wednesday. She had injected herself before sunrise. She had been out for twelve hours. That was double the lethal window for the rats.

"I need water," she said.

"I'll get it."

Brian sprinted down the hall. Mia didn't wait. She turned back into the office, her OCD flaring at the chaos. She began picking up papers, her movements jerky but precise.

She reached for the phone base, which had been kicked under the desk.

It started ringing.

The sound was a physical blow. It wasn't just loud; it vibrated in her teeth. The serum had dialed her senses up to eleven.

"I'm coming, dammit," she muttered.

She lunged for the receiver, her knee slamming into the sharp edge of an overturned metal trash can.

"Ow!"

Pain, sharp and hot, sliced through her leg. She ignored it, grabbing the phone.

"This is Dr. Peers."

"Hello? Is this Mia?"

The voice was male, hesitant. Familiar, but buried under twenty years of static.

"Yes. Who is this?"

"Chris. Chris Holden."

Mia froze. The name pulled a thread from the darkest part of her memory—high school, Unity's boyfriend, the car accident and Chris's unwavering devotion to her sister in a coma. Until the start of college of course, when social worlds swell and high school relationships begin to feel like scrimmages in the game of love.

"Chris?"

"Yeah. I... you remember me?"

"Hard to forget," Mia said. Her brain was processing the call too fast. Why was he calling the lab landline? Why now? "How did you get this number?"

"Your website. I saw the news. The rat... the maze. It was incredible, Mia. It got me thinking about you."

Mia squeezed her eyes shut. The sensory overload was receding, replaced by a cold, crystalline clarity. She could hear the background noise on his end—a coffee shop grinder, low chatter.

"You called to catch up?"

"I know it's out of the blue," Chris said. "But I thought maybe we could get coffee? Catch up properly?"

Mia gaped at the wreckage of her office. She glimpsed the syringe still sitting on her desk. Coffee with her sister's ex-boyfriend seemed absurdly trivial, but maybe that's what she needed. A baseline. A control group to test her new reality against.

"Sure," Mia said, her voice detached. "Sunday. I have a deadline before then."

"Sunday is great. I'll text you the details?"

"Fine." She gave Chris her cell number and hung up.

She sat heavily on the couch, the adrenaline of the waking moment fading into a strange, buzzing hum. She felt... optimized.

Then she noticed her knee.

She remembered the sharp metal. She remembered the sting. There should have been a cut requiring stitches.

She wiped a smear of red blood away with her thumb.

Underneath, the skin was smooth.

Unblemished.

Mia stared. The cut hadn't just clotted; it had sealed. In mere minutes.

Her heart began to hammer again. She gazed at her left forearm, the place where the needle had gone in.

She rubbed the skin. She rubbed it harder.

The tiny, circular birthmark—the single physical flaw that distinguished her from Unity—was gone.

Your Move

Mia

M ia gripped the edge of the heavy oak conference table and heaved.

She strained until her tendons popped and her face flushed crimson. She grunted, putting her back into it, expecting the wood to fly upward like Styrofoam.

The table didn't budge.

Mia let go, gasping for air, and kicked the table leg in frustration. Pain blossomed in her toes—sharp, immediate, and entirely human.

"Useless," she hissed.

She paced the length of the lab, her reflection ghosting in the darkened windows. It had been several days since the injection. Days of hiding, days of staring at the monitors, days of waiting for the superpower to kick in.

There was no super-strength. She couldn't bend metal. She couldn't outrun a cheetah. When she sprinted down the hallway yesterday, she had just looked like a woman late for a meeting, much to Brian's confusion.

The serum had healed her knee instantly. It had erased her birthmark. It had kept her alive past the lethal six-hour window.

But beyond that? Nothing.

She felt like a walking placebo.

Mia stopped at the window, peering through the slats of the new blinds she had installed to replace the ones she'd destroyed. Down on the street across from the parking lot, the black Cadillac sat like a vulture.

The New York crew hadn't left. They rotated shifts—Dylan, Ethan, and the others, except for that big guy... Mason. Mason... his absence worried her for some reason.

These people were patient. They knew she was in the lab, and they knew she had to come out eventually.

The isolation was a physical weight. She was living on vending machine crackers and delivery food that Brian sometimes smuggled in. The lab, once her sanctuary, had become a prison cell.

She headed to the bathroom attached to her office and splashed cold water on her face. She stared at the mirror.

The face staring back wasn't hers.

With the serum, but without the birthmark on her left arm, she resembled Unity exactly. Not the vegetative Unity in the nursing home, but the Unity from twenty years ago—the golden child, the athlete, the perfection.

Mia gripped the sink. The guilt that usually simmered in her gut boiled over.

She had injected herself out of desperation, yes. But deep down, *the choice* whispered to her. The dark, quiet thought that had plagued her since the funeral that never happened: *It should have been me.*

By taking the serum, by erasing the one mark that made them different, was she trying to save her sister? Or become her?

"Stop it," she whispered.

She dried her face. The towel felt rough, like sandpaper.

That was new.

Mia rubbed the fabric between her fingers. It sounded

loud—a dry, rasping *shhh-shhh* that seemed to echo in her ears. She dropped the towel. It hit the floor with a heavy *thump* that shouldn't have been audible over the hum of the air conditioning.

She frowned.

A sudden hunger pang twisted her stomach, sharp as a knife. It had been happening a lot—a metabolic furnace that burned through calories faster than she could consume them. She grabbed a protein bar from her pocket and tore the wrapper open. The sound was like a gunshot.

Mia flinched.

She froze, chewing slowly. The silence of the lab wasn't silent anymore. It was crowded.

She could hear the hum of the refrigerator in the break room, fifty feet away. She could hear the *drip-drip* of a faucet in the chem lab. She could hear the scratch of a pen on paper from Brian's office down the hall.

And then, she heard something else.

Low. Rhythmic. Thumping.

It was coming from outside.

Mia moved to the window again. She pressed her ear against the glass.

The thumping grew louder. *Ba-bump. Ba-bump.*

It wasn't music. It was a heartbeat.

And underneath it, a voice.

"*...bored. How long do we sit here?*"

Mia's breath hitched. The parking lot itself was two hundred yards away. The glass was soundproofed.

"*Until she comes out,*" a second voice answered. It sounded like gravel. Dylan. "*The meeting is Friday. She has to move.*"

Mia backed away from the window, her hands trembling.

She scanned her arms. They weren't bulging with muscle. She wasn't lifting cars. But the "overflow" Sophia had theorized about—the energy diverting to the brain *(and elsewhere?)*

because the body couldn't use it—was real.

It wasn't making her stronger. It was making her *more*.

She could hear them. Which meant she could track them.

Mia glanced at the calendar on the wall. Friday. The investor meeting.

Sunday. The plan to meet Chris. The day she had to leave the fortress.

She wasn't a soldier. She wasn't a killer. But as the voices from the parking lot filtered into her brain with crystal clarity, Mia realized she wasn't a victim anymore, either.

She was a predator who had just opened her eyes.

Board Meeting

Mia

T he video feed stuttered, freezing Telita Johnson's face in a pixelated grimace of disdain.

Mia sat at the head of her conference table, hands clasped tightly in her lap to hide the tremor. On the screen, twelve investors sat in a boardroom in Falls Church, looking like a jury ready to deliver a guilty verdict.

"Let's call this what it is," said Shawn, a man with a voice like grinding gravel. "You're seven months into a twelve-month contract. You promised human trials by Q3. You are still stuck on rodents."

"Projected," Mia corrected, keeping her voice level. "Human trials were a projection."

"A promise," Telita interjected. Her white suit was impeccable, her gaze cold enough to frost the camera lens. "And you've broken it. The point is, Dr. Peers, the score is uncountable dead rats to one survivor. That is not a business model. That is a massacre."

"Lazarus is not just a survivor," Mia argued. "He is an anomaly. His strength, his cognitive function—it's unprecedented. That alone proves the serum has potential."

"Potential doesn't pay dividends," Rick, the tech billionaire in the blue polo, said. "Our money is a sunk cost. We know it. You know it. Let's stop pretending. We're pulling the plug."

Arjun, Mia's liaison, skimmed his notes, refusing to meet her eyes. The silence in the room was deafening.

Mia felt the panic rising, hot and sharp. If she lost funding now, she lost the lab. If she lost the lab, she lost the formula. And if she lost the formula, the New York crew outside might just storm the building and take the current, faulty version.

She reached for the mute button, but Sophia spoke first.

"What if we move to primates?" Sophia asked.

The room erupted. Laughter from Rick. Shock from Shawn. Telita just narrowed her eyes.

"Sophia," Mia hissed, reaching for the mouse. "What are you doing?"

"Saving us," Sophia whispered. She leaned into the camera, her voice smooth, maternal, and utterly convincing. "We are talking about chimpanzees. Not here, of course. Europe. We have suppliers."

"Unethical," Telita said flatly.

"Is it unethical to reverse death?" Sophia countered. "Dr. Peers's formula isn't failing because it's flawed. It's failing because the vessel is too small. The rats are burning out. But a larger physiology? A primate? It could handle the energy load. Lazarus proves it. He survived because he was an alpha—stronger, bigger. Imagine what a chimp could do."

Mia stared at her assistant. Sophia was lying. Lazarus wasn't an alpha; he was a runt. But the lie was elegant. It gave the investors a lifeline—a reason to believe their money wasn't wasted, just misapplied.

"We are talking about billions," Sophia continued. "The next stage of human evolution. You want to walk away from that because you're afraid of a little... regulatory gray area?"

The boardroom went silent. The investors exchanged glances. Greed battled with caution.

"We can't authorize primate trials," Arjun said finally, breaking the silence. "Not officially."

"Then don't authorize it," Sophia said. "Just continue the funding you promised. Let us work. In four months, we will show you something that makes Lazarus look like a parlor trick."

Telita leaned back, tapping a pen against her lips. She stared at Mia, her gaze piercing.

"Four months," Telita said. "But stick to rodents. If you can replicate the Lazarus result—if you can prove it wasn't a fluke—we will discuss renewal. But if you come back with another pile of dead rats, we aren't just pulling funding. We're suing for breach of contract. That little television stunt of yours was amateur hour."

"Agreed," Mia said instantly. "Thank you."

"Four months, Dr. Peers. Clock starts now."

The screen went black.

Mia let out a breath that felt like it had been held for a week. She sagged in her chair, the adrenaline crash hitting her hard.

"You lied to them," Mia said, looking at Sophia.

"I bought us time," Sophia said, closing her laptop. "And I wasn't entirely lying. The primate theory is sound. If you won't do it, maybe the universe will provide."

The relief was intoxicating. Four months. She still had four months to figure out the serum and what it was doing to her.

"I need coffee," she said, eager to get back to work.

She pushed to her feet.

Instead of just standing, she shot upward like a rocket from a launchpad.

Her legs fired with explosive power. Her head slammed into the drop-ceiling tiles, almost ten feet above the floor. She landed lightly on the balls of her feet, dust raining down on her hair.

Silence filled the room.

Sophia stared at her, mouth open. Brian dropped his tablet.

"Did you just..." Brian stammered.

Mia glanced at the hole in the ceiling. She dusted off her head.

"Adrenaline," Mia said quickly, her voice trembling. "Just... adrenaline. Former high jumper, as you know."

She forced a laugh, but it sounded brittle.

Mia shoved her hands into her pockets to hide the shaking and hurried out of the room, leaving a trail of white ceiling dust in her wake.

Safely in her office, Mia locked the door. She leaned against it, breathing hard.

She fixated on her reflection in the window.

The serum hadn't just healed her knee. It hadn't just erased her birthmark. It was rewriting her physics.

She wasn't just a scientist anymore. She was the experiment. And the experiment was starting to succeed.

The Run

Mia

M ia adjusted her hair into a ponytail then checked the clock on the wall. 8:58 AM.

She didn't look in the mirror. She didn't need to see the stranger staring back. She just tightened the straps of her fanny pack, checked the small pistol holstered against her thigh, and opened the rear door of the lab.

The world assaulted her.

The morning air wasn't just warm; it was a tactile pressure against her skin. The chirping of birds sounded like a rhythmic screeching. The smell of pine needles and exhaust fumes was thick enough to taste.

She stepped onto the asphalt.

Two hundred yards away, an engine turned over. To a normal ear, it was background noise. To Mia, it was the distinct, growling idle of a 6.2-liter V8.

They're moving.

She didn't walk. She didn't jog. She launched.

Mia sprinted across the parking lot, her legs eating up the distance with terrifying efficiency. She wasn't running; she was flowing.

Tires screeched behind her.

She crossed the street, weaving through morning traffic, the horns blaring in a Doppler effect of chaos. She glanced back. The black Escalade was tearing across the median, kicking up a cloud of dust.

Mia banked right, cutting through the lot of a tire service center. She could hear the heavy tread of the SUV gaining, the shout of men and a woman inside.

She burst through the employee entrance of the shop.

The smell of vulcanized rubber and grease hit her like a wall. Mechanics gaped, wrenches freezing in mid-turn.

"Hey! You can't be back here," an older man in a blue jumpsuit said.

The service bay door rolled up with a metallic crash. The Escalade screeched to a halt just outside. Dylan, Ethan, and... either Sandra or Bianca bailed out, weapons drawn.

Mia ducked behind a stack of radial tires.

"Mia Peers!" Dylan roared, his voice cracking. "Come out! No more games!"

The older mechanic stepped forward, holding a tire iron. "You folks need to leave. Now."

"Sit down, old man," Dylan snapped. He raised his gun.

"No!" Mia screamed.

She broke cover, grabbing a heavy torque wrench from a workbench. She didn't think; she just reacted. She hurled the tool.

It flew with the velocity of a fastball. It smashed into the Escalade's windshield, shattering the safety glass into a spiderweb of diamonds.

Startled, Ethan spun toward her.

Mia closed the distance. She moved faster than human reaction time allowed. She slammed into Ethan, driving her shoulder into his ribs. *Snap.* The sound of breaking bone was sickeningly loud.

Ethan went down, screaming.

The mechanic, seeing the violence, swung his tire iron at Dylan.

Dylan ducked, a panicked look in his eyes, and fired.

Bang. Bang. Bang.

The shots were deafening in the enclosed space. The mechanic jerked backward, three blooms of red opening on his chest. He hit the concrete with a wet thud.

Time stopped.

Mia gawked at the dead man. An innocent. A bystander.

The wall in her mind—the one she built to protect herself from her parents, from Unity, from the guilt—didn't just crack. It crumbled.

A cold, white rage flooded her system. It wasn't adrenaline. It was the serum, begging for release.

"You killed him," Mia whispered.

Dylan turned his gun on her.

Mia didn't dodge. She grabbed a floor-to-ceiling shelving unit loaded with tires. It was bolted to the concrete, weighing thousands of pounds.

She pulled.

The bolts sheared with a sound like a gunshot. The metal groaned, twisted, and collapsed.

A deluge of heavy rubber rained down on the crew. Dylan shouted, diving for cover. Dylan's female crew member scrambled back, losing her footing.

Mia didn't wait to see the damage. She bolted through the front office, glass shattering in her wake as she slammed through the door.

She hit the sidewalk and kept running. The world blurred at the edges. Her heart wasn't beating; it was vibrating.

She cut through a landscaping lot, vaulting over pallets of stone pavers like they were hurdles. Behind her, the BMW screeched into view. Lucas and... the other lady, the younger one.

She needed to thin the herd. That had been *whole* point!

She saw a convenience store ahead. *Coffee.*

Mia crashed through the door, sending a display of chips flying. "Get down!" she roared at the customers.

She leaped over the counter, grabbing two glass pots of brewing coffee.

The door swung open. Lucas and the woman burst in, guns raised.

Mia threw the pots.

They exploded on impact. The woman screamed, a high, shrill sound as the scalding liquid washed over her face and neck. She clawed at her eyes, dropping her weapon. Lucas slipped in the puddle, crashing down beside her.

Mia vaulted the counter. She landed on Lucas, driving a fist into his jaw. His head snapped back against the tile with a bone-conduction *crack*. He went limp.

"My eyes!" shrieked the Mafia woman, writhing on the floor.

Mia stepped over them. She felt a flicker of horror—*I did that*—but the rage pushed it down. Survival first.

She exited the rear of the store and sprinted toward the massive Cabela's sporting goods store across the lot. It was a fortress of weapons, high ground, and hiding spots.

She kicked the glass doors open.

"Everybody out!" she yelled. "Run!"

The few shoppers froze, then scattered as the remaining members of the New York crew—Dylan, Ethan (hugging his ribs), and the older woman—burst in behind her.

They opened fire.

Bullets shredded the camping displays. A sleeping bag exploded in a puff of down feathers.

Mia scrambled up the fake rock climbing mountain in the center of the store. She moved like a spider, finding holds where there were none. She crested the top, hiding behind a taxidermy mountain goat.

Below, the crew split up, stalking the aisles.

Mia scanned the store. Her vision zoomed in, focusing on the hunting section. *Bows. Knives.*

She dropped from the mountain, landing silently in the archery aisle.

Ethan came around the corner, heaving like he couldn't get enough oxygen.

Mia grabbed a compound bow from the rack. She didn't have arrows. She swung the bow like a bat.

The stabilizers connected with Ethan's wrist. His gun clattered away. He pulled a knife, lunging at her.

Mia caught his wrist. She squeezed.

The bones ground together. Ethan screamed, dropping the knife.

"Sandra, she's here!" he howled.

Sandra appeared at the end of the aisle, raising her pistol.

Mia grabbed Ethan by his jacket. He weighed two hundred pounds. She lifted him like a ragdoll.

Sandra fired.

The bullets thudded into Ethan's back. He jerked in Mia's grip, a human shield absorbing the punishment.

Mia shoved the dying man toward Sandra. The woman stumbled, her gun clicking empty.

Mia closed the gap. She reached for the nearest weapon—a heavy, iron fire poker from a display of camping gear.

Sandra fumbled with a fresh magazine. "You bitch!"

Mia thrust the poker. She meant to push her back. She meant to knock the wind out of her.

She didn't account for the strength.

The iron rod punched through Sandra's chest, exiting her back with a spray of bright arterial blood.

Sandra stared at Mia, her eyes wide with shock. She dropped to her knees, the poker pinning her upright like a butterfly in a display case.

Mia let go, stumbling back. Her hands were slick with blood. *Too strong. Too fast.*

"Mia!"

Dylan stood at the end of the aisle. He was alone. His face was a mask of terror and fury. He raised an automatic rifle.

Mia didn't run. The serum surged, a tidal wave of energy that felt like liquid lightning. Time seemed to slow down. She could see the tension in Dylan's trigger finger. She could see the casing ejecting as he fired.

She moved.

She wove through the bullets, closing the distance.

Dylan's eyes widened as if he couldn't track her.

Mia lunged. She didn't use a weapon. She drove her fist into his stomach.

She felt resistance—skin, muscle, organ—and then she felt nothing.

Her hand passed *through* him.

The sound was wet and final.

Mia pulled her hand back. Dylan regarded the gaping hole in his midsection. He didn't scream. He just collapsed, a puppet with cut strings.

Silence descended on the store.

Sirens wailed outside, growing louder. Blue and red lights flashed against the ceiling.

Mia gaped at her hands. They were covered in gore. She wasn't a scientist anymore. She was a monster.

"Police! Drop your weapons!"

A SWAT team moved into the entrance, shields up.

Mia scanned the skylight forty feet above the atrium.

She crouched. The energy coiled in her legs, burning hot.

She sprang.

She soared through the air, smashing through the tempered glass of the skylight. She landed on the corrugated metal roof, rolling to absorb the impact.

She didn't stop. She ran to the edge of the roof and leaped into the trees behind the store.

———<>———

Three miles away, Mia crashed through the rotting door of an abandoned tobacco barn.

She collapsed onto the dirt floor.

The energy vanished as quickly as it had arrived. The crash was absolute. Her metabolism screamed for fuel. Her stomach cramped so hard she curled into a fetal position, gagging on bile. Her vision grayed out at the edges.

She had won. She had survived.

But as the darkness of unconsciousness swallowed her, Mia realized the terrifying truth. The serum hadn't just fixed her. It had turned her into something that couldn't exist without violence.

She closed her eyes, and the hunger consumed her.

Cuppi Coffee

Mia

M ia woke up fourteen hours later as if she had just had the best sleep of her entire life.

She didn't wake up groggy. Her eyes snapped open, and she was instantly, terrifyingly awake. Her heart rate was slow, powerful, thumping against her ribs like a trapped bear.

She lay on the couch in her office, staring at several water-stained ceiling tiles. Her memory of the previous day felt like a fever dream—the tire shop, the coffee pots, the fire poker, the leap through the skylight.

But the blood under her fingernails was real.

Mia sat up. Her body should have been a wreck. She had jumped off a roof, fought six people, sprinted three miles, and stumbled to safety in the dark of night. Her muscles should be screaming.

Instead, they felt... electric.

She hurried to the small bathroom attached to her office. She stripped off the bloody, torn clothes she had slept in.

She stared into the mirror.

There were no bruises. No scratches. The scrapes on her arms from the skylight glass were gone, replaced by smooth, pale skin. Her birthmark was still missing.

The only evidence of the violence was the jagged cut on her forehead where a glass shard had embedded itself. It was angry and red, sealed but not healed.

"Why you?" she whispered, touching the wound. "Why didn't you fix this one?"

Maybe the serum had limits. Maybe it prioritized internal damage first—taking up all the resources.

Mia turned on the shower. The water felt scalding, but she didn't turn it down. She scrubbed her skin raw, trying to wash away the feeling of the fire poker sliding through Sandra's chest.

I killed them.

The thought should have broken her. It should have sent her spiraling into a panic attack. But her mind felt cold, detached. The wall she had built against her parents was gone, replaced by something harder. Something inorganic.

She dressed in clean clothes from her stash—a pencil skirt and a blouse, trying to look like a scientist, not a killer.

She checked her phone.

Sophia: *Your car is here. You aren't. Where are you?*
Sophia: *Brian is freaking out.*
Chris: *Still on for coffee?*

Mia stared at the last text. Chris. Her sister's high school boyfriend. The coffee date she had agreed to before she was a murderer.

Going out was insane. The police were likely hunting for the "Superwoman" who destroyed a Cabela's. The remnants of the New York crew—Lucas, Bianca, and Mason—were still out there.

But staying in the lab felt like waiting in a coffin.

Mia texted Chris back: *See you in 20.*

———◇———

Cuppi Coffee was a hipster enclave of exposed brick and decently priced pastries.

Mia parked the Porsche, scanning the lot. No black Escalades. No BMWs. Just a silver McLaren Artura.

Chris was waiting by the door. He looked exactly as she remembered, only sharper—the baby fat gone, replaced by the lean, weathered look of a man who ran marathons to outrun his demons. He wore tan slacks and a polo, looking every inch the successful lawyer.

"Hey, stranger," he said, smiling.

Mia hugged him.

The smell of his cologne hit her first—sandalwood and citrus. Then, the sound.

Thump-thump. Thump-thump.

She could hear his heart. It was beating fast.

"Hi, Chris," she said, pulling back.

They ordered coffee and sat at a table by the window. Mia sat with her back to the wall, eyes scanning the parking lot.

"You look... intense," Chris said, taking a sip of his latte. "The news about the rat. Lazarus. Is that why you're so keyed up?"

"Something like that," Mia said. She touched the bandage on her forehead. "Work hazard."

"Sparring injury?" he guessed.

"Sure. Let's go with that."

Chris laughed. It was a warm sound, genuine. "I've been following you, you know. The Olympics. The research. You've had a busy twenty years."

"I keep busy to avoid thinking," Mia said. "What about you? Still saving the world one lawsuit at a time?"

"Hardly. I do estate law now. It's quiet. Pays the bills." He flicked his eyes at his cup. "Alexandria passed away last year.

Cancer."

Mia softened. "I saw that online. I'm so sorry, Chris."

"It happens," he said, his voice tight. "We didn't have kids. Just us. Now... it's just me."

Mia watched him. Her enhanced vision picked up the micro-tremors in his hand, the dilation of his pupils when he mentioned his wife. He was in pain. Real, human pain.

It felt alien to her.

"Why did you call me?" she asked.

Chris looked up. "Honestly? I saw you on TV, and you looked... lonely. Successful, brilliant, terrifying... but lonely. I figured maybe we could be lonely together for an hour."

Mia smiled. It wasn't a fake smile this time. "That's surprisingly honest."

"I'm too old for games." He leaned forward. "You seem different, Mia. Harder."

"I am different," she said. "The world changed me."

"Or maybe you changed the world." He gestured to her coffee. "You haven't touched it."

Mia eyed the black liquid. The smell was overwhelming—burnt beans and acidity. Her stomach roiled. The serum wanted calories, not caffeine.

"I'm taking a break," she said. "Didn't know it until just now."

"From coffee? You?"

"From a lot of things."

They talked for another hour. It was easy, surprisingly so. Chris was safe. He was normal. He was an anchor to a life she used to have, before rats started talking and she started leaping through skylights.

"We should do this again," Chris said as they headed toward their cars. "Dinner? Next week?"

"Dinner," Mia repeated. She thought about the lab. The waiting. The hunger.

"I'd like that," she said.

Chris hugged her again. Mia felt the warmth of his body, the steady rhythm of his pulse. For a second, she felt human.

"Call me," he said.

Mia watched him drive away.

She got into her Porsche. She flipped down the visor mirror to check her face.

She scrubbed at her forehead with her thumb. The bandage peeled away.

She froze.

The gash—the angry, red wound from the glass shard—was gone.

Whatever limit the serum had, whatever priority queue it was running... it was done. The healing was complete.

She wasn't just healed. She was erased. Every scar, every mark, every piece of history written on her skin was gone.

She looked like a blank slate.

She felt like a monster.

Mia slammed the visor shut and started the engine. She needed to get back to the lab. She needed to eat. And she needed to figure out how to get rid of the rest of the Mafia before she lost whatever humanity she had left.

Gelato

Mason

Mason woke to the smell of mildew and old iron. He tried to sit up, but his body refused.

He was strapped to a metal frame—a bed stripped of its mattress—with industrial-grade duct tape. It wound around his chest, his legs, his arms, even his forehead.

He blinked, his eyes adjusting to the gloom. The only light came from a single bulb dangling from a frayed wire, casting long, swinging shadows against the concrete walls.

He was in a basement. Or a bunker. Somewhere deep, somewhere soundproof.

Pain radiated from his left shoulder—a dull, throbbing heat where the bullet had gone in. His mouth tasted of copper and loose teeth.

"I'm going to kill you," he rasped. His voice was a wet gurgle. "I'm going to pull your teeth out one by one."

The silence stretched, broken only by the skittering of rats in the corners.

Then, the heavy steel door groaned open.

Two figures stepped into the light. Siblings... had to be. And Italian. That wasn't good. Probably related to Mia's female assistant, Sophia. Also not good. The woman looked way too similar to Sophia, but younger.

The woman was on crutches, her ankle wrapped in thick gauze. Her face was pale, but her eyes were sharp. The man looked worse—one eye swollen shut, a dark bruise blossoming across his jaw.

They didn't look angry. They looked bored.

They were eating gelato from paper cups.

"Pistachio," the man said, scraping the bottom of his cup with a pink plastic spoon. "It's surprisingly authentic for Virginia."

"The tiramisu is better," the woman said, limping closer. She leaned over Mason, her shadow falling across his face. "Less gritty."

A drop of melting cream fell from her spoon, landing on Mason's cheek. It was shockingly cold against his feverish skin.

"Get this off me," Mason snarled, straining against the tape. The metal frame creaked, but didn't give.

"He's feisty for a man with a hole in his shoulder," the man observed. He stepped up beside his sister, looking down at Mason with clinical detachment. "We know your name, Mason. We know about Dylan. We know about the whole New York crew."

Mason froze. "You don't know jack."

"We specialize in knowing," the woman said softly. "We know you were hired to snatch a scientist. We know you failed. And we know that right now, your remaining friends are probably wondering where to send the flowers."

"My friends will find you. And when they do—"

"They won't," the man interrupted. "Because they're sloppy. You were sloppy. Walking down an alley without clearing your corners? Amateur hour."

He took another bite of gelato, as if savoring every last flavor.

"Now," the man said, his tone shifting from casual to cold. "We have questions. You have answers. If the answers come quickly, we give you morphine. If they don't..." He shrugged. "We leave you with the rats."

"Go to hell."

The man sighed. He handed his cup to the woman.

He strolled to a workbench in the corner and picked up a roll of silver duct tape. He ripped off a six-inch strip. The sound was loud in the small room.

He ambled back to the bed. He didn't go for Mason's face. He went for the shoulder.

He pressed the tape directly over the bullet wound.

Mason screamed. It was a raw, animal sound that tore at his throat.

Sophia's sibling, or whoever he was, smoothed the tape down, sealing the blood inside.

"That's to keep you from bleeding out," he said calmly. "We need you alive for the conversation. But trust me, Mason... you're going to wish we had let you die."

Sophia's younger looking doppelganger licked her spoon. "Start with the buyer," she said. "Who hired you?"

Mason squeezed his eyes shut, breathing hard through the pain. He realized then that these weren't just rivals. They weren't just tough kids.

They were something much worse.

Survivor

Mia

Mia slammed a roundhouse kick into the heavy bag hanging in the corner of her office.

Thud.

The bag didn't swing. It folded around her shin, the leather groaning under the impact.

She stepped back, breathing evenly. No sweat. No fatigue. No ache in her hip flexors. She had been assaulting the bag for an hour, trying to burn off the excess energy coiling in her muscles, but it was like trying to empty the ocean with a teaspoon.

A soft knock interrupted her rhythm.

"Come in," she said, unwrapping her red gloves.

Brian opened the door a crack, peering in like he was checking on a bomb that might explode. Ever since the morning he found her amid the wreckage of her office, he moved around her with a skittish caution.

"I didn't know you brought in exercise equipment," he said, eyeing the dented bag.

"Stress relief," Mia said, grabbing a bottle of water. "What's up?"

"You might want to sit down."

Mia stayed standing. "I'm fine. Tell me."

"We have another survivor."

Mia froze. The water bottle crinkled in her grip. "Alive?"

"Alive. And alert."

"I'll be there in a minute."

Brian hesitated. "I thought you'd be excited."

"I need it to do more than just breathe, Brian. I need data. Close the door."

He nodded and withdrew.

Mia leaned against her desk. Another survivor.

It had been a month since the injection. A month of hiding in the lab, sleeping on a couch, and eating protein bars like they were Tic Tacs to feed the furnace in her gut. She had tweaked the formula a dozen times, desperate to replicate the Lazarus result without killing the host.

But this time, she hadn't tweaked it. She had used the original batch. The Lazarus batch. The batch coursing through her own veins.

She hadn't told Sophia.

Mia grabbed a towel and wiped her face, though she wasn't sweating.

The isolation was taking its toll. The psychiatrist she saw virtually once a week called it PTSD. Mia called it "remembering what it feels like to put your hand through a man's stomach."

Every time she closed her eyes, she saw the spray of blood in the sporting goods store. She felt the wet, sickening resistance of flesh giving way to her fist. She wasn't just a scientist anymore; she was a weapon. And weapons didn't belong in civilized society.

Except when she was with Chris.

They had been dating for almost a month. Coffee. Dinner. Walks in the park. He was safe. He was normal. He didn't know she could hear his heart valves opening and closing. He didn't know she could snap his spine with a hug. He was the only thing keeping her tethered to humanity.

Mia pushed off the desk. *Focus.*

She met Brian and Sophia in the main experiment room. Sophia was beaming, prancing with excitement.

"Show me," Mia said.

Brian pointed to a cage in the center of the row. Inside, a white rat sat on its haunches, grooming its whiskers. It looked... average.

"Vitals?" Mia asked.

"Normal," Brian said. "Heart rate is steady. Respiration is perfect."

"Did it die?" Mia asked. "Rigor mortis? The Lazarus effect?"

"No," Sophia said. "We have it on video. About an hour after injection, it went rigid. seized up. Like Stiff Person Syndrome. It lasted two minutes. Then it relaxed and... well, started grooming. Perhaps that's what happened to Laz, and we pronounced him dead during that two-minute period."

Her assistant's face looked pained, admitting that last sentence.

"So it didn't die," Mia murmured.

"Did the supplier get back to you?" she asked Brian. "About the batch origin?"

"Not yet," Brian admitted. "I'll follow up today."

"Do that. Ask about this one too. Country of origin, genetic markers. Maybe it's the host, not the serum."

"I can't wait to hear what you changed," Sophia said, her eyes shining. "This could be it, Mia. The breakthrough. What did you do differently?"

Mia glanced at her assistant. Sophia was brilliant, loyal, and dangerously curious. If she knew Mia had used the original lethal formula, she would start asking questions Mia couldn't answer.

"Let's get the data first," Mia deflected. "Run the maze test. See if the cognitive enhancement is there."

"You got it, boss."

"I'm going to grab a shower," Mia said, backing out of the room. "I need to clear my head."

In the small bathroom she had recently converted into a living space, Mia turned the shower to scalding. She stood under the spray, watching the water run clear.

She touched her stomach. Under the skin, her muscles were hard as iron. She hadn't aged a day in a month. Her skin was flawless. She was becoming perfect.

And it terrified her.

She stepped out of the shower and dried off. As she was pulling on a fresh blouse, her phone buzzed on the sink counter.

She glanced at the screen.

Caller ID: *Virginia Comfort Care*

Mia's heart skipped a beat—a rare, human reaction. The nursing home never called unless it was an emergency. Or the end.

She picked up the phone, her hand trembling slightly.

"This is Mia."

"Dr. Peers," a nurse said. Her voice was tight, professional. "It's about Unity. You need to come in. Immediately."

Waking Dead

Mia

Dr. Aris, the facility director, wouldn't discuss details over the phone. He insisted on a face-to-face, which usually meant one of two things: a lawsuit or a death certificate.

Mia drove to the facility with her spare Bersa 380 tucked into her waistband. It only held seven rounds, but after the Cabela's incident, she felt naked without the weight of steel against the small of her back.

She found Dr. Aris in Unity's room, staring at a wall of monitors. The room smelled of the usual cleaning carcinogens and decay, but there was a new energy in the air—the hum of machinery working overtime.

"Explain," Mia said, dropping her bag on the visitor's chair.

"I've been a neurologist for thirty years," Dr. Aris said, tapping a tablet screen. "I've never seen this."

He handed her the tablet.

Mia scanned the chart. Her eyes, sharpened by the serum, picked out the anomalies instantly.

Unity's EEG, usually a flat wasteland of delta waves indicating deep coma, was spiking. Not just random noise—patterns. Beta waves. Gamma bursts. The kind of electrical activity associated with complex thought.

"She's dreaming?" Mia asked.

"She's thinking," Dr. Aris corrected. "Look at the cardiac output. Her stroke volume is up twenty percent. Her oxygen saturation is perfect. Her body is... waking up."

Mia examined her sister. Unity still looked like a marble statue—pale, wasted, motionless. But under the skin, the engine was revving.

"When did this start?" Mia asked.

"Days ago," Aris said. "I'll have to check the exact date. But it was around 3:00 AM on a Wednesday."

Mia froze.

A Wednesday. 3:00 AM.

That was the exact moment Mia had injected herself with the serum. The moment she had hallucinated being in this very room, trapped in this very body.

"I'm not suggesting it's a miracle," the doctor said, oblivious to the ice water flooding Mia's veins. "But, whatever it is, it's unprecedented. I want to run an MRI. If the cortical activity continues to climb, we might be looking at an emergence event."

"Do it," Mia said. "But keep my parents out of it for now. I don't want to give them false hope."

"Understood. I'll leave you with her."

Dr. Aris left, closing the door softly.

Mia dragged the chair to the bedside. She sat down, her heart hammering a slow, heavy rhythm against her ribs.

She inspected Unity's hand. The hand she had tried to move in her vision.

"You felt it," Mia whispered. "Didn't you?"

The room was silent, save for the ever-rhythmic *whoosh-hiss* of the ventilator.

"I took the serum, U. I took the stuff that killed the rats. And when I went under... I was here. I was you."

She leaned forward, resting her elbows on her knees.

"Is this overflow?" she asked the silent room. "Sophia thinks the energy has to go somewhere. Maybe it didn't just go to my brain. Maybe it went to yours."

It sounded insane. Quantum entanglement? Psychic bond? Twins were supposed to have a connection, but this was biology, not magic. Unless the serum bridged the gap. Unless the genetic identity they shared was a two-way street.

"I'm changing," Mia confessed. "I healed a cut in seconds. My birthmark is gone. I can hear your heart beating from here. It sounds... strong."

She reached out and took Unity's hand. It was cool and dry, the skin papery.

"I don't know if I'm saving you or haunting you," Mia said. "But I promise, I'm going to figure it out. I have three months. Three months to fix the formula, or I lose the lab. And if I lose the lab... I can't protect you. I'll have to make *the choice*."

She squeezed her sister's hand.

"Chris is back," she added, a non-sequitur to break the tension. "Chris Holden. You remember him? The one who came to the hospital every day until leaving for college? We're getting coffee. It's... nice. Normal."

She stared at Unity's face, searching for a flicker of the sister she used to know.

"I have to go back to the lab," Mia said, standing up. "I have to make sure the new rat survives. If he does... maybe there's hope for both of us."

She leaned down and kissed Unity's forehead.

Mia turned to leave.

Behind her, the sheets rustled.

It was a tiny sound. Barely a whisper of fabric against fabric.

Mia spun around.

Unity's hand—the one Mia had just held—was no longer resting flat on the mattress.

Her pinky finger was twitching.

Twitch. Twitch.

Just like in the vision.

Mia stared, her breath catching in her throat. It wasn't a reflex. It was a signal.

"I see you," Mia whispered.

She backed out of the room, her mind reeling. She wasn't just changing herself. She was changing everything.

And she had no idea how to stop it.

CraftWorx

Brian

Brian stood before the wall of self-pour taps at CraftWorx, analyzing the digital readouts like they were lab results.

He dispensed exactly two ounces of a hazy IPA. He swirled it, checked the turbidity, and took a sip. Notes of citrus, pine, and… betrayal? No, that was just the high IBU count.

He smiled to himself, humming a flat, atonal version of "Sittin' on the Dock of the Bay."

Life was optimizing. For the first time in thirty years, the variables were aligning, despite Mia's eccentricities growing by the day. He had a job at the bleeding edge of science, and he had Bianca.

Bianca. The variable that defied all probability models.

She was beautiful, she was smart, and she didn't look at him like he was a social experiment. She liked his ideas about the tiny house. She liked *him*.

"Hey, Brian."

He turned. Sophia stood there, clutching a glass of Pinot Grigio like it was a stress ball. She looked pale, her usual maternal warmth replaced by a tight, grim line around her mouth.

"Hey, Sophia. Try tap forty-two. The fermentation profile

is—"

"Sit down, dear," she said. It wasn't a suggestion.

Brian followed her to a high-top table in the corner. A man in a Commanders hoodie sat two tables away, watching the door. Brian recognized him—Gabriele, the "cousin" Sophia had mentioned once. He looked less like a relative and more like private security.

Sophia opened her leather satchel. She didn't speak. She just slid a manila envelope across the table.

"What's this?" Brian asked.

"Data," Sophia said softly. "I know you like data."

Brian opened the envelope. He pulled out a stack of glossy 8x10 photographs. They were grainy, blown-up stills from security footage.

The first photo showed a chaotic scene inside a convenience store. Coffee pots shattering. People ducking.

In the center of the frame, a woman was throwing the pot. She was blurry, moving fast, but the profile was unmistakable. The ponytail. The posture.

"Is that... Mia?" Brian asked, his stomach tightening.

"Keep looking."

He shuffled to the next photo. It showed the victims of the coffee attack. A man and a woman on the floor, writhing in pain. The woman's face was turned toward the camera, twisted in agony, skin red and blistering.

Brian stopped breathing.

He knew that face. He had kissed that face in a parking lot three nights ago.

"Bianca," he whispered.

"Look at the timestamp," Sophia said. "This was the day of the Gainesville incident. The day Mia disappeared from the lab. The day before your girlfriend showed up to your date with a 'sunburn'."

Brian stared at the image. The data points crashed into each other, shattering his reality.

Mia is the Superwoman on the news. Bianca was hunting her.

"I don't understand," Brian stammered. "Bianca is... she's into tech. Loves tiny homes. She wants to move to California."

Sophia slid another photo across.

It was high-resolution, taken with a telephoto lens. It showed Bianca walking into a motel room. She wasn't alone. A man was with her—the same man from the convenience store floor. He had his hand on the small of her back. It wasn't a friendly touch. It was possessive.

"That's Lucas," Sophia said. "Her partner. In every sense of the word."

The beer in Brian's stomach turned to acid.

"She's not a tech enthusiast, Brian," Sophia said, her voice gentle but relentless. "She's a cleaner. She works for some people trying to steal Mia's serum. The people trying to *kill* Mia."

Brian gawked at the photos. Bianca laughing. Bianca holding a gun. Bianca screaming as Mia burned her.

He thought about the date. The wine. The way she had touched him, distracted him.

He patted his cargo pocket.

"My badge," he said, his voice hollow. "I thought I lost it."

"She stole it," Sophia confirmed instantly. "She used you to get access. She played you, Brian. I'm so sorry."

Brian glanced over at Gabriele. The man met his gaze and nodded slowly, confirming the intel.

Brian glanced down at the photo of Bianca and Lucas again.

The heartbreak hit him first, a sharp, crushing weight in his chest. But then, something else took over. The cold, hard logic that made him brilliant.

The variable was flawed. The data was corrupted.

Bianca wasn't his girlfriend. She was a contagion. And you didn't mourn a contagion. You isolated it. You neutralized it.

Brian stacked the photos neatly and slid them back into the envelope.

"She has my badge," Brian said, his voice devoid of emotion. "That means they can get in."

"Yes," Sophia said. "Which is why we need to get back to the lab."

Brian stood up. He didn't finish his beer.

"Let's go," he said. "I have some security protocols to update."

Twinning

Mia

The smell of roasted red peppers and balsamic vinegar filled the conference room, but the mood was stale.

"The new rat is impressive," Sophia said, picking at her panini. "But I'm still confused. This was a new version of the formula?"

Mia observed her team. Brian was staring at his sandwich like it was a complex equation he couldn't solve. Sophia was watching her with the intensity of a hawk circling prey.

To lie or not to lie.

"I used the same formula we gave Laz," Mia admitted. "I didn't tell you because I didn't want to discourage the team."

Sophia set her pencil down with a sharp *click*. "So we're going backward?"

"We're replicating results," Mia countered. "That's science."

"Science is transparency, Mia. A one-person team is a liability. You could have hired interns for minimum wage if you just wanted people to hold beakers."

The barb landed. Sophia was usually the peacemaker, the maternal figure. This new edge was sharp, dangerous. It reminded Mia of the woman who had suggested illegal primate testing without blinking.

"We have two survivors," Mia said, keeping her voice level. "Two successes out of a multitude of failures. We need to know *why*."

"We still don't know why it kills everything else," Sophia pointed out. "The investors gave us four months. We've burned one. If we don't have a scalable model by the deadline, you lose the lab and we lose our jobs."

"Brian," Mia said, turning to him. "Weigh in."

Brian peered at Mia. His eyes were red-rimmed, the spark gone. He had been moving around like a man wading through jelly lately, but Mia wasn't sure why.

"The scans," he said flatly. "Laz and the new one—Jaz—are identical to the dead rats. Physically. Genetically. There is no anomaly."

"Jaz?" Mia asked.

"I named him. Laz and Jaz." Brian took a bite of his sandwich, chewing mechanically.

"Cute," Mia muttered. "Just don't teach him your name."

She glanced at the whiteboard where they tracked the batches. Batch 42 (Lazarus). Batch 108 (Jaz).

"Did the supplier get back to you?" Mia asked. "About the litter origins?"

Brian glanced at Sophia.

"I called," Sophia interjected smoothly. "They don't track littermates once they're weaned. They split them for genetic diversity. Standard protocol."

Mia narrowed her eyes. Sophia answered too quickly. And standard protocol usually *did* track genetic lines to prevent inbreeding variables.

"Interesting," Mia said. "Okay. I'll look into alternative rodents. Maybe a different species."

"Like going back to the old formula?" Brian asked. "Going backward seems to be the theme."

Mia stared at him. The bitterness in his voice was new. He

was angry.

"We got a second survivor, Brian. That's progress."

Mia stood up. "Finish lunch. I have work to do."

She retreated to her office and locked the door.

She pulled the files from her desk drawer—Unity's medical records and the batch logs for the rats.

She spread them out on the floor.

Fact 1: Lazarus survived the original formula. Fact 2: Jaz survived the original formula. Fact 3: Mia survived the original formula. Fact 4: Unity began showing brain activity the moment I injected myself.

Mia paced. The "overflow" theory Sophia proposed suggested the energy had to go somewhere. If the body couldn't hold it, it went to the brain.

But what if the body *couldn't* hold it at all? What if it needed an outlet? A ground wire?

Mia scrutinized the batch logs. Rats were born in litters. Large litters.

What if Lazarus and Jaz weren't just random survivors? What if they were connected to each other?

What if the serum requires a close partner?

Mia's heart hammered against her ribs. It was a horrifying thought. A quantum entanglement of biology. One twin absorbs the energy; the other absorbs... what? Or perhaps... one twin acts as a battery for the other.

Mia had injected herself. She had survived. She had healed. She had become stronger.

And Unity... Unity had started to wake up.

"It's a circuit," Mia whispered. "We're a circuit."

She grabbed her phone and dialed the care facility.

"Dr. Aris," she said when he picked up. "It's Mia. I need you to check something on Unity's chart."

"Dr. Peers, I was just about to call you."

"Is she worse?"

"No," Aris said, his voice trembling with excitement. "If

she weren't in a coma, I would swear she preparing for the Olympics."

Mia dropped the phone.

The circuit was live.

Jiffy Lube Live

Mia

T he amphitheater was a cauldron of noise and body heat. Twenty-five thousand people packed the Jiffy Lube Live arena, a sea of flannel shirts and cowboy boots undulating under the overcast Virginia sky.

To an ordinary person, it was a concert. To Mia, it was a sensory strike.

The bass from the speakers didn't just thump; it rattled her teeth. The smell of stale beer, vape smoke, and ten thousand different body odors hit her like a chemical weapon.

She adjusted the earplugs Chris had insisted on buying her. They barely dulled the roar.

"You okay?" Chris shouted over the opening riff of a Blake Shelton song.

"Peachy!" Mia shouted back, forcing a smile.

She glanced down at her outfit—tight jeans, plaid shirt, boots. She looked like every other woman here. She felt ridiculous. She looked ordinary.

But she wasn't.

Under the denim, her muscles were coiled tight enough to snap steel. She could hear the conversation of the couple three rows back (they were arguing about a babysitter). She could track the erratic heartbeat of the security guard twenty feet away (high blood pressure).

She was a tiger hiding in a herd of cattle.

"I know you hate country," Chris said, leaning close so she could hear him without shouting. "My dad used to say if you play a country song backward, you get your wife, your truck, and your dog back."

Mia laughed. It felt good. "I'm just here for the company."

"Liar. You're here because I bribed you with a promise of silence tomorrow."

He took her hand. His palm was warm, rough from weekend yard work. It anchored her. When he touched her, the sensory overload dialed back. The noise faded. The smells dulled. He was a grounding wire for her overcharged system.

They stood in the aisle, swaying as the tempo slowed. The lights dipped, bathing the crowd in a soft, purple glow. The singer started crooning about "Sangria."

Mia watched Chris. He was looking at the stage, but his thumb was tracing circles on the back of her hand. He seemed younger tonight, the weight of his grief lifted by the music and the crowd.

"You're thinking too loud," Mia said.

Chris glanced down at her. "What?"

"I can hear the gears turning," she teased. "Spit it out."

He squeezed her hand. "I was just thinking... this is nice. Being here. With you."

"It is nice."

"I haven't done this in a long time," Chris admitted. "Alexandria... she hated crowds. We stopped going out years before she got sick."

"I'm not Alexandria," Mia said softly.

"I know." Chris turned fully toward her, blocking out the rest of the arena. "You're terrifyingly present, Mia. You make everything else seem... quiet."

Mia's breath hitched. If only he knew.

"Is that a bad thing?" she asked.

"No. It's exactly what I need."

The song swelled into the chorus. Around them, couples were slow-dancing, losing themselves in the moment.

Mia stepped closer. She could hear his heart rate pick up. *Thump-thump. Thump-thump.*

"So," she whispered, looking up at him. "Are we going to stand here like awkward teenagers, or are you going to kiss me?"

Chris's eyes widened slightly. Then, he smiled—a slow, authentic smile that made Mia's own heart skip a beat.

"I was working up to it," he said.

He leaned down.

Mia met him halfway. She had to be careful. She had to be gentle. She was strong enough to crush him, fast enough to break him. She dialed everything back, focusing on being soft, being human.

His lips were warm. He tasted of mint and anticipation.

The kiss was slow, tentative at first, then deeper. Mia closed her eyes. For a moment, the roaring crowd vanished. The sensory data stream shut off. There was just Chris. Just the pressure of his hand on her waist, the scruff of his jaw against her cheek.

He pulled back, breathless.

"Your lips don't taste like sangria," he whispered.

Mia laughed, a genuine, bubbling sound. "I would hope not. We're both sober, remember?"

"Accountability partners," Chris said, resting his forehead against hers.

"We better be more than that," Mia said.

She wrapped her arms around him, burying her face in his chest. She listened to his heart—steady, strong, reliable.

For the first time in months, the hunger in her gut was quiet.

The rage was dormant.

She wasn't a monster tonight. She was just a woman at a concert, holding onto a good man.

But as the song ended and the applause crashed over them like a wave, Mia opened her eyes. Over Chris's shoulder, she scanned the crowd.

Old habits. Predator habits.

She saw a flash of movement near the exit tunnel. A man in a dark jacket, moving against the flow of traffic. He wasn't watching the stage. He was watching her.

Mia stiffened.

"What is it?" Chris asked, pulling back to look at her.

"Nothing," Mia lied, smoothing her expression. "Just... thought I saw someone I knew."

She squeezed his hand tighter. The moment of peace was over. The world was loud again.

And the hunters were back.

Naked and Unafraid

Mason

Mason woke to the familiar sensation of freezing cold metal against his bare skin.

He tried to open his eyes, but they were glued shut. Sticky. Sugary. The smell of pistachio gelato filled his nostrils, masking the underlying stench of mildew and blood.

He strained against the bindings. Duct tape still wrapped his chest, arms, and legs to the rusted bed frame. He was naked, exposed, and shivering violently.

"Get this off me!" he roared, his voice cracking.

He wrenched his head to the side, dislodging the gelato from his left eye. Light flooded in—a dim, yellow bulb swaying overhead.

He examined himself. His body was a roadmap of bruises, centered around the angry, red patch where Gabriele had taped his gunshot wound shut.

"You perverts!"

He tested the bindings. The metal frame groaned, but held. He was strong, but leverage was against him.

From beyond the heavy steel door, he heard sounds. Laughter. Applause. The electronic ding of a game show. *Family Feud*.

They were watching TV while he bled out.

"Hey!" he bellowed. "When I get out of here, I'm going to squeeze your skulls until they pop!"

The laughter abruptly stopped. Footsteps approached. The lock tumbled.

The siblings stepped into the room. The woman leaned on her crutch, looking bored. The young male held a fresh cup of gelato. His eye was healing.

"That's not nice, Mason," the man said. "We saved your life. Twice. And now you're interrupting the lightning round."

"Steve Harvey is a national treasure," the female added. She limped to the bedside, looking down at him with clinical detachment.

"You think this is funny?" Mason spat. A glob of bloody phlegm landed on The woman's boot.

She didn't flinch. She just grinned at the spit, then back at his face.

"You're naked, taped to a bed in a soundproof bunker, and bleeding internally," she said softly. "I think it's hilarious."

She drew a knife from her belt. It was a stiletto, thin and wicked. She traced the tip down his chest, stopping just above his navel.

"Now," she said. "Let's try this again. Who hired you?"

"Go to hell."

She pressed the tip of the blade into his skin. A bead of blood welled up. "We're already there, Mason. We're just the tour guides."

"I don't know!" Mason grunted, arching his back against the pain. "I'm hired muscle. Dylan handled the contract."

"Dylan is dead," the man said, stepping closer. "Mia put her hand through his stomach. Did you know she could do that?"

Mason froze. "That's impossible."

"Is it?" he smirked. "You saw the video of the rat. You know what she's making. And now, your boss is dead, your crew is scattered, and you're the only loose end left."

"If I talk, I'm dead," Mason rasped.

"If you don't talk," the woman said, moving the knife to his eye, "you're going to wish you were dead."

She hovered the blade millimeters from his pupil. Mason stopped breathing. He could see the reflection of his own terror in the steel.

"A woman," Mason whispered. "The buyer is a woman."

"Name?"

"I don't have a name! I swear! But she used a proxy. A messenger. A suit named Arjun."

The woman pulled the knife back and gaped at her partner.

"Arjun," the man repeated. "Mia's liaison?"

"I don't know," Mason said, the words tumbling out now. "He met Dylan in DC. Gave us the files. Gave us the schedule for the investor meeting. He said... someone wanted the serum before the board pulled the plug."

His captors stayed silent.

"I told you everything," Mason pleaded. "Now give me a blanket. It's fucking *freezing* in here."

The man nodded slowly. "Inside job. Sophia isn't going to like this."

"Gabriele! You fool! You just confirmed for him—"

"And you just gave him mine," Gabriele shrugged. "Honestly, Alessia. You know it doesn't matter."

Alessia sheathed her knife. She picked up a bottle of water from the workbench.

She took a long drink, watching him. Then, she upended the bottle over his face.

Water poured into his nose and mouth. Mason sputtered, choking, trying to catch the drops on his tongue.

"That's for the spit," Alessia said.

She turned and sauntered to the door. Gabriele followed.

"Hey!" Mason shouted. "The blanket!"

"No buyer name, no fuzzy blanket," Gabriele said. "Besides. We'll cover your body when you're dead. Won't be long now. Promise."

The heavy door slammed shut, sealing Mason back in the dark with the rats and his despair.

Forgiveness

Mia

Like the concert, the church was a sensory minefield. Mia sat in the third row, gripping the pew until her knuckles turned white.

The worship band was playing a chord progression that clanged in her skull. The drummer's kick pedal felt like a physical blow to her chest.

To the rest of the congregation, it was a Sunday service. To Mia, it was an AC/DC performance.

She adjusted the high collar of her floral dress, trying to hide the fact that the fabric felt like sandpaper against her heightened nerve endings. Chris sat beside her, wearing jeans and a yellow button-down, looking relaxed. Normal as ever.

Mia felt like a wolf trying to pass for a golden retriever.

The music faded, and the pastor took the stage. He was a young man with a wireless mic and an earnest expression.

The message was as boring as Mia feared it would be and she snuck a peek at the large clock with bright red numbers on the back wall. But then Pastor Jack said, "Forgiveness." His voice amplified through the speakers. "It's not just a gift you give to others. It's a gift you give to yourself."

Mia whipped her head around, glaring at the man of God on

the stage.

Forgiveness.

The word tasted like ash.

She thought about the tire shop. The mechanic dying on the floor. She thought about Sandra, pinned to the ground with a fire poker. She thought about Dylan, staring down at the hole in his stomach where her hand had been.

Could you forgive that? Could you forgive yourself for becoming a weapon?

"God wants you to be free," the pastor continued. "But you can't be free if you're holding onto the guilt of what you've done. You have to give it to Him."

Mia's heart hammered against her ribs. *Thump-thump. Thump-thump.* It was so loud she was sure the man in the Ravens hat in front of them could hear it.

She wasn't free. She was bound by a chemical chain reaction. She was tethered to her sister by a biological wire. And she was hunted by people who would be more than happy to cut her open and see how she ticked.

"Amen," Chris whispered beside her.

Mia swallowed bile. She needed to get out.

Twenty minutes later, they were seated at a quiet café down the street.

Mia attacked her turkey avocado sandwich like she hadn't eaten in a week. The serum demanded fuel. She tore into the bread, chewing rapidly, ignoring the crumbs falling onto the table.

Chris watched her, sipping a soda. He seemed serious. The playful banter from the concert a fading memory.

"Okay," Mia said, wiping her mouth. "What was that? You take a girl to a country concert on Friday and a sermon on Sunday? That's quite the pivot."

"You wanted to know me," Chris said. "This is me. Faith is... it's the only reason I'm still here."

"The only reason?" Mia paused, a piece of turkey halfway to her mouth. "That sounds heavy."

"It is." Chris leaned back. "I never told you the whole truth about Alexandria. About the end."

Mia put the sandwich down. Her enhanced hearing picked up the tremor in his voice before he even spoke.

"You told me she died of cancer."

"She did. But before that... we were a disaster, Mia. I was a disaster." Chris ran a hand through his hair. "I married her because she was beautiful. Shallow, right? Just like high school. I wanted the trophy. But trophies don't talk back. We fought constantly. About money. About kids. About nothing."

He glanced out the window at the passing cars.

"I served her divorce papers the day before she got the diagnosis. I wanted out. I was done."

Mia went still. She knew that feeling—the cold detachment of cutting someone loose. She had done it to Music Man. She had done it to Husband One.

"She came home and told me she had Stage 4," Chris continued. "And I felt... trapped. I stayed because I had to, not because I wanted to. And I hated myself for it. That's when the drinking started. Really started."

"Chris..."

"I was drunk at her funeral," he admitted. "I stood there, accepting condolences, and I couldn't feel anything except the whiskey burning a hole in my stomach. I wanted to die, Mia. I thought about driving my car into a bridge abutment every single day for six months."

Mia reached across the table and took his hand. His skin was warm. Human. Flawed.

"What stopped you?"

"My boss took me to that church," Chris said. "I heard a sermon about forgiveness. Not for the people who hurt us, but for the people *we* hurt. For ourselves." He squeezed her hand.

"I had to forgive myself for not loving her enough. For wishing she was gone. It's a daily process."

Mia studied him. He wasn't just a lawyer in a nice shirt. He was a survivor. He carried scars, just like she did. But his scars were healed by faith. Hers were healed by a serum that erased her history.

"I'm glad you're still here," Mia said softly.

"Me too." He stared at her, his eyes searching hers. "I see it in you, Mia. The weight. You carry something heavy. I don't know what it is—the lab, your sister, your parents—but you don't have to carry it alone."

Mia pulled her hand back. The connection was too intense. If she told him the truth—*I killed three people, and I can hear your heart beating*—he would run. Or he would try to save her. And she couldn't be saved.

"I have a lot of regrets," Mia said, deflecting. "But I handle them differently. I work."

"Work is good," Chris allowed. "But it's not peace."

He checked his watch.

"I have a surprise," he said, changing the subject. "For later this month. During lunch."

"A surprise?"

"I want to take you somewhere. It's related to all this." He gestured vaguely at the air. "I think it might help make sense of things."

"Okay," Mia said, forcing a smile. "I'm game."

They cleared the table. Mia finished the last of her sandwich in two bites, the hunger still gnawing at her.

As they headed to their cars, Mia thought about forgiveness.

It was a nice concept. A pretty idea for Sunday mornings. But forgiveness didn't stop bullets. It didn't fix comas. And it didn't keep the monsters at bay.

Sometimes, you didn't need forgiveness. You needed ammunition.

No Secrets in a Tiny Home

Bianca

The "Live Big Tiny Homes" lot was a graveyard of minimalist dreams, parked in neat rows under the Virginia sun.

Bianca squeezed Brian's knee as he steered the car into a gravel space. She felt the familiar knot of guilt in her stomach, tighter than usual.

Since the massacre at Cabela's, the crew was decimated. Dylan, Ethan, and Sandra were dead. Mason was missing. It was just her and Lucas now, pulling double shifts watching the lab, terrified that the "Superwoman" who put her fist through Dylan's stomach would come for them next.

And here she was, playing house with the assistant.

"We're here," Brian said. His voice was flat, devoid of the nervous energy he usually radiated.

He led her to a model called "The Rustic"—a brown shed on wheels with a flower box that looked like an afterthought.

They stepped inside. The air was stifling, smelling of sawdust and chemical sealant.

"It's... really cozy," Bianca lied, suppressing a wave of claustrophobia.

"It's efficient," Brian corrected. "Everything has a purpose.

No wasted space. No hidden corners."

He showed her the combo washer-dryer, the fold-out table, the composting toilet that was uncomfortably close to the kitchen sink. Bianca nodded along, her mind racing. She still had his keycard. She should have used it days ago, but Lucas was spooked. He wanted a plan before they breached the lab.

"Let's check the loft," Brian said.

He pulled a latch, revealing a ladder. He climbed up, his movements precise. Bianca followed, her skirt bunching around her thighs.

The loft was a cramped crawlspace with a mattress and a skylight. Brian lay down, staring up at the glass. Bianca crawled in beside him. There was barely enough room to breathe.

She put a leg over his lap, leaning in close. This was the routine. Distract him. Keep him hooked.

"I bet you can see a lot of stars from here," she whispered, running her hand up his chest.

She went to kiss him.

He turned his head away.

"You're not who you say you are," Brian said.

Bianca froze. Her hand stopped mid-caress. "What?"

Brian turned back to look at her. His eyes were cold, analytical. "You're not a tech enthusiast. You're not an aspiring actress. You're a cleaner."

Bianca's heart hammered against her ribs. She pulled back, hitting her head on the low ceiling. "Brian, that's crazy. Who told you that?"

"Data," Brian said. "Sophia showed me the photos. The convenience store. The motel with Lucas."

Bianca scrambled backward, her head pressing against the angled ceiling. She was trapped in a plywood box with a man who knew everything.

"Brian, I can explain."

"No talking. One finger for yes, two for no," Brian said,

his voice monotone. "You work for people trying to steal the serum."

Bianca hesitated. She glanced at the ladder. Too far.

She raised one finger.

"You stole my badge."

One finger.

"You were planning to use it to break into the lab."

One finger.

"Good," Brian said. "The variables align."

"Brian," Bianca whispered, tears pricking her eyes—real tears this time. "I didn't want to hurt you. I... I started to care. Really."

"Irrelevant," Brian said. "Feelings are variables I can't control. But I can control the outcome."

He sat up, ignoring the cramped space. He studied her, his expression shifting from cold to something darker. Something tired.

"Mia is dangerous," he said. "You saw what she did at the store. She killed your friends. She's not a scientist anymore. She's a demon. And she's making more of it."

"Good," Bianca said. "Our customer wants it."

"You can't stop her," Brian said. "Not from the outside. But you have the badge."

Bianca blinked. "You... you want me to use it?"

"I want this to end," Brian said. "I want the serum destroyed. I want the lab burned down. I want to go to California and live in a box and never think about rats or resurrection again."

He reached into his pocket and pulled out a folded piece of paper. He handed it to her.

"Mia sleeps in her office from 3:00 AM to 6:00 AM. That's your window. The alarms are silent, but they trigger a notification to... my phone."

Bianca took the paper. Her hands were shaking. "Why are you doing this?"

"Because I can't stop her," Brian said softly. "But you can."

He lay back down, staring at the skylight.

"Keep the badge, Bianca. Come to the lab. Bring Lucas. Just make sure when you leave... you finish it."

But as they drove away from the Live Big Tiny Homes lot, Bianca couldn't shake the feeling that something was off. Way off. And that Brian's proposal wasn't a tiny lie. It was a big lie.

Shelter

Mia

The soup kitchen smelled of pasta sauce, body odor, and despair.

Mia stood behind the serving line, ladling noodles onto Styrofoam plates. The steam rising from the pot was hot against her face, but she barely felt it. Her skin, reinforced by the serum, registered the temperature as a mild warmth.

It had been almost four months since the board meeting. Four months of watching rats die. Four months of tweaking the formula, adjusting the viral vectors, and failing.

Laz and Jaz were still alive, thriving in their cages, a constant reminder of what success looked like. But they were outliers. Every other rat—hundreds of them—had perished. The twin theory, the "circuit" idea, was sound in principle, but the application was elusive.

Mia scanned the line of people shuffling past. Hollow eyes. Cracked hands. They were hungry for food. She was hungry for answers.

"You okay?" Chris asked beside her. He was pouring sauce with a rhythmic efficiency, smiling at every person who passed.

"I'm fine," Mia said. "Just... thinking."

"About the lab?"

"Always."

"You needed a break," Chris said gently. "You were driving yourself crazy. And probably driving Brian and Sophia crazy too."

"They're resilient," Mia muttered. She scooped another ladle of noodles.

She watched Chris. He was different here. In the office, he was a lawyer—sharp, guarded. Here, he was open. He touched people on the shoulder. He looked them in the eye. He treated the homeless veterans and the struggling mothers with a dignity they rarely received.

It made Mia's chest ache. She was a killer. And here was Chris, serving noodles on a Tuesday, trying to save the world one plate at a time.

"Why do you do this?" she asked quietly.

"I told you," Chris said, handing a plate to a man in a tattered army jacket. "It helps me."

"You help people for a living."

"I get paid to argue for a living. This is different. This is real."

A man tapped Chris on the shoulder. He was older, with a face like worn leather and eyes that had seen too much.

"Hey, Chuck," Chris said, wiping his hands on his apron.

"Got a minute when you're done?" Chuck asked. His voice was raspy, like he'd swallowed smoke.

"Always. I'll stop by the office."

They finished the shift in silence. The line finally dwindled, the last of the pots scraped clean.

Mia followed Chris to the director's office. It was a closet, really—cramped, smelling of coffee and old paper. The ceiling tiles were stained brown from a leak that had probably started during the Reagan administration.

Chuck sat behind a metal desk that looked like it had been salvaged from a dump. He pushed a manila envelope toward Chris.

"I hate to ask," Chuck said. "But the city is breathing down my neck. Zoning ordinances. They want to shut us down."

Chris opened the envelope. He scanned the documents, his brow furrowing.

"They're citing code violations," Chris murmured. "Sewage line capacity. Fire exits."

"I can't pay you," Chuck said. "I barely pay the electric bill."

"Don't worry about it," Chris said, sliding the papers into his back pocket. "This is right up my alley. I'll handle it."

"You're a good man, Chris."

"I'm just a lawyer with a guilt complex," Chris joked. He shook Chuck's hand. "We'll fix this."

As they made their way to Chris's truck, Mia was silent. Her brain was buzzing, but not with the usual serum-induced static. It was something else. A connection.

"What?" Chris asked, unlocking the truck.

"You said something in there," Mia said slowly. "About the case being right up your alley."

"Yeah? It's an expression."

"Alley," Mia whispered. "Alleles."

"Bless you?"

"No, Chris. Alleles. Genetic variants." Mia's eyes widened. Her enhanced brain spun the data, connecting dots she hadn't seen before. "The rats. The twins. It's not just about sharing a womb. It's about the specific allelic variation in the immune response genes. The serum triggers a cytokine storm in the unmatched subjects. But if the alleles match... if the genetic key fits the lock..."

"I have no idea what you're talking about," Chris said, starting the engine. "But you look like you just won the lottery."

"Better," Mia said. "I think I just figured out how to stop killing them."

She gazed at Chris. The sunlight caught the gray in his hair, the lines around his eyes. He was so painfully, beautifully human.

"If this works," Mia said, "if I get the funding... I'm going to build Chuck a new facility. A real one."

"I'm holding you to that," Chris said, pulling out of the lot.

"Hold me to whatever you want," Mia said, her mind already racing back to the lab. "Just get me to my microscope."

Least Favorite Mistake

Alessia

Alessia limped into the bunker, the rubber tip of her single crutch striking the concrete with a dull, rhythmic *thud*.

She had hurt her foot again kicking a brick wall in another fit of rage arguing with Gabriele.

Mason was awake. He was staring at the ceiling, his breathing shallow and ragged. The newest duct tape bandages on his body were soaked through, dark, wet patches against his pale skin.

How the man was still alive, Alessia had no idea.

"Che piacere," Alessia said, her voice devoid of humor.

She leaned against the wall, taking the weight off her injured foot. Every step was a negotiation with pain. This op had broken her body, but the last few months of babysitting this meathead had broken her patience.

"Are you ready to escape today?" she asked. "The door is unlocked. Please. Make a run for it. Give me a reason."

Mason turned his head slowly. His eyes were sunken, rimmed with red. He looked like a man who had made peace with dying.

"Pathetic," Alessia spat. "Whoever hired you made a bad investment."

Mason chuckled. It was a wet, bubbling sound.

"Investment," he wheezed. "Funny."

Gabriele stepped into the room. He looked tired.

"He's still bleeding from the latest round of being an asshole," Gabriele observed. "Lucky us."

Mason laughed again. He scowled at Alessia, his eyes mocking. "You broke your foot because of me," he rasped. "And you still refuse to kill me."

Alessia snapped.

The professional veneer—the cold, Italian detachedness she had cultivated since childhood—shattered.

She dropped the crutch. She lunged at the bed.

She drove her fist into his wounds.

Mason screamed, his body arching against the restraints. Blood welled up around her knuckles, hot and sticky.

"Alessia!" Gabriele shouted, grabbing her arm.

She thrashed, her ribs screaming, but she didn't stop. She punched Mason in the stomach, then the face.

"Die!" she screamed. "Just die, you useless piece of garbage! You know nothing! You are nothing!"

Gabriele hauled her back, pinning her arms to her sides. "Alessia, stop! You're killing him!"

"Let him die!" she panted, her chest heaving. "He's a dead end, Gabriele. He gave us Arjun. That's all he has. We're wasting time in this hole while Sophia is alone out there."

She glared at Mason. He was moaning, blood trickling from his nose and the reopened wounds.

"We need to get back to the lab. We need to protect Sophia."

Gabriele released her. He eyed Mason, then at the blood on the floor.

"We can't just leave him," he said.

"Why not?" Alessia wiped her bloody hand on her pants. "He's not going anywhere. Look at him. He'll be dead in two days from sepsis anyway."

"Mother wants him alive."

"Mother isn't here," Alessia snapped. "I am. And I am making a command decision. We are leaving."

She picked up her crutch.

"We go back to the hotel," she said. "We shower. We eat real food. And then we go help Sophia. If Mason survives, fine. If not... problem solved."

Gabriele hesitated. He regarded the prisoner like he was calculating the odds. Finally, he nodded.

"Fine."

He went to the bed and checked the bindings one last time. He added fresh strips of tape around Mason's arms.

"Don't go anywhere," Gabriele said.

They exited, leaving the single bulb burning overhead.

Alessia paused at the heavy steel door. She glanced back at Mason one last time.

"I hope the rats get hungry," she whispered.

She slammed the door and threw the deadbolt.

Waves

Mia

The beach at Assateague Island was a desolate strip of white sand and crashing waves, bitten by a forty-degree wind coming off the Atlantic.

Mia zipped her jacket to her chin. To a regular human, the cold would be biting. To her, it was just data—ambient temperature forty-two degrees, wind speed fifteen knots. Her body adjusted instantly, rerouting blood flow to her extremities.

She watched Chris. He was huddled in a low beach chair, bundled in a parka and a sun hat, reading a Louis L'Amour paperback. He looked ridiculous and comforting all at once.

It had been months since the massacre at the sporting goods store. Months of therapy sessions where she lied about why she couldn't sleep. Months of scrubbing her hands, trying to get the phantom sensation of Dylan's internal organs off her skin.

The ocean helped. The relentless noise of the surf drowned out the memories.

"Ready to go?" Chris asked, marking his page.

"No. Finish your chapter. I want to see the sunset."

Mia stood up. She needed to move. The energy in her muscles was a constant hum, a coiled spring waiting to snap.

She strolled toward the water line, her phone buzzing in her pocket. She pulled it out, intending to silence it.

Subject: FDA Notice of Action - NDA 2035-004 (Moratusom)

Mia froze.

Her thumb hovered over the screen. It had been eleven months. This was it. The verdict on her life's work before the serum took over. If *Moratusom* failed, she was financially ruined. If it passed... she had resources. She had power.

She opened the email. Her eyes scanned the dense legalese, skipping to the bottom.

...we have completed our review of this application, as amended. It is approved, effective on the date of this letter...

Approved.

The word hit her like a physical blow.

Mia dropped the phone into her pocket. A laugh bubbled up from her chest, raw and unbidden.

She started to run.

She didn't mean to sprint. But the joy, the relief, the sheer kinetic energy of the moment took over. She pushed off the sand, and the world blurred.

The wind roared in her ears. The dunes whipped past like a film reel on fast forward. She wasn't running; she was skimming the surface of the earth.

She reached the end of the beach in seconds—a distance that should have taken minutes.

She stopped, skidding in the wet sand, and spun around. She screamed into the wind, a primal shout of victory.

"Yes!"

She dropped to her knees, the adrenaline crash hitting her hard. Tears—hot, human tears—spilled over. She buried her face in her hands, sobbing.

Footsteps pounded behind her.

"Mia!"

Chris was running toward her, his face pale with worry. He reached her, dropping to his knees in the surf.

"What is it? Are you hurt?"

Mia grabbed him, pulling him down into a hug. She buried her face in his neck, soaking his parka with tears.

"It's approved," she choked out. "The FDA. They approved it."

Chris went still. Then he squeezed her tight, lifting her off the sand. "Oh my god. Mia. That's... that's incredible."

He pulled back, framing her face with his hands. "I'm so proud of you."

Mia laughed through her tears, handing him her phone. He read the email, grinning like a fool.

"Let's celebrate," he said. "Dinner. Champagne. The works."

"No champagne," Mia reminded him, wiping her eyes. "But dinner sounds good."

They headed back to the truck, the sun dipping below the horizon, painting the sky in bruises of purple and orange.

As Chris unlocked the doors, he paused, surveying the stretch of beach she had just covered.

"Mia," he said slowly. "How fast did you run that?"

"What?"

"I was watching you," Chris said. He wasn't smiling. "One second you were by the chairs. The next, you were... gone. It was like watching a video skip."

Mia's heart skipped a beat. She had been careless.

"The light is tricky out here," she said, forcing a laugh. "And I was a track star, remember? I still have some kick left."

"No," Chris said, shaking his head. "I ran track in high school. That wasn't track speed. You were... blurring."

Mia opened the passenger door. She needed to shut this down. Now.

"You need to get your eyes checked, old man," she teased, poking him in the ribs. "Low light and small print are getting to you."

Chris studied her. He didn't look convinced. But he let it go.

"Maybe," he said. "Or maybe you're just Superwoman."

Mia froze. The nickname the press had given the killer in the sporting goods store.

"Come on," she said, her voice a little too sharp. "You have a girlfriend to impress with a celebration dinner."

Chris blinked. The tension broke. A slow smile spread across his face.

"Girlfriend?"

Mia reached out and grabbed the lapels of his jacket, pulling him in for a kiss. It was fierce, possessive, a claim staked in the sand.

"Yes," she whispered against his lips. "Girlfriend."

Chris wrapped his arms around her, lifting her against the truck.

Mia held on tight. She had the FDA approval. She had the money. She had the man.

But as she looked over his shoulder at the darkening beach, she knew the truth. She wasn't Superwoman. She was something else entirely. And she was running out of time to hide it.

Tournament

Mia

M ia bounced on the balls of her feet, the mat yielding slightly under her weight.

The arena noise—the cheers, the whistles, the slap of flesh on pads—was a dull roar in her ears. Her focus was absolute. Time seemed to stretch, the seconds elongating until the referee's hand signal looked like it was moving through molasses.

Her opponent, a woman ten years her junior with a fierce scowl and a black belt, lunged.

To the crowd, it was a lightning-fast strike. To Mia, it was a telegraphed plea for a concussion.

She saw the shift in the woman's weight, the rotation of the hip, the extension of the leg. Mia didn't block. She slipped inside the guard, her movement a blur of efficiency.

She cocked her fist.

The urge to let go—to unleash the energy coiling in her shoulder—was intoxicating. It would be so easy. One strike to the solar plexus. One strike to end it.

But she remembered the tire shop. She remembered the sickening wet sound of her hand passing through Dylan.

Mia pulled the punch. She transformed a lethal blow into a scoring tap, her fist grazing the woman's chest protector with barely a pound of force.

"Point!" the referee shouted.

The buzzer sounded. Game over.

Mia bowed. She didn't feel triumphant. She felt like a tiger forced to play with a ball of yarn. She had fulfilled the pact with Unity—she had conquered the sport—but the victory tasted like ash. She wasn't an athlete anymore. She was a predator pretending to be prey.

She trotted toward the locker room, pretending to wipe sweat from her neck.

A flash of movement in the stands caught her eye.

High up, near the exit tunnel, a woman with dark hair stood motionless in the sea of cheering fans. She wasn't clapping. She was watching.

Sophia?

Mia blinked, her enhanced vision trying to lock on. But a group of fans stood up, blocking her line of sight. When they sat down, the woman was gone.

Mia shivered. It wasn't the air conditioning. It was the feeling of eyes on her back, a sensation she hadn't been able to shake since the Cabela's massacre.

The rain turned the world into a gray smear against the windshield of Chris's truck.

Mia eyed the wipers beat a hypnotic rhythm—*thwack-hiss, thwack-hiss*. She was exhausted, not from the tournament, but from the effort of pretending to be normal for three hours.

Chris drove with one hand on the wheel, the other resting warmly over hers on the center console.

"You barely broke a sweat," he said, breaking the silence.

"Good conditioning," Mia murmured.

"You looked... bored."

"I'm retiring," she said. "That was the last one. I promised myself I'd win it for Unity, and I did. Now it's done."

Chris squeezed her hand. "What's next? The Olympics again?"

"No. Just the lab."

The mood in the cab shifted. The lab was the third wheel in their relationship—a silent, demanding presence that consumed Mia's nights and secrets.

"When are you going to sleep at home?" Chris asked softly.

"Soon," Mia lied. "We're close. I have one more thing to run. A genetic variation. If it works..."

"If it works, you save the world," Chris finished. "I know. But you can't save the world if you burn yourself out."

He pulled the truck up to the security gate of the industrial park. The rain drummed on the roof, a relentless staccato.

"You want to come in?" Mia asked, trying to keep the desperation out of her voice. "Celebrate the win?"

Chris glanced at her. The dashboard lights cast shadows across his face, highlighting the lines of worry around his eyes.

"I want to," he said. "But I don't think that's what you need right now. You're itching to get back inside. I can feel it."

Mia glared at the looming brick building. He was right. The allele theory was burning a hole in her brain. She needed to test the new batch. She needed to know if she had fixed the flaw or if she was just a monster making more monsters.

"I'm complicated," she whispered.

"I like complicated."

Chris put the truck in park. He turned to her, unbuckling his seatbelt.

"Mia."

"Yeah?"

"I love you."

The words hung in the damp air, heavy and absolute.

Mia's breath hitched. She had been waiting for this, dreading it, craving it. She didn't deserve this man.

"Say something," Chris said, a nervous smile touching his lips.

Mia didn't speak. She lunged.

She grabbed his face, pulling him in. The kiss wasn't gentle. It was fierce, a collision of need and fear. She kissed him like it was the last time, like she was trying to imprint his humanity onto her own DNA.

Chris groaned, wrapping his arms around her, pulling her across the console. The rain hammered the roof, sealing them in a private world of heat and breath.

Mia pulled back, her forehead resting against his. Her heart was racing—*thump-thump, thump-thump*—syncing with his.

"I love you too," she whispered.

She meant it. It terrified her, but she meant it.

Chris kissed her again, softer this time. "Go. Save the world. Then come home to me."

"I will."

Mia grabbed her gym bag and opened the door. The cold rain hit her instantly, soaking her blouse. She ran to the lab entrance, her keycard already in hand.

She paused at the door, looking back. Chris's truck was still there, idling in the mist, taillights glowing red.

The warmth of his confession was there, a shield against the cold.

Mia swiped her card. The lock buzzed.

She stepped into the darkness of the lab. The warmth faded, replaced by the sterile chill of science. She had a love to fight for now. But first, she had a rat to save.

Taking Care of Business

Mia

Mia sat at the head of the conference table, her hands clasped so tightly together the flow of blood to them had stopped.

On the screen, the investors in Falls Church were discussing Q4 projections for a subsidiary she had never heard of. It had been forty minutes. They were ignoring her.

"I feel like I'm waiting for the warden to throw the switch," Mia muttered.

To her left, Sophia tapped a pen against her legal pad, a rhythmic *click-click-click* that echoed in Mia's enhanced ears like a metronome of doom. To her right, Brian sat motionless, staring at the screen with the dead-eyed focus of a man who had seen too much.

"And that brings us to Dr. Peers," Arjun said finally.

The room on the screen went silent. Twelve heads turned toward the camera.

"Mia," Arjun said. "Can you hear us?"

"Loud and clear," Mia said. She resisted the urge to say *I can hear your heartbeat through the microphone.*

"We apologize for the delay. We felt it was important you understand the broader financial picture before we... address your situation."

Mia's stomach dropped. *Here it comes.* The axe. The lawsuit. The end of the lab.

"As you can imagine," Arjun continued, "we saw the FDA's decision regarding *Moratusom.*"

Mia braced herself. She expected them to claim ownership. To say the sleep drug belonged to them because they presently funded the lab that birthed it.

Instead, the room erupted.

The investors stood up. All twelve of them. They were clapping.

"Congratulations, Dr. Peers," Telita Johnson said, actually smiling. "It's a monumental achievement."

Mia blinked. The applause washed over her, surreal and disorienting.

It triggered a memory, sharp and unbidden.

High school auditorium. Senior year. The air smelled of floor wax and cheap perfume.

Mia sat in the front row, waiting for her name. "Student of the Year," Mr. Littlejohn had whispered. A guarantee.

She glanced back at her parents. They were in the middle section. They weren't looking at the stage. Their heads were bent together over a phone, their faces illuminated by the blue glow of a screen.

When her name was called, Mia hurried up the stairs. She stumbled, her heel catching on the carpet. The audience laughed. Her parents didn't look up.

Unity would have been paying attention. The pact. Always support each other to the very end. That's what they had promised each other.

Mia shook the memory away. She forced a smile at the camera.

"Thank you," she said. "It's... been a long road."

"We believe the CDC approval is a formality at this point," Arjun said, sitting back down. "Which brings us to our offer."

"Offer?"

"We want to secure your future, Mia. And ours. We are unanimously offering you a seat on the board."

Sophia gasped. Brian's eyes widened.

"A board seat?" Mia repeated.

"And," Arjun added, "effective immediately, we are extending your funding for the enhancement project. Two years. No strings attached. Full autonomy."

The room went silent.

Two years.

Two years to fix the serum. Two years to figure out how to stop being a monster.

"Dr. Peers?" Arjun asked. "Did we lose the connection?"

"No," Mia whispered. "I'm here. I... I accept. Thank you. I don't know what to say."

"Say you'll get it done," Telita said. "We know about the second survivor. The rat named Jaz. We know you're close."

"I am," Mia said, her voice strengthening. "I've discovered a variable. A genetic key. I believe it explains the fatality rate."

Sophia turned to look at her, eyes sharp.

"I will get this across the finish line," Mia promised. "You have my word."

The rest of the meeting was a blur of legal talk. When the screen finally went black, the silence in the lab was heavy.

Then, it broke.

"Two years!" Sophia screamed, jumping up to hug Mia. "Two years and a board seat! Mia, you're set for life!"

Mia hugged her back, relief flooding her system. "I know. I can't believe it."

Brian remained seated, a small, grim smile on his face. "Congratulations, boss."

"What did you figure out?" Sophia asked, pulling back. "The variable you mentioned to the board?"

Mia hesitated. She eyed Sophia—her friend, her rock. But

also the woman who lied about the rat supplier.

"I'm not sure yet," Mia lied. "It's just a theory. I need to run the data before I share it."

Sophia's smile faltered. Just for a second. But Mia saw it. A flicker of cold calculation behind the warmth.

"Of course," Sophia said. " rigorous science. I understand."

"I need to tell Chris," Mia said, grabbing her bag. "He's going to lose his mind."

She bolted from the room, desperate for fresh air, desperate to tell the man she loved that they had a future.

Sophia watched her go. She stood there for a long moment, staring at the empty doorway.

Then she turned to Brian.

"She knows," Sophia said quietly. "She knows exactly how to fix it. And she's cutting us out."

Brian didn't look up. "Variables change, Sophia. We just have to adjust the equation."

Leverage

Sophia

Sophia stood by the window, watching the parking lot. Her reflection in the glass was calm, composed—a mask she had perfected over years of navigating family politics.

Mia burst into the office, flushed with victory. She looked younger, lighter, the weight of the funding deadline lifted.

"Oh, Sophia," Mia said, breezing past her, sitting in the desk chair. She shoved the meeting notes into a drawer. "What are you doing in here?"

Sophia turned. She didn't smile.

"We need to talk about the formula, Mia."

Mia leaned back, crossing her arms. The glow of the board meeting was still on her face, but her eyes hardened.

"I told you," Mia said. "I'm not ready to share it. The situation is complex."

"The situation isn't complex," Sophia said, pulling a chair out and sitting down. "The situation is you."

Mia froze. "Excuse me?"

"We're ordering primates," Sophia said calmly. "My contacts in Europe are processing the shipment. Orangutans. They'll be here in three days."

Mia bolted upright. "Like hell they will. We have funding for two years. We don't need to break the law."

"We aren't breaking the law, dear," Sophia said, a thin smile touching her lips. "You are."

She reached into her pocket and pulled out a flash drive. She set it on the desk.

"What is that?" Mia asked.

"Insurance," Sophia said. "It contains the security footage from the convenience store in Gainesville. The photos of the body at the tire shop. And your personal medical scans I pulled from your trash can—the ones showing your accelerated healing."

Mia went very still. The color drained from her face.

"You injected yourself with the Lazarus batch," Sophia said. It wasn't a question. "You killed three people with your bare hands. You jumped off a roof and walked away."

"Get out," Mia whispered.

"No," Sophia said. "I don't think I will. Because if I leave, that drive goes to the FBI. And the FDA. You'll be in a black site before dinner."

Mia sank back into her chair. The predator was caged.

"So," Sophia continued, "here is how this works. You are going to give me the full ingredient list. You are going to approve the primate trials. And I am going to run this lab."

"Why?" Mia asked, her voice trembling with suppressed rage. "Why are you doing this? We have the money. We have the time."

"You have... *some* time," Sophia corrected. "I don't. My family... they have needs. Specific medical needs. They can't wait two years for you to find your conscience."

"Your family?" Mia spat. "I've proven it works on humans," Mia argued. "I'm living proof."

"You're an anecdote," Sophia shot back. "One subject is a fluke. Six orangutans is a study. If the serum works on them, we ship it. Immediately."

"It will kill them," Mia said. "Without a genetic match... without a twin... it will burn them out."

Sophia's eyes narrowed. "A twin?"

Mia clamped her mouth shut.

"Is that the situation?" Sophia asked, leaning forward. "A genetic link? Interesting. We'll test that on the apes too. Siblings. Parents."

"You're a monster," Mia whispered.

"I'm a pragmatist," Sophia said, standing up. "Unlike you. You play god with your own body because you have a martyr complex. I'm trying to save lives."

Mia looked at the flash drive. She looked at Sophia's throat. It would be so easy. One quick movement. A crushed windpipe.

"Don't even think about it," Sophia said, reading her mind. "The drive is encrypted. If I don't enter a code every twelve hours, the files are automatically emailed to the Department of Justice. If you kill me, you end yourself."

Mia's hands curled into fists on the desk. She was trapped. Outmaneuvered by the woman who brought her coffee.

"Fine," Mia said through gritted teeth. "You get your monkeys. But if this goes south... if the Feds come knocking... I'm telling them everything."

"They won't come," Sophia said, walking to the door. "Because unlike you, Mia, I know how to clean up a mess."

She paused at the threshold.

"Have the formula ready by morning. And Mia? Don't try to be a hero. You're not Superwoman. You're just a lab rat who learned a few tricks."

Sophia closed the door.

Mia stared at the wood grain, listening to her assistant's footsteps fade down the hall.

She picked up the flash drive. It was light, plastic, insignificant. But it held her life.

She crushed it in her hand, the plastic shattering into dust.

It didn't matter. Sophia had copies.

Mia stared at her reflection in the darkened window. The monster was trapped. But monsters were dangerous when cornered.

"Orangutans," she whispered.

If Sophia wanted a study, she would get one. But she might not like the results.

To the Rescue

Bianca

Bianca sat in the rental car, binoculars pressed to her eyes, watching the dilapidated warehouse through a gap in the chain-link fence.

It had taken her three weeks to find this place. Three weeks of hacking traffic cam footage, tracking the license plate of a rental Yaris that had been spotted near the alley where Mason disappeared.

The Yaris was parked by the loading dock.

For hours, she watched. A man and a woman exited the building. They looked like siblings—dark hair, sharp features. The woman limped, favoring her left leg. The man held a roll of duct tape.

They argued by the car, then got in and drove away.

Bianca waited ten minutes. Then twenty. When they didn't return, she made her move.

She slipped through the fence and crossed the cracked asphalt, her Glock drawn. The silence of the industrial park was heavy, broken only by the hum of the nearby highway.

She reached the side door. The handle was smeared with something dark and dry. *Blood.*

It was unlocked.

Bianca pushed it open with her shoulder, leading with the gun. The interior smelled of rot and damp concrete. Fast food wrappers littered the floor. A TV sat on a metal table, silent.

She moved deeper, her footsteps soft on the dusty floor.

A hallway stretched ahead, lined with heavy steel doors. The dust on the floor was disturbed in front of only one—Door 3.

Bianca pressed her ear against the cold metal.

Inside, she heard a sound. A wet, rattling wheeze.

"Mason?" she whispered.

The wheezing stopped.

"Mason, if that's you, make a noise."

A weak thump against the other side of the door.

Bianca tried the handle. Locked. A deadbolt.

She holstered her gun and pulled a lockpick set from her pocket. Brian's "tech girl" persona wasn't a lie. Plus, she knew her way around a tumbler.

Thirty seconds later, the lock clicked.

Bianca threw the bolt and shoved the door open.

The smell hit her first—a wall of ammonia, infection, and unwashed body.

"Holy shit," she breathed.

Mason was strapped to a metal frame in the center of the room. He was naked, his body a canvas of tattoos and bruises. But the tattoos were pale, stretched over skin that clung to his ribs. He had lost at least fifty pounds.

His eyes were sunken pits. His lips were cracked and bleeding. A mound of silver duct tape covered his left shoulder, the edges black with old blood.

"Bianca?" he croaked. It barely sounded human.

"I'm here," she said, rushing to his side. She pulled a knife and started sawing at the tape binding his wrists. "I've got you."

"Water," he rasped.

"In the car. We have to go."

She freed his arms, then his legs. Mason tried to sit up, but collapsed back onto the frame, groaning.

"I can't," he whispered.

"You have to," Bianca said. She grabbed his good arm and hauled him up. He was dead weight, a mountain of crumbling stone. "If they come back, we're both dead."

She dragged him out of the room, his bare feet leaving streaks in the dust. They stumbled down the hallway, Mason leaning on her so heavily she thought her knees would buckle.

They burst out into the sunlight. Mason hissed, squeezing his eyes shut against the glare.

Bianca shoved him into the passenger seat of her car. He slumped against the window, shivering violently.

She got in and keyed the ignition, tires spinning as she peeled out of the lot.

"Who did this?" she asked, glancing at his ruined body.

"Italians," Mason whispered. "Siblings. They work for Sophia."

Bianca's blood ran cold. "Sophia? Mia's assistant?"

"Yeah." Mason coughed, a wet, rattling sound. He glowered at her, his eyes filled with a terrifying clarity. "She knows everything, Bianca. She knows about the buyer. She knows about Arjun. And she's not protecting the lab."

"What is she doing?"

"She's taking over."

Shawshank

Mia

M ia sat in the dark of her office, staring at the glowing numbers on the digital clock. 4:00 AM.

She hadn't slept. Every time she closed her eyes, she saw Sophia's face—calm, maternal, holding a flash drive that could end Mia's life.

Six orangutans.

The shipment was two days away. Two days before she had to inject a lethal serum into an endangered species, or risk being handed over to the FBI as a mass murderer.

But Mia wasn't beaten yet. She was a scientist. And scientists solved problems.

She inspected the whiteboard where she had sketched out the new formula. She had isolated the genetic marker—the specific allele sequence in the epigenome that triggered the "circuit" between twins. If she could synthesize a chemical mimic, a "dummy twin" for the serum to latch onto, maybe she could bypass the need for a biological partner.

She had injected twelve rats with the new batch four hours ago.

If they lived past the six-hour mark, she had a solution. If they died... she was out of options.

CRASH.

The sound came from the back of the lab—the main experiment room.

Mia was off the couch instantly, the Bersa in her hand. She racked the slide, a round chambering with a metallic *clack.*

Her heart rate didn't spike. The serum regulated it, keeping her calm, lethal.

Sophia? The Mafia?

She moved to the door, listening. Her enhanced hearing picked up the *skitter-scratch* of movement on tile. The clang of metal hitting metal.

It sounded like a search. Someone tearing the place apart.

Mia checked the monitors. The external cameras showed an empty parking lot. No Escalades.

Whoever was inside had bypassed the perimeter alarms.

Professionals.

Mia moved down the hallway, silent as a ghost. She didn't need the lights. Her pupils dilated, pulling in the ambient glow from the exit signs.

Another crash. Glass shattering.

And then, a high-pitched squeal.

Mia frowned. That didn't sound like a person.

She reached the double doors of the experiment room. The noise inside was chaotic—a frenzy of motion.

She took a breath, centered her aim, and kicked the doors open.

"Don't move!" she shouted, sweeping the room with her gun.

She froze.

There were no people. No hitmen. No Sophia.

The room was a wreck. Cages were toppled. Beakers were smashed.

But the cages weren't just knocked over. They were *open.*

Mia lowered her gun, her mind struggling to process the scene.

The twelve rats she had injected four hours ago weren't dead. They were loose.

And they were organized.

On the far side of the room, three rats were working together to push a heavy metal stool toward the ventilation grate near the ceiling. Two others were gnawing at the rubber seal of the grate, their teeth stripping the material with industrial efficiency. Several were throwing themselves against a window.

Another rat—larger, faster—was perched on the counter, watching the door. When Mia entered, it chattered a warning.

The rats froze. Twelve pairs of black, intelligent eyes turned to look at her.

"No way," Mia whispered.

The large rat on the counter stood on its hind legs. It pointed a claw at the ventilation shaft.

Go.

The rats moved as one. They didn't scurry; they flowed. They swarmed the stool, using it as a ladder to reach the vent. The grate clattered to the floor, the screws stripped.

"Stop!" Mia lunged, holstering her gun and grabbing a net from the wall.

She wasn't fast enough. The serum-enhanced rats moved with a blur of speed that rivaled her own. One by one, they vanished into the ductwork.

The last rat—the leader—paused at the lip of the vent. It stared back at Mia.

It didn't look afraid. It looked... calculating.

It launched itself through the window. Then it was gone.

Mia stood in the ruined lab, listening to the *scritch-scratch* of tiny claws fading into the building's infrastructure.

She had solved the problem. The formula worked.

It worked too well.

Pause

Mia

Mia stood in the center of the experiment room, the cold morning air pouring through the shattered window.

She had spent the last four hours cleaning up the wreckage of the escape. She had swept up the glass, gathered the mangled cages, and wiped down the counters. But she couldn't wipe away the facts.

Fact 1: Fourteen serum-enhanced rats were now loose in the Virginia ecosystem. Fact 2: They were intelligent, coordinated, and possibly apex predators. Fact 3: Laz and Jaz—the originals—were among them.

If they bred... if they passed the genetic alterations to the local population... Mia hadn't just created a super-soldier serum. She had engineered an invasive species event.

She popped two *Moratusom* pills, chewing them dry. She needed the clarity. She needed a lie.

The electronic chime of the front door echoed down the hall.

Mia checked her watch. 7:00 AM. Too early for Sophia.

Rubber soles squeaked on the linoleum. Brian appeared in the doorway, holding a travel mug. He stopped, his eyes widening as he took in the room.

"So," he said, lowering his sunglasses. "I see we're going for the open-air concept."

"They're gone," Mia said flatly.

"Who?"

"The rats. Laz. Jaz. The new batch. All of them."

Brian stepped into the room, crunching on a stray shard of glass. He stepped toward the window and inspected the frame. The metal mesh was torn outward, shredded like wet paper.

"Gone?" he repeated. "Or stolen?"

"Stolen," Mia lied. She leaned against the counter, crossing her arms to hide the tremor in her hands. "A crew broke in last night. The same people who tried to grab me after the gym."

"And they took... the rats?"

"They didn't know which one was valuable," Mia said. "So they took them all. Smashed the place up for good measure."

Brian ran a finger along the jagged edge of the window frame. "Reinforced polycarbonate," he murmured. "Shatter-resistant. Bulletproof. And yet... it looks like it was punched out from the inside."

Mia's heart skipped a beat.

"The glass is out in the parking lot."

He turned to look at her. His expression wasn't fearful anymore. It was cold. Analytical. Like he was dissecting a frog.

"Did you call the police?"

"I will," Mia said. "After I assess the damage. I don't want them trampling the crime scene before I verify the data is safe."

"The data is in the cloud," Brian said. "Encrypted. Did they get your laptop?"

"No."

"Then they have nothing. Just a box of rats that will hopefully be dead in six hours."

"Except for Laz and Jaz," Mia corrected.

"Right. The 'Wonder Twins.'" Brian took a sip of his coffee. "Strange that the alarms didn't trip. I usually get a notification."

"They must have jammed the signal," Mia said quickly.

"Must have."

The silence stretched between them, heavy and suffocating. Brian knew. He didn't know *what* exactly, but he knew she was lying.

"Where's Sophia?" he asked.

"I don't care."

Brian's head jerked.

"I mean, I don't know. I'm not thinking straight. No sleep."

"Maybe she ran into traffic." Brian checked his watch. "Or maybe she ran into something else."

He set his mug down.

"I'm going to head out," he said. "I need to... check the backups. Remote server access is better from home."

"Take the day," Mia said, relieved to have him gone. "I'll handle the window problem."

"Sure. Sorry about the rats, boss."

Brian strolled out. Mia watched him go. He didn't look back.

As soon as the front door chimed, Mia sagged against the counter. That was too close. Brian was suspicious. Sophia was a con artist. And fourteen super-rats were currently terrorizing Northern Virginia.

She squinted through the broken window.

In the distance, near the tree line, a crow landed on a fence post.

Suddenly, a blur of brown fur shot up the post. The crow didn't even have time to squawk. It was snatched, pulled down into the tall grass, and silenced.

Mia gripped the windowsill.

They weren't running. They were hunting.

And they were hungry.

True Lies

Mia

M ia found her father in Unity's room, sitting in the dark. He was asleep in the visitor's chair, head lolling against the wall, looking small and frail.

The ever-present rhythmic *whoosh-hiss* of the ventilator was the only sound in the room.

Mia didn't wake him. She tiptoed to the bedside and examined Unity.

Her sister's skin was still the pallid gray of her long-term comatose.

Mia touched Unity's arm. The muscle underneath still atrophied.

"She's changing," Jeff said.

Mia jumped. Her father was awake, watching her with eyes that were sharp and lucid, belying his frailty.

"Her vitals are up," Mia said, keeping her voice neutral. "Brain activity is spiking. Dr. Aris thinks she might be waking up."

"I know," Jeff said. "I saw the charts."

He stood up, his joints popping. He moseyed to the window and closed the blinds, plunging the room into deeper shadow.

"We need to talk, Mia."

"About what? Your parenting style?" Mia crossed her arms. "I don't have the energy for a guilt trip today, Dad."

"No guilt," Jeff said. "Just facts. You asked me once why we treated you differently. Why we protected you."

"You didn't protect me. You ignored me."

"We kept you separate," Jeff corrected. "Because we had to."

He headed back to the chair but didn't sit. He gripped the back of it tight.

"Close the door," he said.

Mia hesitated, then pushed the door until it clicked shut. The silence in the room deepened.

"This stays in this room," Jeff whispered. "If anyone finds out... the people we worked for... they will kill us all."

"Who did you work for?"

"It doesn't matter. What matters is what we did." Jeff fixated on Unity, his expression a mixture of love and horror. "We lost a son before you were born. Milo. Spinal Muscular Atrophy. It broke us."

"I didn't know," Mia said, softening slightly.

"We vowed it wouldn't happen again. We were geneticists. We thought we could fix it. When your mother got pregnant with Unity, we... intervened. In utero. We spliced the gene. We removed the marker for SMA."

Mia stared at him. "That's illegal. And dangerous."

"It was necessary. But the procedure was risky. We knew the fetus might not survive the edit. Or the disease might return. We needed... insurance."

A cold dread settled in Mia's stomach. "Insurance?"

Jeff looked at her. Really looked at her. "We induced a split, Mia. We took the edited zygote and divided it. One became Unity. The other... became you."

"We're identical twins," Mia said. "That happens naturally."

"Not like this," Jeff said. "We didn't just copy her. We *edited* you. We enhanced your physical resilience. We tweaked your neural pathways for analytical processing. We made you stronger. Smarter. Because if Unity failed... if the disease took her... we needed a backup who could finish the work. Who could cure her."

The room spun. Mia grabbed the edge of the bed to steady herself.

"You... you made me to be her doctor?"

"We made you to be her savior," Jeff said. "And something else. The contract we were under... they were interested in something called *Animae*. Soul replication. They believed that twins shared a quantum link. A biological circuit."

Mia's breath caught. *The circuit.* The overflow. It wasn't just a theory. It was the design.

"You built the connection," Mia whispered. "You wired us together."

"We didn't know if it worked," Jeff said, tears tracking down his cheeks. "Until the accident. When Unity went under... you felt it. You changed. You became even more obsessed with science. You signed up for her sports and started winning fights. You stepped into the role we designed for you."

"I'm a spare part," Mia said, her voice trembling. "I'm not a person. I'm a backup hard drive."

"You are my daughter," Jeff said, reaching for her.

Mia recoiled. She scrambled back, hitting the wall.

"The birthmark," she gasped. "On my arm. The dot."

Jeff glanced away. "The injection site. From an extraction. It scarred."

Mia clawed at her sleeve, ripping it up. Her arm was smooth. Flawless. The serum had erased the scar because it wasn't part of the original blueprint. It wasn't *her*.

"I'm a clone," she whispered.

"You are an *Animae*," Jeff said. "A soul copy. And you are the only reason she is still alive. You're feeding her, Mia. Whatever you've done to yourself... it's waking her up."

Mia glanced at Unity. Her sister. Her twin. Her original.

She wasn't just saving Unity. She was somehow *charging* her.

Mia backed toward the door, her heart hammering a frantic rhythm against her ribs.

"You're monsters," she said.

"We're parents," Jeff said. "We did what we had to do."

Mia ripped the door open and ran. She ran down the hallway, past the nurses' station, past the reception desk. She burst out into the cold air, gasping for breath.

She wasn't real. Her memories, her drive, her "reason"—it was all code. Programming.

She was a weapon built to save a ghost.

And now, the weapon was loose.

Apes Rising

Brian

Brian watched the unmarked box truck back up to the loading dock. The hydraulic lift whined, lowering six large, draped cages onto the concrete.

He moved to help, but Sophia stepped in front of him.

"I'll handle the paperwork," she said. Her voice was crisp, authoritative—no longer the kindly aunt, but the foreman of a job site.

Brian stepped back, watching as the "delivery team" unloaded the cargo. A man and a woman. They moved with efficient, predatory grace. The woman favored her left leg, limping slightly. The man, Gabriele, was Sophia's so-called "cousin."

As Gabriele leaned over to secure a wheel lock, his jacket fell open. Brian caught the glint of a shoulder holster.

Brian pushed a dolly toward the ramp. As he passed the woman, he noticed her eyes—dark, sharp, identical to Sophia's.

Family.

He wheeled the first cage into the storage room, the heavy casters rumbling on the tile. He peeked under the drape.

A pair of intelligent, mournful eyes stared back. An orangutan.

"Hey there, big guy," Brian whispered. "Welcome to the jungle."

The ape reached out a long, hairy arm, gripping the bars. Its fingers looked eerily human.

"Brian," Sophia said from the doorway.

He jumped. She was watching him, her expression unreadable.

"Leave them," she said. "Go get Mia."

Brian nodded and hurried down the hall. The lab felt different today. Colder. The air was thick with secrets he wasn't supposed to know.

He found Mia in her office. She was sitting at her desk, staring at a blank monitor. She looked shattered—pale, hollow-eyed, like someone who had just seen a ghost. Or become one.

"Mia?"

She glanced up. For a second, he saw terror in her eyes. Then, the mask slipped back into place.

"The shipment is here," Brian said.

Mia stood up slowly. She didn't look excited. She looked resigned. Like a prisoner walking to the gallows.

"Okay," she said.

They trudged back to the storage room. Sophia was waiting by the cages, flanked by the two delivery people—her siblings. The muscle.

"The specimens are secure," Sophia said. "We begin the trials tonight."

Mia stared at the cages. "Tonight?"

"We're on a schedule," Sophia said. Her tone wasn't a request. It was an order.

Mia nodded, her shoulders slumping. "Fine. I need to prep the serum."

Brian watched the exchange. The dynamic had shifted. Mia wasn't the boss anymore. She was the asset. And Sophia was the handler.

He slipped away, retreating to his office.

He sat at his computer and brought up the security logs.

Bianca hadn't tried the badge yet. She was waiting. But why?

Brian opened the code for the scanners. He typed quickly, his fingers flying across the keys.

If Badge ID #4402 is scanned: 1. Disable silent alarm. 2. Trigger lockdown protocol Level 4 (Internal containment). 3. Send alert to [Phone Number].

He paused at the phone number field. He entered a number.

He executed the script. The cursor blinked, confirming the trap was set.

Brian leaned back in his chair. He thought about the tiny house. The way she had kissed him. The way she had lied to him.

He pulled up his phone. He still had the Tinder app open.

He swiped left. Left. Left.

He wasn't looking for a date. He was looking for a distraction.

Because soon, the lab was going to turn into a war zone, and he needed to be ready to pick a side.

Missed Opportunities

Bianca

B ianca adjusted the focus on her binoculars, the lenses cutting through the fog hovering over the asphalt.

A white semi-truck was backed up to the lab's loading dock. No markings. No logos. Just a ghostly slab of metal.

"What are you seeing?" Lucas asked over the comms. He was parked a mile away, coordinating the perimeter.

"Movement," Bianca said. "They're unloading crates. Big ones. Draped in canvas."

She watched as Brian pushed a dolly up the ramp. He seemed different—tenser, his movements jerky. He wasn't the awkward nerd she had kissed in his car. He looked like a man walking through a minefield.

Two other figures were helping him. A man and a woman. They moved with military precision, scanning the perimeter as they worked.

"I've got two new players," Bianca said. "Male, female. Tactical movement. They're carrying under their jackets. Mason, they look like the two who..."

In the passenger seat, Mason stirred. He was a patchwork of healing bruises and fresh anger. His new teeth—a row of porcelain veneers so white they looked like piano keys—glinted in the sun.

"Let me see," Mason growled.

Bianca handed him the binoculars.

Mason peered through the lenses. His jaw tightened, the muscles bunching like steel cables.

"It's them," he whispered. "The Italians." He lowered the binoculars. His eyes were cold, dead things. "Alessia and Gabriele. The ones who taped me to the bed."

Bianca felt a chill. The siblings who worked for Sophia. The ones who had tortured Mason. They weren't just security. They were moving in.

"They're bringing something in," Mason said. "Those cages aren't for equipment. They're for something alive."

Bianca's phone buzzed.

She picked it up. A text from Brian.

Brian: *I know you have the badge. If you want to use it, do it soon. Things are changing here. I can't protect the perimeter much longer.*

Bianca stared at the screen. It was the opening she needed. Or the trap she feared.

"What is it?" Mason asked.

"Brian," Bianca said. "He wants to meet. He says the window is closing."

"It's a trap," Mason said immediately.

"Maybe," Bianca said. "Or maybe he's scared. He saw the cages too. He knows what's happening inside that lab."

She texted back: *Want to meet?*

Brian: *Sure. The house. One hour.*

Bianca eyed Mason. "I'm going."

"Take your gun," Mason said. "And if you see the Italians... tell them I'm coming."

Bianca nodded. She started the car.

The game was accelerating. The Italians were digging in. Brian was turning—maybe. And somewhere inside that fortress, Mia Peers and Sophia Romano was building an army of monsters.

This was a fork in the road. But how would Lucas react if she chose the wrong path?

Last Chance

Bianca

The tiny house sat on a trailer in a storage lot, looking like a monopoly piece dropped into the real world. It was painted a cheerful, rustic yellow that clashed violently with the pewter industrial skyline.

Bianca parked her car next to Brian's truck. She sat for a moment, gripping the steering wheel.

This was it. The meeting point.

She got out. Brian was waiting by the door. He looked different—not the bumbling assistant she had seduced, nor the cold analyst who had confronted her in the model home. He looked determined.

"You bought it," Bianca said, gesturing to the house.

"I did," Brian said. "It's fully off grid. Solar panels. Composting toilet. Rainwater collection."

He unlocked the door and ushered her inside.

It was even smaller than the model. The walls pressed in, smelling of fresh pine and desperation. A fold-out table served as the dining room. A ladder led to the cramped loft like the one where she had admitted her duplicity.

"Why are we here, Brian?" Bianca asked, crossing her arms. "You have information?"

"I do," Brian said. "But first, I have a proposition."

He sat on the tiny bench at the table. Bianca sat opposite him, her knees bumping his.

"The Italians have taken over the lab," Brian said. "Sophia is running the show now. Mia is a hostage. They're starting primate trials tonight."

"Tonight?" Bianca felt a surge of panic. If the Italians got the formula first, she was a dead woman.

"Yes. And once they have the data, they'll burn the place down. With Mia inside."

"So let us in," Bianca said. "We'll use the badge. You disable the gate and all the alarms. Let us take them out."

"No," Brian said.

"Brian, Mason is... people are going to die."

"People are already dead," Brian countered. "Your friends. The mechanic. The people at the store. This isn't a heist anymore, Bianca. It's a war. And you're on the losing side."

He reached into a drawer and pulled out a thick envelope. He slid it across the table.

"What is this?"

"Cash," Brian said. "Ten thousand dollars. And a title for the truck outside."

Bianca stared at the envelope. "I don't understand."

"I'm leaving," Brian said. "As soon as the chaos starts at the lab, I'm hooking this house to the truck and driving west. I'm not stopping until I hit the Pacific Ocean."

He stared at her, his expression open and terrifyingly earnest. "Come with me."

Bianca laughed, a short, sharp sound of disbelief. "You want me to run away with you? To live in a shed?"

"I want you to live," Brian said. "Look at your options. You stay, you fight the Italians. Best case scenario? You get the serum, give it to your boss, and spend the rest of your life looking over your shoulder. Worst case? You end up like

Mason."

Bianca flinched. She thought of Mason, strapped to the bed, broken and bleeding.

"The Mafia doesn't let people just walk away," she whispered.

"They won't look for you," Brian said. "Not if they think you're dead."

He leaned forward. "When the lab goes up... there will be bodies. Unidentifiable bodies."

Bianca gawked at him. He had thought this through. It was a clean exit. A restart.

"Why?" she asked. "After everything I did. I used you. I stole from you."

"Because you're not a killer," Brian said. "You're just trapped. I can see it. You hate this life."

Tears pricked Bianca's eyes. He was right. She hated the blood. She hated the fear. She hated Lucas' cold ambition.

She looked at the envelope. Then she looked at the door.

"I can't," she said. "Lucas... he's my partner."

"Lucas is dead weight," Brian said coldly. "He'll get you killed."

Bianca stood up. The walls were closing in. She needed air.

"I have to go," she said. "We're making a move soon. If you're not going to help us... stay out of the way."

Brian stood too. He didn't try to stop her. He just looked sad.

"Keep the badge," he said. "Use it if you have to. But remember... once you go through that door, there's no coming back."

Bianca fled. She ran to her car, her heart pounding.

She drove away, leaving the tiny yellow house behind. She told herself she was loyal. She told herself she was a professional.

But as she merged onto the highway, heading back to the hotel where a mutilated Mason and a desperate Lucas waited, she couldn't stop thinking about the ocean.

And she realized, with a sinking dread, that Brian was the only person in her life who had ever offered her a logical choice.

Signs

Mia

Mia buzzed Chris in. He strode into the lab carrying a paper bag from Katerina's, the smell of roasted lamb and garlic cutting through the sterile scent of floor wax.

He kissed her cheek as he passed. "Lunch is served."

"Conference room," Mia said, her voice tight. "First door on the right. I forgot something in my office."

She waited until he turned the corner, then bolted for her desk. She grabbed the spare Bersa pistol from the drawer and shoved it into the holster at the small of her back. She pulled her blouse down to cover it.

She scanned the office. Suitcases lined the wall like soldiers. The punching bag hung in the corner, dented and sad. The broken picture frame on her desk, held together with more duct tape, that she had rescued from the trash bin.

This wasn't a workplace. It was a bunker.

She joined Chris in the conference room. He had already laid out the food—Styrofoam containers of gyro meat, pita, and Greek salad.

"You okay?" he asked, handing her a Diet Coke. "You look like you're pulsating."

"Just busy," Mia lied. She sat down, grateful for the food. Her metabolism was a constant, demanding furnace. "Thanks for this. Katerina's is life."

"Where's Brian?"

"Errand," Mia said around a mouthful of pita. "He's testing his new truck."

Chris watched her eat. He didn't eat much himself. He was observing.

"So," he said casually. "I saw the luggage in the hall. Moving day?"

"Finally going home," Mia said. "I'm going to sleep in my own bed tonight."

"That's good. And the gun?"

Mia froze. She hadn't realized her shirt had ridden up.

"Protection," she said, pulling the fabric down. "There have been... incidents. Break-ins in the area."

"Incidents involving reinforced glass being punched out from the inside?" Chris asked.

Mia looked up. Chris wasn't smiling. His lawyer eyes were locked on her.

"You saw the window," she said.

"Hard to miss. And the fact that you're carrying a concealed weapon in a secure facility." He leaned forward. "Mia, talk to me. What is going on here?"

Mia put down her fork. The food turned into guilt in her mouth.

"The rats escaped," she said.

"Escaped?"

"Fourteen of them. Including Lazarus. They... broke out."

Chris glanced at the window, then back at her. "Rats broke through bulletproof glass?"

"They're enhanced, Chris. Stronger. Smarter."

"How smart?"

"Smart enough to coordinate. Smart enough to unscrew a vent."

Chris was silent for a long moment. "And the primates? You mentioned approval for primate studies."

"In the back," Mia said. "Sophia is handling it."

"Sophia," Chris repeated. "The assistant you haven't mentioned in a while."

"She's... taking lead."

Chris stood up. He went to the window, looking out at the parking lot.

"You're scared," he said. "I can see it. You're terrified of your own lab."

Mia joined him at the window. She wrapped her arms around herself, feeling the cold weight of the gun against her spine.

"I've lost control," she admitted. "The formula works, Chris. It works too well. I've created something I can't contain. And now I have people pushing me to do it again. On bigger subjects."

"Sophia?"

"The Mafia. And now Sophia and her family. Unless they're working together."

Chris turned to her. He put his hands on her shoulders.

"We need to get you out of here," he said. "Leave the lab. Leave the formula. Come with me."

"I can't," Mia whispered. "I have to fix it. I have to know if the genetic variable works. If it does... I can save myself."

"Save yourself from what?"

Mia diverted her eyes from Chris. *From being a spare part. From being a monster.*

"From *the choice*," she said cryptically.

Chris didn't push. He pulled her into a hug. Mia melted into him, listening to the steady *thump-thump* of his heart. It was the only real thing in her life.

"I love you," he said into her hair.

"I love you too."

She pulled back, forcing a smile. "Hey. You wanted to drive

the Porsche."

Chris blinked. "What?"

"The Taycan. You asked for a ride. Let's go. Right now."

"Mia, we're in the middle of a crisis."

"Exactly," she said, grabbing his hand. "Which is why we need to drive fast. Please, Chris. Just for an hour. Let me pretend to be normal."

Chris regarded her for several seconds, then glanced at the door. He sighed.

"Okay. One hour."

They stepped out onto the parking lot. The sun was shining, birds were chirping. It looked like an ordinary day.

But as Mia unlocked the Porsche, she saw a crow land on the fence post near the woods.

It didn't stay long. A dark blur shot up the post, snatching the bird in a explosion of feathers.

Chris didn't see it. He was looking at the car.

Mia got in, her heart racing. The rats were hunting. The Italians were waiting. And she was going for a joyride.

Chris pressed the button and revved the engine.

"Hold on," he said.

And he floored it, allowing Mia to leave the monsters behind for just a little while longer.

Déjà vu

Mia

The Porsche Taycan hummed like a spaceship, devouring the asphalt of Route 29.

Chris drove with a relaxed confidence, one hand on the wheel, the other resting on the gear selector. He looked exuberant, free, the weight of the world momentarily lifted by the horsepower at his command.

"So far, so good," he said, weaving through traffic. "You think I should get one of these?"

"We could start a club," Mia teased. She leaned back in the passenger seat, watching the trees blur into a green smear. For the first time in months, the knot of anxiety in her chest loosened. She still had the funding. She still had the man. She just had to survive Sophia.

"I'm serious," Chris said, slowing for a red light at a major intersection. "What if I call off work tomorrow? We go cruising. Skyline Drive. Just us."

Mia glanced at him. The sun caught the white in his stubble. He looked so hopeful. So natural.

"You don't have to ask me twice," she said.

The light turned green.

Traffic started to move.

Directly ahead, a black Cadillac Escalade—the same model that had stalked her for weeks—lurched forward, then slammed on its brakes, stalling in the middle of the intersection.

"Idiot," Chris muttered. He checked his mirror and pulled the wheel right to go around.

A black BMW i5 shot out from the cross-street, screeching to a halt directly in their path, blocking the escape lane.

Mia's enhanced brain processed the geometry instantly.

Escalade front. BMW right.

It wasn't traffic. It was a kill box.

"Chris, stop!" Mia screamed.

Chris slammed the brakes, but they were already in the intersection.

Mia stared to her left.

A heavy-duty dump truck was barreling through the red light, its grill growing larger by the millisecond. It wasn't slowing down. It was accelerating.

Déjà vu.

The universe had a sick sense of humor. Twenty years ago, a truck had ended her childhood. Today, a truck was coming to finish the job.

But this time, time didn't just slow down. It stopped.

The serum flooded Mia's system. She saw the terror in Chris's eyes as he turned his head. She saw the rivets on the truck's bumper. She saw the individual shards of glass as the side window began to bow inward before it even shattered.

She didn't brace for impact. She reached for Chris.

CRUNCH.

The world turned into noise and violence.

The Porsche didn't just crumple; it was punted. The impact lifted the 5,000-pound car into the air like a toy. Mia felt the G-force slam her against the door, shattering her ribs. Her head whipped sideways, snapping against the B-pillar.

The car rolled. Once. Twice. Three times.

Metal screamed. Glass turned to dust. The roof collapsed.

Through it all, Mia was conscious. She felt every bone break. She felt her organs shift. The serum was trying to knit her back together even as the car was tearing her apart.

The Porsche finally came to rest in the grassy median, upright but ruined. Smoke hissed from the battery pack.

Silence fell, heavy and ringing.

Mia coughed. Blood sprayed the dashboard. Her lungs were punctured. Her spine felt like it was on fire.

She forced her head to turn.

"Chris?"

He was slumped over the steering wheel. Blood matted his hair.

He wasn't moving.

"Chris!" Mia wheezed. She reached out with a broken hand, touching his shoulder.

Thump... thump...

His heart. It was faint, erratic, but it was beating.

"Hang on," she whispered. "Help is coming."

The passenger door groaned. Metal peeled back with a shriek.

Sunlight flooded the cabin.

Mia squinted upward, expecting a paramedic. Expecting a Good Samaritan.

Instead, a mountain of a man filled the frame.

He was shirtless under a leather jacket, his chest a tapestry of tattoos and healing scars. His face was a mask of bruises. When he smiled, his teeth were a blinding, unnatural white.

Mason.

"Found you," he growled.

He reached in, grabbed Mia by her shirt, and yanked.

Mia screamed as he dragged her from the car. Her broken ribs ground together. He threw her onto the grass like a sack of trash.

The world spun dizzily. Mia stared at the sky. It was a beautiful, clear blue.

Mason stood over her. He pulled a heavy revolver from his belt.

"No," Mia gasped, raising a hand. "Please. Chris..."

Mason didn't look at the car. He looked at her.

"This is for Dylan," he said. "And for Sandra."

He aimed at her stomach.

BANG.

The bullet hit her like a sledgehammer. It tore through her abdominal muscles, shredding intestines, lodging in her spine.

BANG.

The second shot hit her chest, blowing out her right lung.

BANG.

The third shot hit her hip, shattering the pelvis.

"Enjoy hell, bitch," Mason spat.

He turned and swaggered away. Tires squealed. The Escalade and the BMW peeled out, leaving the scene of the execution.

Mia lay on the grass.

She couldn't breathe. She couldn't move. The pain was a white-hot ocean, drowning her.

She turned her head toward the wreck. She could see Chris's hand hanging out of the broken window.

I'm sorry, she thought. *I'm so sorry.*

Her vision narrowed to a pinprick. The sounds of the world—the distant sirens, the wind in the grass—faded into a high-pitched whine.

The darkness rose up to meet her.

In the Ether

Mia

The sun was a white-hot coin pressed against the sky, baking the empty seats of Nationals Park as the Nats played the Angels.

Mia sat in Section 134, squinting at the field. Beside her, Unity cracked a peanut shell, the sound echoing like a gunshot in the silent stadium.

"I don't even like baseball," Mia said.

"It's not baseball," Unity replied, tossing a peanut into her mouth. "It's accounting."

Mia peered at the Jumbotron.

HOME: 36 VISITORS: 0

"We're winning," Mia said.

"Are we?" Unity pointed to the field. "Top of the ninth. Bases loaded. Two outs."

The pitcher wound up. The batter swung.

CRACK.

The sound wasn't wood on leather. It was bone snapping.

Mia flinched, clutching her chest. A sharp, stabbing pain bloomed under her sternum.

"Grand slam," Unity narrated flatly. "Four runs."

On the field, the runners circled the bases. But they weren't baseball players.

First base was her mother, Theresa, looking lost and frail. Second base was her father, Jeff, staring at his phone. Third base was Chris, blood matting his hair.

And heading for home plate was a massive, shirtless man covered in tattoos. Mason.

He stomped on the plate.

THUD.

Mia gasped, doubling over. The pain in her stomach flared white-hot.

VISITORS: 4

"You need to catch up," Unity said. She looked different. Older. Her skin was papery, her eyes sunken. She looked like she did in the hospital bed, but standing up. "You're lagging."

"I'm tired," Mia whispered.

"You're dying," Unity corrected. "Look at yourself."

Mia pulled a compact mirror from her pocket. The face staring back wasn't hers. It was a woman in her eighties. Deep wrinkles. Thin, whitish hair.

"The serum," Mia realized. "It's eating me."

"It's fixing you," Unity said. "But repairs cost money. And you're overdrawn."

CRACK.

Another grand slam. Another pain, this time in her hip. Her pelvis felt like it was grinding together.

VISITORS: 8

"Make it stop," Mia pleaded.

"I can't," Unity said. "You built the machine, Mia. You wired the circuit. You're the battery."

She leaned in close, her breath smelling of decay.

"Do you want to know the secret?" Unity whispered. "The one Dad didn't tell you?"

"What?"

"You aren't the backup," Unity hissed. "You're the fuel."

CRACK.

That hit was the worst. Her lungs burned. She couldn't breathe. She was drowning in dry air.

VISITORS: 12

The stadium lights flickered. The sun vanished, replaced by a swirling darkness. The crowd and its noise—which had been absent—suddenly roared to life. But it wasn't cheering. It was screaming.

"Time to go," Unity said. She stood up and traipsed away, fading into the shadows.

"Wait!" Mia reached out. "Where are you going?"

"To die," Unity called back. "You made your *choice*, remember?"

Mia was alone. The pain was a tidal wave now. She fell out of her seat, tumbling down the concrete stairs.

One. Two. Three.

Every impact was a shock to her heart.

Thirty-five. Thirty-six. Thirty-seven.

"Clear!"

The world exploded in white light.

Mia arched off the grass, gasping. The air tasted of fuel and fumes.

"We got a rhythm!" a voice shouted. "Sinus tach, but it's holding."

Mia blinked. A paramedic hovered over her, sweat dripping from his nose. His hands were on her chest.

"Thirty-seven compressions," he panted. "I thought we lost her."

"She took three rounds," another voice said. "How is she even intact?"

Mia tried to speak, but her throat was full of blood. She turned her head.

Ten feet away, another team was working on a body. They were loading him onto a stretcher. His arm hung limp off the side.

Chris.

"Is he…" Mia choked out.

The paramedic regarded her. "Ma'am, don't try to talk. You've lost a lot of blood."

"Chris," she wheezed.

"He's alive," the paramedic said.

Mia let her head fall back against the ground.

Alive.

She closed her eyes. Chris would survive. But would their relationship, if he knew about the *choice* she had made ten years ago?

Tell All

Mia

The light was blinding. Mia tried to blink, but her eyelids felt heavy, taped shut by sleep and drugs.

She could hear voices—muffled, urgent, clinical.

"...never seen anything like it. The tissue regeneration rate is logarithmic."

"Is it a mutation? A reaction to the trauma?"

"It's a miracle."

Mia forced her eyes open. The room spun, then snapped into focus. She was in an ICU. Machines beeped and hissed around her. A group of people in white coats stood at the foot of her bed, staring at her like she was a specimen in a jar.

A doctor leaned over her, shining a penlight into her eyes.

"She's tracking," he announced.

"Impossible," a woman's voice said. "Her GCS was three an hour ago."

Mia tried to sit up. Her body protested—not with pain, but with a strange, buzzing resistance, as if her muscles were vibrating at a different frequency than the rest of the world.

She glanced down. Her hospital gown was on backward, open, revealing her abdomen.

There were several pink scars on her stomach. Fresh, shiny,

but sealed.

Three bullets.

She remembered the shots. The heat. The pain.

"Take that final bandage off," the doctor ordered.

A nurse peeled back the gauze covering her chest.

Gasps rippled through the room. A camera shutter clicked.

"My God," the woman whispered. "The lung puncture is gone. It's just... healed."

Mia sat up fully. The movement was fluid, powerful. She ripped the IVs from her arm, ignoring the spray of blood that clotted almost instantly.

"Where are my clothes?" she asked. Her voice was rasping, but strong.

The medical team recoiled. Two orderlies stepped forward, hands raised.

"Dr. Peers, please," the lead doctor said. He was an older man, overweight, sweating profusely. "You need to lie down. You've suffered massive trauma. Gunshot wounds. A skull fracture."

"I'm fine," Mia said. She swung her legs over the side of the bed. Her feet hit the cold tile. "I want my clothes. And my purse."

"Your clothes were destroyed," the doctor said. "Cut off in the ER. The police have your belongings. Everything from the wreck."

Mia processed this. Police. Evidence. Her gun.

"The police?"

"They're waiting outside," the doctor said nervously. "They want to talk to you. About the shooting. About the car."

Mia stood up. The room seemed to shrink. She was trapped. A medical anomaly in a room full of scientists with cameras.

"I'm leaving," she said.

"You can't," a security guard said, stepping in front of the door. He was big, but to Mia, he looked slow. "We have orders to keep you contained."

Contained.

The word triggered something primal. The rage she had felt in the sporting goods store. The cold calculation of the predator.

Mia sauntered toward the guard. He put a hand on her shoulder.

She didn't hit him. She just grabbed his wrist and squeezed. The guard yelped, dropping to his knees.

"Don't touch me," Mia said softly.

The room went dead silent.

She scowled at the doctor. "Scrubs. Now. And shoes. If I don't have them in thirty seconds, I'm walking out of here naked, and I'm taking your badge with me."

The doctor stared at her, his face pale. He studied the guard on the floor, then noticed Mia's unblemished skin.

"Get her some scrubs," he ordered.

"But doctor—" a nurse started.

"Just do it!" he shouted. "Discharge her against medical advice. Just get her out of here."

Five minutes later, Mia strolled out of the ICU wearing blue scrubs and surgical booties. She moved through the hospital corridors, head down, avoiding eye contact.

She passed a waiting room TV. The news was playing.

"Miracle survivor of Route 29... Dr. Mia Peers... sources say she took three rounds to the chest..."

Her face was on the screen.

Mia pulled the surgical cap lower. She wasn't just a scientist anymore. She wasn't just a killer. She was a headline.

She pushed through the emergency exit doors and into the cool night air. She didn't have a phone. She didn't have a wallet. She didn't have a car.

But she had legs that could run forever.

Mia started jogging, her pace increasing with every block. She needed to get to the lab. She needed a story for Chris.

And she needed to feed.

Fallout

Mia

Mia sat at Chris's dining room table, staring at a bowl of soup she hadn't touched.

Her brain felt... crowded.

It had been twenty-four hours since she escaped the hospital for Chris's house. He hadn't asked questions. He just let her in, cleaned her up, and gave her his bed.

But while her body healed, her mind was undergoing a renovation she hadn't authorized.

It started as a hum—a low-frequency vibration at the base of her skull. Then, it became a sensation of physical restructuring. Synapses firing. Neural pathways rerouting.

It was like watching a defrag program run on a corrupted hard drive.

Memory: High school prom. Deleted. Irrelevant data. Memory: First kiss with Husband #1. Compressed. Emotional redundancy. Analysis: Fear response to loud noises. Inefficient. Suppressed.

Mia gripped the edge of the table. "Stop," she whispered.

The optimization didn't stop. It categorized her personality traits as bugs in the code. Sarcasm? Inefficient communication. Vulnerability? Tactical weakness. Love? Biological imperative, override recommended.

"Stop!" Mia slammed her hand on the table.

The wood cracked.

Chris appeared in the doorway, holding a towel. He looked tired, his arm in a sling, bruises still fresh on his face.

"Mia? You okay?"

Mia glanced at him. Her enhanced brain cataloged him instantly: *Male. 38. Left clavicle fracture, healing. Cortisol levels elevated. Threat level: Zero.*

She shook her head, forcing the cold logic back into its cage.

"I'm fine," she lied. "Just... a headache."

"You haven't eaten."

She had. Before arriving.

"I'm not hungry."

That was a lie too. She was starving. But she was afraid if she started eating, she wouldn't stop.

———◆———

For a week, Mia hid in Chris's house while the world outside burned.

She still slept in his bed; he still took the couch. At night, she lay awake, listening to the house settle, listening to the neighbors breathe through the drywall.

The PTSD she expected didn't come. The serum had scrubbed it. The memory of Mason shooting her wasn't a trauma anymore; it was just data. A tactical error she wouldn't repeat.

The real horror came from the TV.

Chris tried to keep it off, but Mia found his iPad.

The news cycle had moved past the "miracle survivor" angle. Now, they were asking questions.

CNN: *"Sources at Virginia General confirm Dr. Peers suffered three fatal gunshot wounds. Yet she walked out of the ICU under her own power less than 48 hours later. Experts are calling it medically impossible."*

FOX: *"Video from a local sporting goods store shows a woman matching Peers' description leaping forty feet into the air. Is this the result of her controversial research?"*

ESPN: *"Olympic Committee launches investigation into Mia Peers' gold medals. Doping allegations surface amid rumors of genetic enhancement."*

She wasn't a victim anymore. She was a subject. A curiosity. A threat.

"Don't watch that," Chris said, taking the iPad from her hands.

He sat on the edge of the bed. He gazed at her with a mixture of love and fear that made Mia's chest ache.

"They don't know the truth," he said.

"They know enough," Mia said. Her voice sounded strange to her own ears—flat, devoid of inflection. Optimized. "They know I'm different."

"You're alive," Chris said. "That's what matters."

"Is it?"

Mia inspected her hands. They were perfect. No scars. No calluses. Even her fingerprints looked faint, as if the serum was smoothing away her identity.

"I'm changing, Chris," she whispered. "My brain... it's fixing things that weren't broken."

Chris reached out and took her hand. His skin felt rough, warm, *human.*

"You're still you," he insisted. "You're the woman who loves terrible coffee and hates country music. You're the woman who saved me."

Mia stared at him. She wanted to believe him. But the cold voice in the back of her head—the voice of the serum—was already analyzing his statement.

Love: Chemical reaction. Oxytocin dump. Temporary.

"I need to go back to the lab," Mia said, pulling her hand away.

"Mia, you can't. The police or media might be watching it."

"I have to," she said, standing up. "I have to stop the primate trials. If Sophia injects those orangutans... if she creates more things like me..."

"You'll be arrested the second you step foot on the property."

"No," Mia said. She headed to the window and stared into the night. Her reflection stared back—cold, perfect, alien.

"They won't arrest me," she said. "They can't catch me."

She turned to Chris.

"Please," Chris said. "Just wait one more day. We can talk about it tomorrow."

Mia analyzed the request. What would one more day give her?

No. That wasn't the right question.

The right question was, what was Chris hiding?

Consequences

Mia

M ia woke to the smell of coffee and the sound of silence. For a week, mornings had been a symphony of domestic noise—eggs frying, Chris humming, the clatter of plates.

Today, the house was quiet.

She entered the living room. Chris was sitting on the couch, still in his pajamas, staring at his phone. He didn't look up.

"What's the matter?" Mia asked.

"Coffee is on the table," he said. His voice was flat.

Mia picked up the mug. The ceramic was warm, grounding. She caught her reflection in the window—a woman who looked rested, healed, and utterly terrified. The serum had fixed her body, but her mind felt like a dam holding back a flood.

"Okay," she said, sitting in the armchair opposite him. "Lay it out. You're using your lawyer face."

Chris finally looked at her. His eyes were red-rimmed. "It's time for the truth, Mia."

"I told you the truth."

"You told me a version of it." He set his phone down. "Let me tell you what I see. Someone is hunting you for the formula. You slept at the lab with an arsenal. You tested the drug on yourself.

That's why you healed. That's why you're... different."

Mia gripped the mug. "Go on."

"The Cabela's massacre," Chris said softly. "That was you."

Mia didn't flinch. The serum wouldn't let her. It suppressed the shame, categorizing it as *inefficient emotional data*.

"Guilty as charged," she said. The words tasted bitter.

"You killed three people."

"They were going to kill me. They killed an innocent mechanic."

Chris leaned forward, resting his elbows on his knees. "I'm not judging you, Mia. I'm terrified for you. You're healing, yes. But you're also disappearing. I look at you, and sometimes... I don't see the woman I met at the coffee shop. I see a soldier."

"I am a soldier," Mia whispered. "I have to be."

"I wish you had trusted me."

"I couldn't risk you."

"I'm already at risk," Chris said. He took a breath, a ragged sound. "But that's not the only reason we need to talk. I have a confession."

Mia's enhanced hearing picked up the spike in his heart rate. *Thump-thump-thump.*

"What is it?"

"Your dad," Chris said. "He called me."

Mia froze. "At the hospital?"

"No. Over a year ago. After your second divorce." Chris stared at the floor. "He tracked me down. He told me he knew about Alexandria. He asked if... if I would consider reaching out to you."

The room seemed to tilt. The "optimization" in Mia's brain stuttered, unable to process the data.

"My father set us up?" she asked.

"Not exactly. He didn't tell me to date you. He asked me to... steer you." Chris swallowed hard. "He wanted me to encourage you to work on the cure. For Unity. He thought if you had a stable partner, someone who supported the 'right' kind of science, you'd go back to the original research."

Mia stood up. The mug slipped from her hand, shattering on the floor. She didn't hear it.

"It was a job," she whispered. "I was an assignment."

"No," Chris said, standing up and reaching for her. "Mia, no. I fell in love with you. The call was just the catalyst. Everything after that... the coffee, the concert, the beach... that was real."

Mia backed away, holding up a hand.

Analysis: Betrayal. Source: Father. Instrument: Chris. Conclusion: Trust is a vulnerability.

"He engineered me," Mia said, her voice trembling. "He cloned me to be her spare parts. And then he engineered my love life to make sure I stayed on task."

"Mia, please—"

"Stop."

She glowered at him. She saw the pain in his eyes, the sincerity. She believed he loved her. But it didn't matter. The foundation was rotten. Her father's fingerprints were on everything she touched.

"I have to go," she said.

"I'm not letting you leave," Chris said. "We can fix this."

"You can't fix what I am," Mia said. She beelined to the hook by the door and grabbed the keys to his truck.

"Mia, put the keys down."

"I can't be here, Chris. I'm dangerous. And now... now I know I'm alone."

"You are not alone!"

"Yes, I am," she said coldly. The serum surged, locking down her emotions, turning her heart into a stone. "I need to finish this. And I need to do it without distractions."

She opened the door. The morning air rushed in, cool and clean.

"I love you," Chris said, his voice breaking.

Mia paused. She glanced back at him one last time.

"I know," she said. "That's why I'm leaving."

She walked out, closing the door on the only normal life she would ever know. She climbed into his truck, the engine roaring to life.

She wasn't Mia Peers anymore. She was the asset. And it was time to clear the board.

Threats

Mia

Mia stepped out of the gun shop carrying a duffel bag heavy with ammunition and a new custom AR-15.

The paparazzi were waiting.

A dozen cameras flashed, a strobe light effect in the afternoon sun. Microphones were shoved into her face like spears.

"Dr. Peers! Is it true you survived three gunshot wounds?" "Are you enhancing yourself?" "Are you human?"

Mia stopped. She lowered her sunglasses. She stared directly into the lens of the nearest camera, her eyes cold and unblinking.

"I'm evolution," she said.

She let the soundbite hang there, heavy and arrogant. She wanted the New York crew to see it. She wanted Sophia to see it. She wanted them to know that the woman they tried to kill had crawled out of the grave and bought a bigger gun.

She pushed through the crowd, her movements fluid and terrifyingly precise. She didn't need a bodyguard. *She* was the danger.

Back at the lab, Mia poured a shot of bourbon. Then another. Then another.

The bottle was empty in ten minutes.

It was a biological arms race. Her liver processed the alcohol almost as fast as she could swallow it, neutralizing the toxin before it could reach her brain. She had to drink lethal amounts just to feel a buzz, just to dim the cold, white light of the "optimization" running in her head.

She smashed the empty bottle against the wall. The glass shattered, but the noise barely registered.

Analysis: Empathy levels critical. Compassion subroutine offline. Objective: Survival.

The lab phone rang.

Mia stared at it. Chris had stopped calling two days ago. He knew she was gone.

She picked up the receiver.

"Speak."

"Hello, Dr. Peers."

The voice was familiar. Lucas. The boyfriend. The one she had punched in the convenience store.

"It seems you're having trouble dying," Lucas said. "I bet your parents won't."

Mia leaned back in her chair, propping her boots on the desk. "Is that supposed to be a threat?"

"We have them," Lucas said. "Jeffrey and Theresa. We took them from the care facility an hour ago."

Mia waited for the panic. She waited for the fear, the daughterly instinct to protect her creators.

It didn't come.

Instead, her brain ran a cost-benefit analysis.

Subject: Parents. Value: Low. Risk: High. Status: Expendable.

"Go on," she said, inspecting her fingernails.

"We'll kill them," Lucas said, his voice tight. "Unless you bring us the formula. The one you used on yourself."

Mia laughed. It was a dry, humorless sound.

"You're threatening me with the people who made me?" she asked. "The people who designed me to be spare parts? You really didn't do your research, did you, Lucas?"

Silence on the other end.

"Let me get this straight," Lucas said slowly. "You're willing to let them die?"

"I'm saying I don't negotiate with dead men," Mia said. "And you are a dead man, Lucas. You just don't know it yet."

"We'll send you a message," Lucas snarled. "Just to show we're serious."

"Send whatever you want," Mia said. "It won't change the outcome."

She hung up.

She sat in the silence of the lab, waiting for the guilt. Waiting for the horror of what she had just done.

It never arrived.

She picked up the AR-15 from the duffel bag. She stripped it down, checking the action, oiling the bolt. Her hands moved with mechanical precision.

They had her parents. Good. That meant they were in one place. That meant she knew where to find them.

Mia didn't need to save her parents. She needed to clear the board. And if Jeffrey and Theresa were collateral damage in the war they started... so be it.

She loaded a magazine.

Optimization complete.

Parricide

Mia

T he sirens weren't just noise. They were physical pressure, drilling into Mia's skull like an auger.

She pressed a pillow over her face, trying to block out the cacophony. Her enhanced hearing picked apart the layers of sound: the wail of police cruisers, the lower warble of an ambulance, the excited chatter of a crowd gathering on her lawn.

And underneath it all, a single, erratic heartbeat. *Thump... thump... silence.*

Mia sat up. The pillow hit the floor.

She didn't have a hangover. Her body had processed the lethal dose of alcohol in under an hour. She was sober, alert, and terrified.

She hurried to the window and peered through the blinds.

Her front lawn was a sea of blue uniforms. Police tape fluttered in the wind. An ambulance was backed up to the porch, but the medics weren't rushing. They were standing around a covered shape on the grass.

Mia grabbed her pistol from the nightstand, shoved it into her waistband, and threw on a hoodie.

She opened the front door.

Three officers turned, shotguns raised.

"Dr. Peers!" one shouted. "Hands where I can see them!"

"What happened?" Mia demanded, stepping onto the porch. "Who is that?"

"Ma'am, get on the ground!"

Mia ignored them. She trotted down the steps. The officers moved to intercept her, but she brushed past them. It wasn't a shove; it was a displacement of mass. They bounced off her like children running into a wall.

She reached the body.

A medic tried to stop her. Mia grabbed his arm and moved him aside, gentle but with intention.

She pulled back the sheet.

Her mother stared up at the sky, a single bullet hole in the center of her forehead. Her eyes were open, glazed with the final surprise of death.

Theresa Peers. The woman who made her. The woman who abandoned her.

Mia didn't scream. She couldn't. The sound was trapped in her throat, blocked by a wall of cold logic.

Analysis: Cranial trauma. Immediate cessation of life functions. Time of death: Less than one hour.

"Dr. Peers, down! Now!"

A heavy hand clamped onto her shoulder.

Mia spun. The rage flared, hot and bright. She grabbed the officer by his vest and threw him. He flew ten feet, landing in the rhododendrons.

"Don't touch her!" Mia roared.

Then the world collapsed.

A dozen officers piled onto her. She felt the weight of bodies, the bite of cuffs, the impact of knees on her spine. She could have thrown them off. She could have snapped the cuffs like paperclips.

But she didn't.

Because looking at her mother's dead face, Mia realized something terrifying.

She didn't feel sad. She felt... relieved.

The horror of that relief broke her. She went limp, letting them drag her to the armored van.

Memory: Summer.

The swing set creaked rhythmically. Mia and Unity, five years old, matching pink bows.

"Underdog!" Mia screamed.

Her mother laughed, running under the swing, pushing Mia higher. "Hold on tight, baby!"

"I'm going to jump!" Mia yelled.

"No!" her father shouted from the patio.

Mia glanced at Unity. Unity smiled. It wasn't a child's smile. It was knowing. Ancient.

Mia gaped at her own arm. The birthmark was gone. She peered at Unity's arm. There it was. The dot.

"One," Unity whispered.

"Two," Mia said.

"Three!"

They jumped. For a second, they floated, defying gravity. Just two little girls, flying forever as one.

The interrogation room was cold. Stainless steel table. Two-way mirror. The smell of stale coffee and fear.

Mia sat with her head on her arms, staring at the table. The cuffs chafed her wrists, but the skin didn't break.

The door opened. Two men in suits entered.

"Dr. Peers," the older one said. "I'm Agent Smith. This is

Agent Hadley. FBI."

Mia didn't look up. "I want my lawyer. Call Chris Holden."

"We're calling him," Smith said, sitting down. "But we need to talk about your mother."

"Did you check the cameras?" Mia asked, her voice muffled by her arm. "My house has security."

"The system was disabled," Hadley said. "Wiped clean. Professional job."

"It was the New York crew," Mia said. "Lucas. Mason. Bianca."

"We're looking into them," Smith said. "But right now, we're looking at you. You were found at the scene. Armed. Aggressive."

"I was grieving," Mia said flatly.

"Were you?" Hadley slid a folder across the table. "Because you don't look like a grieving daughter. You look like a woman bent on destruction."

Mia sat up. She opened the folder.

Photos from Cabela's. Grainy shots of her throwing a man through a display case. Leaping through a skylight.

"This isn't about my mother," Mia said.

"It's about everything," Smith said. "Three dead in Gainesville. One dead at a tire shop. And now your mother. Bodies are piling up around you, Dr. Peers. And you seem to be the only one walking away without a scratch."

"Where is my father?" Mia asked.

The agents exchanged a look.

"He's missing," Hadley admitted. "Taken from the facility. We think it's connected."

"You think?" Mia laughed, a harsh, barking sound. "They took him to make me comply. They killed my mother to send a message."

"Who?"

"I told you. The people who want the formula."

"And what formula is that?" Smith asked, leaning forward. "The one that turns a scientist into a super-villain?"

Mia stared at him. He knew. Or he suspected.

"I want my lawyer," she repeated.

"You're being held until arraignment on Monday," Smith said, standing up. "Enjoy the weekend, Dr. Peers."

They walked out.

Mia stared at the mirror. She could hear the hum of the recording equipment behind it. She could hear the agents talking in the hall.

"*She's cold as ice,*" Hadley said.

"*She's not human,*" Smith replied.

Mia glanced at her hands. No birthmark. No scars. No mother.

They were right. She wasn't human. Not anymore.

She was an experiment that had outlived its creator. And now, she was the only one able to finish the job.

Arraignment

Mia

The courtroom smelled of floor wax and old wood. Mia stood at the defendant's table, her hands clasped behind her back to hide the tremors—not from fear, but from the sheer effort of holding her strength in check.

The judge, a man with a face like a bulldog, glared down at her.

"Three million dollars," he boomed. "Dr. Peers is a flight risk and a danger to the community. I'm setting bail high."

Chris stepped forward. He was wearing his best suit, his posture rigid. He didn't look like a grieving widower or a heartbroken ex. He looked like a shark.

"Your Honor," Chris said, his voice smooth as glass. "My client has no criminal record. She is a victim of a violent home invasion that left her mother dead. The prosecution's case relies on grainy footage and conjecture. We have the funds ready for transfer."

Mia stared at him. Three million dollars.

Analysis: Debt incurred. Obligation established.

The gavel banged. "Bail granted."

Mia stepped out of the courthouse, cameras flashing like lightning. She didn't blink. She didn't shield her face.

She got into Chris's truck and stared straight ahead.

"Where did you get the money?" she asked as they pulled away.

"Does it matter?" Chris asked. His knuckles were white on the wheel.

"It matters to the ledger."

"There is no ledger, Mia. Just stay alive."

———◇———

The funeral was a study in gray. Sleet fell in sheets, coating the black umbrellas in ice.

Mia sat alone under the tent. The casket was closed. A mercy, considering the caliber of the round that had taken Theresa's face.

She felt... nothing.

The optimization was working. Grief was inefficient. Tears were a waste of hydration.

She watched the casket lower into the ground with the detachment of a scientist observing a chemical reaction.

Subject: Mother. Status: Terminated. Emotional impact: Negligible.

Chris stood outside the tent, shivering in his coat. He gazed at her with eyes full of pity.

Mia hated it. She didn't need pity. She needed ammo.

The ceremony ended.

Mia strode to Chris. She hugged him, careful not to crush his ribs.

"Thank you," she said.

"I'm sorry about your dad," Chris said. "The police still have no leads?"

"They're looking in the wrong places," Mia said. "But I'll find him."

"Mia," Chris started, grabbing her arm. "Come home with

me. Let me help you."

"I can't." She pulled away. "I have work to do."

She got into her Highlander and drove home. The house was a crime scene, but the police tape was gone.

She parked in the driveway, unable to enter the garage because of the boxes scattered across the concrete floor she had been rummaging through —her parents' hoarding.

She entered the garage. The smell of dust and old paper filled her nose.

She started kicking through the boxes, looking for anything—a clue, a safe house, a contact.

Her foot struck something hard. A leather-bound book.

She picked it up. *Project Animae - Log 1999.*

Her father's handwriting.

Mia opened it. She scanned the pages, her enhanced brain processing the text in seconds. It was all there. The genetic splicing. The failed embryos. The creation of the "spare."

Subject M demonstrates higher aggression levels than Subject U. Recommend conditioning to suppress volatility.

"Conditioning," Mia whispered. "You didn't raise me. You programmed me."

Her phone buzzed.

Unknown Number.

Mia answered. "Speak."

"Daddy's next," Lucas's voice said. "Unless you bring it."

"Bring what?"

"The formula. The one that turned you into a freak."

"Where?"

"The mountain," Lucas said. "Cabela's. Where you killed my friends. Meet me at the base of the indoor rock wall. Noon. Come alone."

"Bring him," Mia said coldly. "If he's not there, I burn the formula."

"He'll be there. Don't be late, Dr. Peers."

The line went dead.

Mia looked at the journal. She looked at the boxes of her childhood—toys, clothes, memories. All props in a stage play.

She tossed the journal into a trash can. She didn't need memories. She needed a weapon.

Mia drove to the lab. The window was repaired, but the scars of the rats' escape were still visible on the floor.

She went to the secure storage. She didn't just pull out one vial; she grabbed a rack of three.

She wasn't going to give Lucas the new formula. She wasn't going to give him the key to the kingdom. She was going to give him the Twin Variant. The one that required a genetic match to survive. The one that burned out the host in six hours if the circuit wasn't complete.

She mixed the solution in three separate vials. They were identical to the Lazarus batch.

"Here's your miracle," Mia whispered, tucking the three vials into her tactical vest. One for the trade. Two for insurance.

She wasn't going to Cabela's to negotiate. She was going to deliver her own message. And the enemy was going to understand it six hours too late.

The Deal

Mia

Mia stood in the atrium of Cabela's sporting goods store. The place was closed for "renovations" following the massacre months earlier.

Caution tape crisscrossed the aisles. The air smelled of stale popcorn and industrial cleaner.

She stood at the base of the massive artificial mountain, the taxidermy goats staring down at her with glass eyes.

She checked her watch. 11:59 AM.

The front doors were forced open. Lucas strode in, flanked by Bianca and two men Mia didn't recognize. They were armed with rifles, holding them low but ready.

Then, they dragged him in.

Jeff Peers stumbled forward. He looked frail, his skin colorless, his wrists bound with zip ties. A bruise bloomed on his cheek.

"Dad," Mia whispered.

"Stay back," Lucas warned, raising a hand. "Show me the vial."

Mia reached into her vest. She felt the three cold glass tubes. She pulled out one.

"Here," she said. "Let him go."

"Not yet," Lucas said. "We need to know it's real. We know you're smart, Mia. We know you're tricky."

He gestured to Bianca. She inched forward, holding a syringe.

"Inject yourself," Lucas said.

Mia froze. "What?"

"Prove it," Lucas said. "If it's the real deal, it won't kill you. If it's poison... well, then we kill your dad anyway."

Mia stared at the vial. It *was* poison to anyone else. But to her? She was already enhanced. She was already part of the circuit.

She didn't have a choice. She handed the vial to Bianca, who drew the liquid into the syringe.

Mia took the needle. She jammed it into her arm and depressed the plunger.

Cold fire flooded her veins. Her vision sharpened. Her heart rate dropped, then hammered a slow, powerful rhythm. The energy surge was intoxicating.

She didn't die. She got stronger.

Lucas smiled. "It works."

"Let him go," Mia said, her voice vibrating with the force of the serum.

Lucas nodded to the men holding Jeff. They shoved him forward.

"Mia," Jeff gasped, stumbling toward her. "Mia, I'm sorry."

She reached for him. "It's okay, Dad. We're going."

"No," Lucas said.

He raised his hand. "Kill them both."

From the upper level, a dozen more men emerged. They weren't locals. They were tactical. Professional.

The air erupted.

Mia didn't think. She moved. She grabbed her father and threw him to the ground, covering his body with her own.

She was fast, faster than bullets, but she wasn't bulletproof.

The rounds hit her. One. Two. Five. Ten.

They punched through her back, shredding muscle and

organ. Pain, white-hot and blinding, tore through her.

But the serum was working overtime. It was knitting her back together as fast as she was being torn apart.

But the bullets didn't stop at her. They passed through.

She felt her father jerk beneath her. Once. Twice.

"No!" Mia screamed.

The firing stopped. The echo rolled through the cavernous store.

Mia pushed herself up. Her back was a ruin of blood and healing tissue.

She glanced down.

Jeff Peers lay on the linoleum. His eyes were open, staring at the ceiling. A smile was frozen on his lips.

"Mia," he whispered, blood bubbling from his lips. "I'm so proud... of you."

The light left his eyes.

Mia stared at him. The man who made her. The man who used her. The man who loved the original more than the copy.

Dead.

"Finish her," Lucas ordered.

Mia leered at her foes. Her eyes weren't human anymore. They were black pits of rage.

She stood taller. The bullets pushed out of her skin, clinking onto the floor.

Lucas took a step back. "Shoot her again!"

Mia moved.

She was a blur. She reached the first gunman and snapped his neck before he could raise his rifle. She grabbed the second and threw him into a display case.

The others scattered, firing wildly.

Mia didn't chase them. She grabbed her father's body. She lifted him effortlessly, cradling him against her chest.

She ran.

She sprinted through the shattered front doors, moving

faster than a car, leaving the carnage behind.

The funeral was small like her mother's had been. Closed casket. Security perimeter.

Mia stood by the grave, watching them lower her father into the ground next to his wife.

She didn't cry. She couldn't. The serum had burned away her tears.

"Goodbye, Dad," she whispered. "You made me a monster. I hope you're happy with the result."

She stared across the cemetery. Chris stood by the gate, watching her. He waved, a sad, tentative gesture.

Mia waved back after commanding an override of the serum's central optimization program. She could risk involving him. He was worth it. That important to her. Her lifeline. Her everything. Besides, Dr. Jeffrey, her so-called "father," was only a memory now.

She got into her Highlander. Her phone rang.

Arjun.

"What?" she answered.

"Mia," Arjun said. His voice was cold. "The board has met."

"And?"

"With the recent... publicity. The violence. The legal issues. We are terminating the contract."

Mia gripped the phone. "You can't. The formula works. I proved it."

"You proved you are unstable," Arjun said. "We are cutting ties. The funding is pulled. Effective immediately."

"You owe me," Mia snarled.

"We owe you nothing. Goodbye, Dr. Peers."

The line went dead.

Mia stared at the phone.

No money. No lab. No parents. But she had Chris.

She was *not* alone.

And she still had the Secret Serum, the one from ten years ago. She still had *the choice*. A sister to potentially save.

Mia started the car.

Better Together

Mia

The clock on the microwave read 3:17 AM. Mia sat at the kitchen island, staring at the grain of the granite countertop.

Her hands were steady—unnaturally so. Her heart rate was a slow, rhythmic thud, pumping blood that was more chemical than biological.

She hadn't slept. The serum didn't let her. It kept her in a state of suspended readiness, like a sentry gun waiting for a target.

She heard the floorboards creak upstairs. Then, the soft pad of footsteps.

Chris stood in the doorway. He looked older in the dim light, the lines around his eyes deepened by the last few weeks. He wasn't wearing a shirt; the bruise on his chest from the seatbelt was fading to a sickly yellow.

"You seem energized," he said, his voice rough with sleep.

"I can't turn it off," Mia whispered. "The engine is running hot."

He headed into the kitchen. He didn't turn on the light. He moved to the coffee maker, the domestic ritual a stark contrast to the violence clinging to Mia like smoke.

"I lost the funding," she said. "Arjun called yesterday. They pulled the plug."

"I figured," Chris said. He pressed the brew button. The machine hissed. "Dead bodies are bad for business."

"I have nothing, Chris. No lab. No money. No parents." She stared at her hands—the hands that had snapped necks and punched through flesh. "Just this."

Chris turned around. He leaned against the counter, crossing his arms. He didn't look afraid. He looked resigned.

"You have me," he said.

"Do I?" Mia asked. "You know what I am now. You saw the news. You saw the bodies."

"I saw a woman trying to survive."

"I didn't just survive," Mia said coldly. "I exterminated them. And I didn't feel a thing."

She stood up, the chair scraping harsh against the tile.

"My father... he made me this way. He edited me. He stripped out the fear and the weakness so I could save Unity. I'm not a person, Chris. I'm a biological contingency plan."

Chris strode over to her. He stepped into her personal space, fearless.

"You're Mia," he said. "You hate mediocrity. You drink terrible coffee. You cry when you think no one is looking."

"That's just programming."

"No," Chris said. He reached out and took her face in his hands. His palms were warm. "That's a soul. And it's bruised, and it's bleeding, but it's there."

Mia leaned into his touch. The contact sent a jolt through her system, quieting the static in her brain.

"I can't be what you need," she whispered. "I'm too dangerous."

"I don't need safe," Chris said. "I need you."

He kissed her. It wasn't a desperate kiss like in the truck. It was slow, deliberate. A sealing of a pact.

Mia closed her eyes. For a moment, she let herself be human. She let herself believe that forgiveness was possible.

The cold, hard logic of the serum tried to take over. She pushed it away.

Chris loved her. And because he loved her, he was a target. Sophia knew about him. The Italians knew about him. If Mia stayed, he died.

No, he wouldn't die. Mia would burn the world down before that happened.

"Go back to bed," she said softly. "I'll be there in a minute."

"You promise?"

"I promise."

Chris hesitated, searching her eyes. He wanted to believe her.

"Okay," he said. "Don't stay up too late."

He trekked back toward the bedroom.

Mia waited until she heard the bedroom door click shut. She waited until she heard the rhythm of his breathing slow down to a sleep state.

She went to the sink and poured the coffee down the drain.

She didn't need caffeine. She needed leverage.

She hurried to the living room and grabbed her bag. She checked the load in her Bersa. Seven rounds. Not enough for a war, but enough for an extraction.

She took a piece of paper from Chris's notepad and wrote two words.

I'm sorry.

She left it on the counter next to his keys.

Mia didn't take his truck. She didn't want them tracking him. She slipped out the back door, melting into the darkness of the suburbs.

She began to run.

Her destination wasn't the lab, but she had to go there first.

The funding was gone. Time was up. For whoever had hired the Mafia. Because Mia had the location. The vial exchange for her father had been a double cross in more ways than one.

And after that, it was time to fix *the choice*. Or rather, to make it.

Mia's pace increased, her legs eating up the miles. She wasn't a scientist tonight. She wasn't a girlfriend.

She was a cleaner. She was going fix everything that had gone wrong in her life or she was going to take everyone down with her.

Point Blank

Bianca

The Escalade smelled of stale smoke, sweat, and rage. Bianca lowered the binoculars, rubbing her eyes.

The lab was a fortress of brick and tinted glass, silent under the Virginia moon.

"Wake up," she said, nudging Lucas.

He jerked awake, his hand instinctively going for the pistol in his lap. "What?"

"Movement," Bianca said. "Brian just left."

In the backseat, Mason shifted. He was eating gelato again—pistachio, a dark obsession since his torture. The sound of his spoon scraping the cup was grating.

"Is he alone?" Lucas asked, rubbing his face.

"Alone. Getting into his truck."

"Good," Lucas muttered. "One less distraction."

The mood in the car was toxic. Since the ambush on the mountain—where Mia had not only survived but slaughtered a portion of their backup team—Lucas had been unraveling. He was no longer the cool professional Bianca had fallen for. He was a cornered animal.

"We can't wait anymore," Mason growled. "We go in tonight."

"Mia might have slipped back in there. You know how fast she is." Bianca warned. "You saw what she did to Dylan. You saw what she did on the mountain. If we go in while she's there, we die."

"She's not invincible," Mason spat. "She bleeds. I saw it."

"And then she healed," Bianca countered. "She took thirteen rounds, Mason. Thirteen. And she walked away carrying her father like a bag of groceries."

Lucas turned to her. His eyes were bloodshot, manic. He pointed his gun at her face.

"Stop talking," he whispered.

Bianca froze. The barrel was inches from her nose.

"Lucas?"

"You're scared," he said. "I get it. But the drug she gave us killed the client's associate. And if I hear one more word about how scary the scientist is, I will put a bullet in your leg and leave you here. Clear?"

Bianca nodded slowly. Her heart hammered against her ribs. This wasn't her boyfriend. This was a stranger.

Lucas lowered the gun. "We wait until Mia's whereabouts are confirmed. Then we breach. We take the real serum, we take the data, and we burn the place down."

"And the Italians?" Mason asked. "Alessia and Gabriele?"

"If they're in there," Lucas said, checking his magazine, "you can have them."

Mason smiled. His new veneers glinted in the dashboard light. "Good."

They waited. Hours dragged by. The moon climbed higher.

Finally, the side door of the lab opened.

"Movement," Bianca whispered.

Mia stepped out. She was wearing a hoodie, carrying a duffel bag. She moved with a predatory grace that made Bianca's skin crawl. She didn't look around. She headed straight toward the forest and disappeared into the darkness.

"Smart. Harder to track," Bianca said. ""She's gone.""

"Gear up," Lucas ordered.

They pulled tactical vests from the trunk. Lucas handed Bianca an MP5. The weight of it felt wrong in her hands. She was a tech specialist, a grifter. Not a soldier.

"What about Sophia?" Bianca asked as she strapped on the vest. "She's still inside."

"She's leverage," Lucas said. "Or a casualty. Depends on how much trouble she gives us."

Bianca surveyed the lab. She touched the pocket where Brian's keycard was hidden. She could get them in quietly. She could prevent a firefight.

But if she opened that door, she was letting monsters in. Including her.

"Let's go," Lucas said.

Mason racked the slide of his shotgun. "Time to pay the rent."

Bianca told herself she was doing this to survive.

But as they approached the silent, looming fortress, she knew the truth.

She wasn't surviving. She was just prolonging the inevitable.

Welcome to the Jungle

Sophia

Sophia stood over the centrifuge, watching the serum spin into a blur of electric white.

It was late. The lab was silent, save for the occasional hoot from the storage room where the six orangutans were staged.

Gabriele and Alessia were patrolling the hallway, bored and restless. They were soldiers without a war, pacing the perimeter like caged tigers.

Sophia checked the readout. The batch was stable. It was Mia's new formula—the Twinless Variant—mixed with the specific genetic markers of the alpha male orangutan.

She strode to the storage room. The alpha, a massive male named Thor by the supplier, watched her from his cage.

His eyes were intelligent, mournful. He knew what she was. He remembered the needles.

"Don't look at me like that," Sophia whispered. "You're going to save lives."

Suddenly, Gabriele shouted from the lobby.

"They're here!"

Sophia bolted to the front. The black Cadillac Escalade was idling outside the glass doors, its headlights blinding in the dark.

Mason stepped out. He was a ruin of a man—shirtless, covered in tattoos and scars, moving with a stiff, mechanical gait.

He held up a badge. Pressed it to the scanner.

The light flashed red. A harsh buzzer sounded.

"Access Denied," the electronic voice chirped.

Mason frowned. He tried again. Red.

"Brian," Sophia muttered. "Smart boy."

Mason shrugged, returning to the Escalade. The reverse lights flared.

"They're going to ram!" Alessia shouted. "Take cover!"

The siblings scattered into the side offices. Sophia sprinted down the hall, diving behind the reception desk just as the SUV roared backward.

CRASH.

The world exploded in a shower of glass and twisted metal.

The Escalade plowed through the lobby, smashing the front desk and coming to rest in a cloud of dust and debris.

Gunfire erupted immediately.

Alessia and Gabriele opened up from the offices, their pistols popping in the enclosed space.

The rear doors of the Escalade flew open. Lucas and Bianca rolled out, clad in tactical gear, firing MP5s.

But it was Mason who stole the show.

He stepped out of the driver's side, probably fueled by enough painkillers to drop a horse.

His eyes were clear. Manic.

He held two huge red cans. He didn't shoot. He poured.

Gasoline splashed across the floor, soaking the carpet, the debris, the demolished front desk.

Mason lit a cigar. He took a long drag, the cherry glowing bright orange. The bullets whizzing past him didn't seem to faze him.

He tossed the cigar.

WHOOSH.

The lobby turned into an inferno.

"To the back!" Sophia screamed. "Protect the serum!"

She scrambled down the hall, coughing as the black smoke rolled in. Her siblings followed, firing blindly into the flames.

They reached the experimentation room. Sophia grabbed the nearest vial of serum and shoved it into her pocket.

Behind them, the fire roared. And through the smoke, a shadow emerged.

Mason.

He broke through the flames like a demon.

He reached out with massive arms and grabbed Alessia and Gabriele by their necks.

He slammed their heads together. *Crack.*

They dropped to the floor, dazed.

Mason straddled Gabriele. He reached into his pocket and pulled out a handful of pink plastic spoons—the same kind they had used to eat gelato while he bled.

"Dessert time," he growled.

Sophia watched in horror as he plunged the spoons into Gabriele's eyes.

Her brother screamed, a high, thin sound that was cut short as Mason drove his fist into his throat.

Alessia tried to crawl away. Lucas stepped out of the smoke, leveling his gun at her.

Bang.

Sophia dove under a lab table as another bullet sparked off its metal leg. She was alone. Her family was dead. The lab was burning.

"Come out, Sophia," Lucas called. "We know you have it."

She clutched the vial in her pocket. She scanned the area desperately.

Her eyes landed on the cages.

The alpha male was thrashing against the bars, howling in

terror at the fire.

Sophia crawled toward the cage. She reached up and unlatched the lock.

The door swung open.

The orangutan burst out. He didn't run for the exit. He turned toward the source of the noise.

Lucas saw the ape and raised his gun. "What the—"

The orangutan roared—a sound that thundered in Sophia's chest—and charged.

Lucas fired. The bullets hit the ape's chest, but the serum-enhanced muscle absorbed the impact. The beast didn't stop.

He slammed into Lucas, picking him up and throwing him across the room.

Lucas hit the wall with a sickening *crunch* and slid down, motionless.

Mason turned from the corpses of the siblings. He saw the ape. He saw Sophia cowering under the table.

He smiled. He raised his gun.

"Two birds," he said.

"Kill him!" Sophia screamed at the ape.

The orangutan grinned at her. For a second, Sophia thought he would kill her instead. He remembered the needles.

But then he turned toward Mason. He saw the fire. He saw the violence.

He recognized a predator.

The ape charged.

Mason fired until his clip was empty. The orangutan took the hits and kept coming.

He leaped, tackling Mason to the ground.

The screams that followed were human. The tearing sounds were not.

Sophia didn't watch. She scrambled out from under the table and ran for the back door.

The heat was intense, the smoke blinding.

She burst out into the cool night air, gasping for breath.

Behind her, the lab was a bonfire. Sirens wailed in the distance.

She touched her pocket. The vial was safe.

She was alive.

Sophia started to run toward her car, leaving the fire, the bodies, and the monster she had created to burn together in the dark.

Off Grid

Bianca

B ianca lay prone in the tree line, the stock of the sniper rifle pressed against her shoulder.

Through the scope, the world was green-tinted night vision. She saw the flames licking the lobby of the lab.

And then, she saw Sophia.

The woman burst out of the rear exit, coughing, soot streaked across her face. She clutched a single vial in her hand like a holy relic.

Bianca centered the crosshairs on Sophia's chest.

Breathe in. Breathe out. Squeeze.

It was a clean shot. One hundred yards. No wind. Sophia's family had put the hit on Mason. She was the reason Lucas was probably dead inside that burning building.

Bianca's finger tightened on the trigger.

She thought about her father, the Ranger. He had killed for his country. She was about to kill for... what? A vial of liquid? A paycheck from a boss who considered her expendable?

Lucas had pointed a gun at her face. The crew was probably dead. There was no way they had survived that fire. Except for her. She had gone to the trees instead of inside the building as planned.

If she pulled the trigger, she wasn't a soldier. She was just another monster in the dark.

Bianca exhaled. She lifted her finger off the trigger.

Sophia reached her car, threw the vial into the passenger seat, and peeled out of the lot, tires screeching. Seconds later, blue lights flooded the entrance as the first police cruisers arrived.

Bianca watched them. She lowered the rifle.

She sat up, her back against the rough bark of an oak tree. She pulled Brian's keycard from her pocket. The badge that didn't work. The trap.

Brian had played them. He had tried to stop them. He was smarter than she gave him credit for.

She pulled out her burner phone.

To Brian: *The badge didn't work. Nice play. The police arrived way too fast. You were right about the Mafia life. I'm done. Don't look for me. I'm going to disappear.*

She hit send.

Then she took the SIM card out and snapped it in half. She threw the phone into the brush.

Bianca stood up. She left the rifle where it lay. She didn't need it anymore. She wasn't a cleaner. She wasn't a tech specialist. She was a ghost.

The Customer

Mia

T he tracker on Mia's phone pulsed a steady red dot. It led to the Old Post Office Pavilion, now a luxury hotel and residence.

It was fitting. The man or woman who wanted to burn her life down lived in a monument to power.

Mia parked her Highlander two blocks away. She checked her reflection in the rearview mirror.

She wore black cargo pants, a dark blouse, and a tactical vest filled with magazines. She looked like a soldier. She looked like the predator she had become.

But her hands were shaking like they never had before. Something was wrong because it wasn't fear. This was something foreign. Maybe the serum. She wasn't sure and she couldn't focus on it.

The task she set for herself demanded her all.

She got out of the SUV. She moseyed to the building, head down, blending into the evening crowd. She slipped through the resident entrance as a tenant left, flashing a confident smile she didn't feel.

"Police," she muttered to a startled man in the lobby. He nodded and glanced away.

Mia took the stairs. Third floor. Room 304.

She paused in the stairwell, listening. Her enhanced hearing picked up three heartbeats in the hallway. *Thump-thump. Thump-thump. Thump-thump.*

Private security.

She opened the fire door.

Three men in suits stood outside the apartment. They saw her. Their hands went to their jackets.

Mia raised her pistols.

Kill them, the serum whispered. *Eliminate the threat. Clear the board.*

Her fingers tightened on the triggers.

Then she stopped.

She saw their faces—fear, surprise, the realization that they were about to die. She saw herself in the mirror of their eyes. A killer. A weapon.

No.

She wasn't her father's experiment. She wasn't Sophia's lab rat. She was Mia Peers. And she was done killing.

She holstered the guns.

"Let's dance," she said.

The men fired and charged. Mia moved. Dodged. She didn't shoot. She didn't punch through chests. She struck pressure points, shattered knees, delivered concussive blows. It was surgical. Precise.

In ten seconds, they were unconscious on the floor.

Mia stepped over them and kicked the door open.

Arjun Kasudia sat on the edge of the bed, holding a suitcase. He looked up, his face pale.

"Hello, Mia," he said.

"Arjun."

"I knew you'd come," he said. "I saw the news. I saw the bodies."

"You hired them," Mia said, walking toward him. "You hired

the crew. You gave them the intel. You killed my parents."

"I didn't want them dead," Arjun said, his voice trembling. "I just wanted the formula. The board... they were going to cut you loose. I needed the serum before they shut you down."

"Why?" Mia asked. "Greed? Power?"

"Life," Arjun whispered.

A cry came from the adjoining room. A baby.

Mia froze.

Arjun stood up. "Please. Let me show you."

He went into the other room and came back carrying a car seat. Inside was a baby girl, pale and lethargic, her head lolling to the side.

"This is Natasha," Arjun said. "My granddaughter. She has Spinal Muscular Atrophy. Type 1."

Mia stared at the child. The same disease that killed her brother.

"You wanted to save her," Mia said.

"I saw what you did," Arjun said. "The rats. You nearly cured death, Mia. I couldn't let that disappear because of a budget cut."

"So you destroyed my life instead."

"I was desperate," he said, tears tracking down his face. "I'm sorry."

Mia stared at the baby. Then at Arjun.

She reached into her pocket and pulled out one of the two remaining vials of Twin Variant she had saved from the Cabela's exchange.

"This would have killed her," she said.

Arjun blanched. "I know. We... found out."

"It requires a genetic match," Mia said. "A twin. A circuit. Without it, the energy burns the host alive. You would have watched her melt."

Arjun sank back onto the bed, clutching the carrier. "Oh god."

"You owe me," Mia said. "You owe me for my parents. You

owe me for my life."

"Anything," Arjun said. "Name it."

"You still have money," Mia said. "You still have connections."

"Yes."

"Good. Because I'm done hiding. I'm finally going to work on cures for real diseases. And you are going to help fund them."

"But the board—"

"Forget the board," Mia snapped. "You work for me now. You get me a new lab. A secure lab. And you get me the best SMA specialists in the world. For Natasha."

Arjun gawked at her. He probably saw the monster in her eyes. But perhaps he also saw the scientist.

"Okay," he whispered. "Okay."

"And Arjun?" Mia leaned in close. "If you ever cross me again... I won't be this nice."

She turned and walked out, stepping over the unconscious guards.

She left the building and headed into the cool night air.

The war was over. The hunters were dead or broken. She had lost her parents, her humanity.

But she had one final mission.

Mia got into her Highlander. She didn't go to Chris. She didn't go to the police.

She drove home. She was Mia Peers. And she was just getting started.

Turncoat

Mia

Mia threw the deadbolt. The steel tumblers slid into place with a heavy *thunk* that echoed through the foyer.

She leaned her forehead against the cool wood of the door, exhaling a breath she felt she'd been holding since Cabela's. She had done it. Arjun was handled. Funding was secured. The war, for a brief, beautiful moment, felt over.

She pushed off the door and headed for the kitchen. There was a hole in her stomach the size of the Grand Canyon.

"Hello, dear."

Mia spun.

She tried to dive, but her reflexes betrayed her. A sharp pinch stung her neck.

She slapped a hand to her jugular, her fingers brushing against plastic fletching, but her legs were already turning to water. The room tilted violently. The refrigerator slid sideways, and the floor rushed up to meet her cheek.

The kitchen dissolved into a wash of psychedelic static. Above her, a figure swam into focus.

Sophia.

She looked like a wraith. Her clothes were stained with soot. Her hair was wild, singed at the ends, and she smelled of acrid smoke and burnt plastic.

"Look what the cat dragged in." Sophia grinned, her face distorting like a reflection in a funhouse mirror. Her teeth looked impossibly white against her soot-streaked skin.

She leaned down, ripped the dart from Mia's neck, and pried Mia's eyelid open with a rough thumb. "Or is it a rat? I always get that idiom mixed up."

Mia tried to thrash, to sweep Sophia's legs, but her body was a stone. The paralytic was fast—military grade. *Move*, she commanded her arm. *Move, damn it.*

Her fingers didn't even twitch.

"What's the matter, Mia? Not the smartest person in the room anymore?" Sophia reached into Mia's pocket and fished out the vials. She held them up to the light, swirling the amber liquid.

"I managed to save the new version from the fire," Sophia rasped, her voice rough from smoke inhalation. "But having a spare 'twin' set seems ironic." She slipped them into her jacket. "I'm a scientist too, you know. Mother and I have years more experience than you."

"Buh..." The sound was a wet gurgle on Mia's lips.

Sophia tsked and tapped the barrel of her suppressor against Mia's forehead. The cold steel sent a shock through the numbness.

"You have such an attitude. We have your father to thank for that." Sophia sighed, looking around the kitchen as if bored. "Oh... wait. Daddy told you, didn't he? That naughty little scientist. You all should have been dead long ago."

She scowled down at Mia, her expression mocking. "When did you find out you were a clone? As a teenager? No... I think it was more recent. It doesn't matter. He's dead now, so at least Mother doesn't have to clean up another one of Cesaro's messes."

Chris. The name flashed in Mia's mind.

"And your boyfriend?" Sophia continued, as if reading the panic in Mia's dilating pupils. "Lovers can't keep secrets. He has to go, too. And Unity... well, she won't survive long after you're gone. You never understood what I meant by 'overflow.' It was never a twin thing. Laz and Jaz are clones. They came from our family factory. You're welcome. I'm betting one of your formulas will make Mother happy. If not, I'll fix it. We've had decades of attempts to find—well, a cure. You'd understand if you lived to be forty. Too bad you won't."

Sophia stood, towering over Mia like a titan.

"We could have been a great team. If only you weren't such a self-centered, know-it-all Barbie bitch. It's a miracle I lasted as long as I did at your lab." Sophia leaned close, her voice dropping to a whisper. "I had no choice. Mother said to remain there, and no one crosses Mother. Not even me."

Sophia's boot slammed into Mia's ribs.

The pain was distant, dull, like it was happening to someone else. Another kick to the stomach. A stomp to the thigh. Mia felt her body jerk with the impacts, but the paralysis kept her limp. She was a ragdoll.

Her vision tunneled. The kitchen lights began to strobe.

Memories bled into the present. She and Unity on a swing set. Her mother applying brown lipstick in the rearview mirror. Sophia, dressed as a laughing circus clown, beating the shit out of her. Her dad handing her a baby that looked exactly like her.

Sophia stopped kicking. She raised the gun.

"Goodbye, Mia."

The muzzle flashed. Two distinct *thwips*.

Mia didn't feel the bullets. She heard an umpire yell, "Play ball!" and the world went black.

———◆———

Time lost its meaning. It could have been seconds; it could have been centuries.

A vibration buzzed against her hip.

Mia opened her eyes. The ceiling was white, textured like popcorn. Why was she lying on the red carpet at her parents' retirement home? They were dead. She shouldn't be here.

She tried to inhale, but her throat was full of copper.

Move.

Her right arm twitched. A minor victory.

The carpet beneath her cheek was wet. Soaked.

She shifted her gaze.

Okay—not carpet. Not carpet at all. Not a retirement home either.

Her kitchen. Floor covered in blood. The baseboards splattered with red.

Her vision fractured. One eye focused on a dead fly on the light fixture; the other drifted lazily to the left. The phone in her pocket buzzed again, a lifeline dragging her back to the surface.

Mia jolted her body, forcing a roll.

Her face slapped into a puddle of tacky, cooling liquid. The shock of it—the smell of iron—triggered a primal alarm. She hacked, spewing blood and saliva across the floor tiles. The paralytic was wearing off, replaced by a searing agony in her chest and abdomen.

Sophia. The gun. The shots.

She dragged herself backward, leaving a smear of red in her wake. Her hand found the leg of the table. She pulled, her muscles screaming, her breath coming in ragged, wet gasps.

The front door burst open.

"Mia!"

Chris.

She tried to call out, to warn him, but only a wheeze escaped. He was there in a second, sliding on his knees through the blood, his hands hovering over her, afraid to touch.

"Oh god. Oh god, Mia." His face was pale, his eyes wide with terror. He pressed his hands to her chest, trying to stem the flow. "Stay with me. You hear me? Stay with me!"

Sirens wailed in the distance, growing louder.

Mia stared at him. She wanted to tell him it was okay, that the serum was already knitting the holes in her lungs, that the monster inside her refused to die. But the darkness was heavy, and it pulled her down again.

The hospital room was sterile and white, the smell of antiseptic burning her nose.

Mia sat on the edge of the bed, her legs dangling. The gown was drafty, but she didn't care. She watched the door.

"I heard about her," a doctor whispered to a nurse in the hallway. "Didn't believe it. But she completely healed. It's medically impossible. Two gunshot wounds to the torso. The liver was nicked. The lung collapsed. And now? There's not even a scar. Just... pink skin. Did you hear her lab burned down? With people inside. You think she did it?"

"Don't ask questions you don't want answered," the nurse replied, her voice shaking.

So Sophia destroyed the lab too. Figures. At least Mia had Arjun now.

She touched her stomach. Smooth. The serum had worked overtime. It had burned through her reserves—she was starving, her metabolism roaring like a furnace—but she was whole.

The door opened. Chris stepped in, looking like he hadn't slept in a week, though it had only been six hours. He stopped, staring at her sitting upright.

"You're up," he said, his voice thick with emotion.

"We have to go," Mia said. Her voice was raspy but strong. "Sophia thinks I'm dead. If she finds out I'm here..."

"She won't get near you," Chris said, stepping aside.

Two men in dark suits entered the room behind him. They didn't look like doctors. They didn't look like friends. One held up a badge.

"Dr. Peers," the agent said, his eyes quickly scanning her unblemished skin with cold calculation. "We're with the FBI. And we have a lot of questions."

Mia glanced at the badge, then at the window. The sun was rising. The war wasn't over. It had just changed battlefields.

Someone Like You

Mia

Mia refused to talk to the FBI at the hospital. So instead, a caravan of agents followed them to Chris's house like a presidential convoy.

Three agents stood in the living room. Chris tried to stall, citing Mia's medical trauma, but Mia waved him off. She sat on the couch, the fabric groaning under the tension in her frame.

The lead agent, a man with a hairline in full retreat and eyes like flint, placed a laptop on the coffee table.

"Watch," he said.

Mia didn't argue. She leaned forward as the screen flickered to life.

"In tonight's top story, we go live via satellite to Dr. Sophia Romano, a former associate of the fugitive scientist Dr. Mia Peers. Dr. Romano claims to have insight into the arson at the Peers Laboratory and the deadly shooting at Cabela's."

Sophia appeared on screen. She looked impeccable—calm, professional, and radiating concern. The perfect witness.

"Thank you for having me, David."

"Let's get straight to it," the anchor said. "You worked with Dr. Peers on a performance-enhancing drug. Is that correct?"

"It is," Sophia said, her voice dropping to a somber register.

"We called the prototype 'Lazarus.' It was meant to help stroke victims, but Dr. Peers... she had other applications in mind."

"You're referring to the violence in Gainesville?"

"I am. I arrived at the lab the morning of the attacks. Mia's car was there, but she was gone. I believe that was the moment she fully snapped. The pressure to succeed—combined with her illegal self-experimentation—turned her into something unstable."

Mia's hands balled into fists. The leather of the couch creaked loudly. Chris placed a hand over hers, his grip tight.

"The security footage seems to back that up," the anchor said. Split screens appeared. On the left, Mia in the lab. On the right, Mia in Cabela's, throwing a man through a display case. "Dr. Romano, critics are saying the woman in the video displays impossible strength. Some are even suggesting the video is doctored."

"It's not doctored, David. Physics still apply, but Mia has altered her own biology. She escaped that store through a skylight while surrounded by fifty officers. She survived being shot multiple times just yesterday. She has become a danger to the public, and frankly, I'm terrified."

"God damn it," Mia growled, standing up.

The two junior agents by the door instantly reached for their holsters. The lead agent held up a hand.

"Sit down, Dr. Peers."

Mia ignored him, eyes glued to the screen.

"What about the fire?" the anchor asked.

"Arson," Sophia said smoothly. "Mia realized she couldn't control the test subjects—rats and apes that she had illegally modified. They escaped into the wild. She burned the lab to cover up the disaster she created. I tried to stop her, but..." Sophia glanced away, feigning tears. "I'm heading back to Italy. I can't stay here knowing what she's capable of. I just hope the authorities stop her before she hurts anyone else. And... we still haven't found our colleague, Brian Carter."

"Brian?" Mia whispered. The blood drained from her face.

"Thank you, Dr. Romano."

The agent snapped the laptop shut. The silence in the living room was heavy, suffocating.

"Most of that is lies," Mia said, her voice shaking with rage.

"We know," the lead agent said. He didn't reach for cuffs. He sat on the edge of the coffee table, invading her space. "We're not here to arrest you, Dr. Peers. We're here because we have a problem that standard law enforcement can't solve."

"What problem?" Chris asked, stepping between the agent and Mia. "This isn't procedure. If you have charges, file them. Otherwise, get out of my house."

The agent ignored Chris. He stared directly at Mia. "We've been tracking the Romano family for a decade. They aren't just scientists. They act as a pipeline, supplying experimental... *things* to terrorist cells in Eastern Europe. This is the first time we've had concrete proof of the grandfather, Cesaro, operating on U.S. soil. Sophia is his proxy."

"Cesaro?" Mia asked.

"He's a ghost. But Sophia is very real. And as of a few hours ago, intelligence suggests she is also... enhanced."

Mia froze. "She used the serum."

"We believe so. And that's the problem. We can't send a SWAT team after someone who can punch through concrete and heal from gunshot wounds. The collateral damage would be catastrophic. We need an equalizer."

"You need a monster to kill a monster," Mia said coldly.

"We need you."

"Why should I help you?" Mia crossed her arms. "You people hunted me. You let my parents die."

"Mr. Holden," the agent said, glancing at Chris. "You're a lawyer. Explain to her that if she doesn't cooperate, she goes to a black site for the rest of her unnaturally long life. Or, she helps us, and the slate is wiped clean."

Chris eyed Mia, his expression torn. "Mia, if that family has Sophia... if she's really like you..."

"She is," Mia said. She faced the agent. "I have terms."

The agent sighed. "I'm listening."

"First, total immunity. For me, for Chris, and for Brian if he's still alive. Second, you extract my sister, Unity. You take her to a secure medical facility of my choosing. Third, the formula remains mine. You don't get a drop."

"The White House won't like the third one."

"Screw the White House," Mia snapped. "I'm the only one who can stop Sophia. Take the deal or get out."

The lead agent headed over to the two men at the door. They huddled close, whispering.

Mia concentrated. The room faded. The sound of the refrigerator hum dropped away. She focused her hearing like a laser.

"...*Director said secure the asset at all costs,*" the tall agent whispered. "*We can seize the formula later, once Romano is neutralized,*" the lead agent replied. "*Just get her to say yes.*"

Mia smiled grimly. They thought they were playing her.

"Deal," the lead agent said, turning back to her. "We'll make arrangements to have Unity moved."

"One more thing," Mia said, walking toward him until she was inches from his face. She let a fraction of the predator slip through, her pupils dilating, the air around her seemingly vibrating with potential violence. "If you double cross me—if you try to take the formula after I do your dirty work—I won't just break your arm. I'll break the Bureau."

The agent swallowed hard. He nodded. "Understood. Now, what do you need?"

"Guns," Mia said. "Big ones."

She turned to Chris. He was staring at her, looking pale and nauseous. He went to the kitchen and braced himself against the counter.

"I'm gonna need a Xanax," he muttered.

Mia strolled up behind him and rested her hand on his back. She could feel his heart hammering against his ribs.

"No Xanax," she whispered. "Get your keys, Chris. The pact isn't over. I have a sister to save, and a bitch to kill."

The Scientist

Mia

The sunlight outside was insulting. It was the kind of pristine Virginia spring day that demanded convertibles and mimosas, not a life-and-death decision that should have been made a decade ago.

Mia drew the curtains, cutting the day into ribbons of shadow. She pulled the vinyl chair close to the bed, the friction against the linoleum screeching like a dying bird.

Jon had given them privacy, though he didn't know the extent of what was about to happen. Chris had offered to come, but Mia had declined. This was the final secret. The rot at the center of the onion.

She observed Unity's condition. The ventilator hissed—*inhale, exhale*—a mechanical rhythm that had measured the last twenty years of their lives.

"Hey, U," Mia whispered.

She reached into her pocket and pulled out a small, sparkling blue vial. It wasn't the serum that made monsters. It was something older. Something Mia had synthesized ten years ago, tested illegally, then hidden behind a wall of frozen peas in her refrigerator, and never spoken of again.

Neuro-Regen.

It was supposed to be Unity's cure. She had tested it on a control group of TBI patients in a shadowy clinic in Mexico. It worked. It rewired damaged pathways, jump-started dormant synapses. It was a miracle.

And Mia had buried it.

She uncapped the syringe, her enhanced hands trembling with a very human fear.

"I used to tell myself I was waiting for FDA approval," Mia said, her voice cracking. "Then I told myself the side effects were too risky. But those were lies."

She brushed a strand of hair from Unity's forehead.

"The truth is, I liked being the only one. I became the queen. I was the smart one. The strong one. If you woke up... I was just the afterthought again."

Tears hot as acid tracked down her cheeks. The "choice" that had haunted her wasn't about medical ethics. It was about jealousy. She had sentenced her sister to a decade of silence because she didn't want to share the stage.

"I'm so sorry," Mia sobbed, the guilt finally breaking her. "I robbed you of your life because I was too afraid to live mine. But the pact... the pact says I was supposed to protect you. Even from myself."

She found the vein in Unity's arm. The skin was papery, translucent.

"It's time to wake up, U."

Mia depressed the plunger. The amber liquid disappeared into the IV line.

For three seconds, nothing happened. The ventilator hissed. The heart monitor beeped its steady, sluggish rhythm.

Then, Unity gasped.

Her eyes flew open—wide, terrified, and shockingly blue. Her back arched off the mattress, straining against the sheets.

The heart monitor screamed.

Beeeeeeeeeeeeeep.

The line went flat.

"No." Mia dropped the syringe. The room spun, a sudden, violent vertigo. "No, no, no!"

She vaulted onto the bed, straddling her sister's hips. She interlaced her fingers and slammed her palms into Unity's chest.

Crack.

Mia flinched. Her strength. She had to be careful. She couldn't punch through her sister's chest; she had to restart her heart.

"Breathe, damn it!" Mia screamed. "Don't you dare die on me now! Come on!"

She pumped. Hard. Fast. *Stayin' Alive* tempo. Tears dripped from her chin onto Unity's hospital gown.

The door burst open.

"Code Blue!" Jon yelled, charging in with a crash cart. Two other nurses were right behind him.

"Get off her!" a nurse shouted, grabbing Mia's arm.

Mia didn't move. She pumped again. "I've got her! She's just stunned!"

"Dr. Peers, move!" Jon commanded, his voice cutting through her panic. He shoved a defibrillator paddle toward the bed.

Mia scrambled off, backing into the corner, her chest heaving. She watched the team descend on her sister like a flock of white birds. They cut the gown. They applied the pads.

"Clear!"

Thump.

Unity's body jerked.

Mia held her breath. Her enhanced hearing picked up the silence between the seconds.

Beep.

The team froze.

Beep... Beep... Beep.

"Sinus rhythm," Jon said, exhaling loudly. "She's back. BP is stabilizing. What the hell just happened?"

He turned to look for Mia, but the corner was empty.

Mia stood in the hallway, pressing her back against the cool wall. Inside the room, she could hear the steady, strong rhythm of her sister's heart—stronger than it had been in years. The Neuro-Regen was aggressive, but it worked. Unity wasn't just alive; she was rebooting.

The FBI tactical team was coming down the corridor, their boots heavy on the tile.

Mia wiped her face with her sleeve. The guilt was still there, but the secret was gone. She had made *the choice*. She had saved her sister.

Now she had to save the world.

She pushed off the wall and aimed for the agents. Her tears were gone, replaced by a cold, hard resolve.

"Is the package secure?" the lead agent asked, glancing at the medical commotion behind her.

"She's alive," Mia said. "She'll need some time, then get her out of here. Take her to the secure site."

"And you?"

Mia checked the magazine in her pistol and slid it back into the waistband of her pants. She glanced toward the exit, where the spring sun was waiting.

"I have a playdate with a former colleague."

The Hangar

Mia

Mia knew she wasn't dead, but the sensation was eerily familiar.

She stood in a world of white fog, the mist swirling around her ankles like dry ice. There was no sky, only a diffused, white light that cast no shadows. Beside her, Unity *walked*. They were sixteen again, dressed in matching blue jumpsuits, their blonde hair swaying in perfect sync.

Mia squeezed her sister's hand. It was warm. Solid.

"You're tapped out," Unity said, her voice cutting through the silence like a bell. She didn't look at Mia; she stared straight ahead into the nothingness. "Are you sure this is a good idea?"

"I don't have a choice," Mia said. "I never did."

"That's the lie you tell yourself to sleep at night." Unity stopped walking. The fog rose, obscuring their waists. She turned to face Mia. Her eyes were clear, devoid of judgment but full of a terrible knowing. "We aren't promised a happily ever after, Mia. The story doesn't end with a feast. It ends with a sacrifice."

"What do I do?" Mia asked, her voice sounding small in the vast white.

Unity smiled, sad and sweet. "You let go."

The sisters hugged. As their chests touched, Unity dissolved into mist, slipping through Mia's arms like smoke.

Mia's phone buzzed against her hip, waking her.

GREEN LIGHT.

Mia stared at the text message in the dim light of the guest room. A knock sounded on the door, followed by Chris's urgent whisper.

"They're here."

Twenty minutes later, Mia sat in the back of an unmarked tactical van. The air smelled of gun oil and nervous sweat. Across from her, nine agents in full heavy armor checked their weapons. They were the best the government had to offer, yet they couldn't stop staring at the woman in the running clothes.

The briefing had been short. Sophia had been tracked to a private airfield in Manassas. She had a hostage—Brian—and a small jet fueled on the tarmac.

The lead agent, a man whose face was mostly scar tissue, handed Mia a heavy assault rifle.

"Standard issue," he said. "Armor-piercing rounds."

Mia eyed the weapon, then at her own hands. They were out of control again. A low-frequency tremor that baffled her.

"I don't want it," Mia said.

The van went silent.

"You can't take her hand-to-hand," the agent said. "Intel says she's enhanced."

"If she's like me, your guns are noise," Mia said. "Just be ready with the containment unit."

The van slowed. Gravel crunched under the tires.

"We're a go," the driver announced. "Target is in the main hangar. Sophia's extras are... neutralized."

"Neutralized?" Chris asked, gripping Mia's knee.

"Dead," Mia corrected. "They're already dead."

The doors swung open.

Sunlight flooded the compartment. Mia didn't wait for the

"clear" signal. She stepped out onto the tarmac, ignoring the tactical team flanking out behind her.

The hangar doors were open. Inside, it was a charnel house. Bodies in expensive suits littered the polished concrete floor. Sophia hadn't enhanced these poor souls; she had discarded them.

Mia stepped over a man whose chest had been caved in. The silence in the cavernous space was heavy, broken only by the distant whine of a jet engine spooling up.

"Come out, Sophia," Mia called out. Her voice echoed off the steel rafters. "Mommy isn't here to save you."

A crack of thunder.

Mia stumbled, her shoulder exploding in a spray of red. She didn't fall. She gritted her teeth, feeling the muscle fibers already knitting together, pushing the bullet out.

She scanned the room. Movement on the catwalk.

Sophia stood twenty feet up, holding a suppressed submachine gun. She looked like a dark mirror of Mia—same height, same build, but her eyes were black voids of cruelty.

"You have Brian," Mia said. It wasn't a question.

Sophia laughed, the sound bright and sharp. "If I don't leave this building, neither does he."

She vaulted over the railing.

It was a drop that should have shattered legs. Sophia landed in a crouch and sprang forward in a blur.

Mia met her in the center of the room.

The impact was like two freight trains colliding. The shockwave knocked the wind out of Mia. Sophia was fast—faster than Mia expected. A fist slammed into Mia's jaw, snapping her head back. A knee drove into her gut.

Mia tumbled backward, skidding across the concrete. She tasted surprise.

"You're a prototype, Mia," Sophia sneered, stalking forward. "You're a rough draft. I'm the final edit."

Sophia raised a pistol. Not a standard gun—a tranquilizer pistol. The same one she'd used in the kitchen.

"I know you're burning out," Sophia said. "And look at your hands. You're shaking. I know what that is. Seen it before. Hundreds of times. It's the Syndrome."

Mia glanced at her trembling fingers. Suddenly unsure of herself. What syndrome?

"Where is he?" Mia gasped, struggling to her knees.

"Back office. Bleeding out." Sophia aimed the dart gun. "Say hello to Unity for me."

Time slowed.

Sophia pulled the trigger.

Mia didn't dodge. She moved *into* the path. Her hand lashed out, moving faster than thought, faster than physics should allow.

She caught the dart inches from her neck.

Sophia's eyes widened.

Mia didn't hesitate. She spun, dropping low, and jammed the dart into Sophia's thigh.

Sophia shrieked, slapping at her leg, but the drug was already deploying. She stumbled back, her face slack with shock.

"Prototype," Mia whispered, standing up.

She didn't wait for Sophia to fall. She turned toward the office. Sophia was the government's problem now.

Whirrrrrrrr.

The sound of turbine engines hit a piercing shriek.

Mia spun around. The hangar doors on the far side were opening. A sleek white Learjet was rolling, picking up speed.

Sophia wasn't on the ground. The spot where she had stumbled was empty.

"No," Mia breathed.

She ran to the back office. Brian. Tied to a chair. Not bleeding out. "Go! Go get her, Mia!"

Through the back window, she saw the jet turning onto the

runway.

"Command, target is going airborne!" an agent screamed over the radio. "We have a runner!"

"Weapons free!" came the order. "Take out the engines!"

Gunfire erupted from the tarmac. Bullets sparked harmlessly off the fuselage. The jet roared, accelerating.

Mia gaped at the plane. It was three hundred yards away and gaining speed.

She felt the fire in her chest—the last of the serum, the final energy she had been hoarding. It demanded release.

She didn't think. She ran.

She burst out of the hangar, her legs pumping like pistons. She wasn't running; she was soaring. The world smeared into streaks of brown and green. Her heart hammered against her ribs like a trapped bird, 200 beats per minute, then 250.

She hit the runway. The jet was lifting its nose.

Mia screamed, a primal sound of pure exertion, and launched herself into the air.

Her fingers hooked onto the rear stabilizer. The metal burned her skin. The G-force tried to rip her arms from their sockets as the plane left the ground.

She dangled over the runway, watching the ground drop away. Fifty feet. Hundred feet.

She swung her legs up, hooking a heel over the wing. The wind was a physical weight, a hurricane trying to peel her off the hull. She crawled, inch by agonizing inch, toward the cockpit.

She reached the pilot's window.

Inside, Sophia gawked at her, eyes bulging with madness and fighting the sedative. She banked the plane hard left, trying to shake Mia off.

Mia slammed her fist into the reinforced glass. A spiderweb of cracks appeared.

She hit it again. The glass gave way.

The wind roared into the cockpit. Mia reached in, grabbing the yoke.

"Let go!" Sophia screamed, clawing at Mia's arm, her nails tearing skin.

"Look!" Mia shouted over the wind, pointing with her free hand.

In the distance, a trail of white smoke arced into the sky from the treeline. A Javelin missile. Heat-seeking. Locked on.

"You killed us!" Sophia shrieked, aiming a gun. Bullets ripped through Mia that didn't register.

The missile was closing fast. Three seconds.

Mia stared at Sophia.

Then, she glanced at the ground, two thousand feet below.

Unity's voice whispered in her ear. *You let go.*

Mia tracked the missile, then grinned at the pilot.

"Not us," Mia said. "You."

She let go of the yoke. She let go of the plane.

Mia fell backward into the empty sky, watching as the missile slammed into the engine.

Gone

Mia

Pain wasn't a sensation; it was a universe. Mia existed in a fractured reality of mud, shattered branches, and the smell of pine.

She didn't remember hitting the ground. The last thing she remembered was the missile, the explosion, and the freefall into the Virginia canopy.

Then, the world became a strobe light of consciousness.

Flash.

Blue lights spinning against metal walls. The whine of a siren. The metallic taste of blood in her throat.

Flash.

"She's flatlining again! Charge to three hundred!"

Chris's face, contorted in a scream she couldn't hear, hovered above her. He looked like a ghost.

Flash.

The *thump* of the defibrillator kicked her chest like a mule. Her back arched off the stretcher. Air rushed into her collapsed lungs, burning like fire.

"We got a pulse! It's thready, but it's there."

Mia stared at the ceiling of the ambulance. Her body was a war zone. She could feel the serum scavenging every calorie, every ounce of energy to knit her bones back together. It was a violent, consuming hunger.

She scanned her body. Her stomach was a mess of torn flesh and road rash, but beneath the gore, the skin was rippling.

Clink. Clink.

Two flattened bullets, pushed out by regenerating muscle, fell onto the stretcher. A piece of shrapnel from the plane followed, ejected from her thigh.

The medic staring at her turned green and looked away.

"Chris," she croaked.

He pushed past the medic, gripping her blood-slicked hand. "I'm here. Don't talk. Just stay with me."

"Unity," she whispered. "She's not in the fog."

"What?"

"The dream," Mia gasped, fighting the darkness encroaching on her vision again. "She left the dream."

"Mia, save your strength."

The ambulance lurched to a halt. The doors flew open, revealing the blinding white bay of the hospital trauma center.

Chaos erupted. A swarm of doctors and nurses descended, shouting vitals, cutting away her clothes, hooking up lines. They wheeled her fast, the ceiling lights passing overhead like dashed lines on a highway.

Chris ran alongside the gurney, refusing to let go of her hand. On the other side, the lead FBI agent jogged to keep up, his face grim, a phone pressed to his ear.

Mia locked eyes with him.

"My sister," she demanded, her voice gaining strength as her vocal cords healed. "Take me to the secure facility. Now."

The agent pulled the phone away from his ear. He didn't look at the doctors. He looked at Mia, and the expression on his face stopped her heart more effectively than the fall had.

"We can't, Dr. Peers."

"What do you mean?" Chris shouted over the noise of the

gurney wheels. "You said you had a team moving her!"

The agent grabbed the rail of the bed as they hit the double doors of the trauma room.

"We did," the agent said, his voice low. "Our team arrived at the care center ten minutes ago. The room was empty."

Mia tried to sit up, snapping a plastic restraint. "Empty?"

"The medical staff was unconscious," the agent said. "Someone got there before us. Your sister is gone."

"No." The denial ripped out of her.

"Dr. Peers, please!" a doctor shouted, trying to push her back down. "You have internal bleeding!"

"Get off me!" Mia snarled, her eyes flashing with a terrifying intensity.

Unity wasn't dead. Mia knew it. The connection she had felt in the dream, the sudden absence of her sister in the white fog—it wasn't death. It was separation. Unity was awake. Unity was alive. And someone had taken her.

The realization hit her with more force than the pavement. The war hadn't ended in the sky above Manassas. It had just begun.

The doctors pinned her arms, injecting a sedative into her IV. The room began to spin.

Mia studied Chris. He was crying, broken by the violence of the day, but he was still standing. Still there.

"Come here," she whispered, fighting the drug.

He leaned in, his forehead resting against hers, his tears mixing with the grime on her face.

"We find her," Mia hissed, her voice dropping to a lethal register. "We find her and start a new life."

Chris nodded, a hardened look replacing the fear in his eyes. "We'll find her."

Mia let the darkness take her, not as a victim, but as a soldier resting for the next battle.

Seeing Clearly

Mia

T he heat rising off the asphalt range distorted the air, turning the distant targets into wavering ghosts.

Mia lay prone on the shooting mat, the familiar smell of gun oil and cordite grounding her. Behind her, the bleachers buzzed with a low-frequency hum of whispers. It had been six months since the Manassas airfield attack, since the world learned that Dr. Mia Peers was more—and less—than human.

"Quiet on the line," the range officer commanded.

The hush that fell over the crowd was heavy. To her left, a few zealots held signs that read *Cheater* and *Abomination*, though security had pushed them back to the perimeter. To her right, a sea of fans wearing "Team Mia" shirts leaned forward, breathless.

Mia ignored them all. She focused on the scope.

Her hands were shaking.

It was a subtle tremor, a parting gift from her father's meddling or perhaps from too much serum. Mia hadn't seriously considered Sophia's comments about it being some kind of syndrome. She was bluffing. Mia just didn't know why.

She adjusted her grip, breathing through the tremor. *Inhale. Exhale. Pause.*

This was it. The final shot of the National Championship. She was tied with the reigning champion, the young woman who still looked at Mia with awe and now fear.

Win or lose, this was the end.

The Olympic Committee had let her keep her medals—mostly because she hadn't had the serum when she won them—but other plastic trophies on her mantle at home were gone. She had cleared them out weeks ago, sending bags of accolades to the landfill. They belonged to a woman who needed applause to feel whole.

That woman died falling from an airplane.

Mia lowered the rifle for a moment, breaking her stance. A murmur rippled through the crowd. Was she choking? Was the "Superwoman" failing?

Mia looked past the judges, past the press pit where shutters clicked like a swarm of cicadas, and found Chris.

He sat in the front row, wearing sunglasses and a grin that said, *I know who you are.* He didn't care about the score. He didn't care about the government liaisons waiting in the VIP tent to beg for the formula again. He didn't care that they were living in an FBI safe house, moving every few weeks to dodge the paparazzi and the threats.

He just saw her.

Mia winked.

She returned her cheek to the stock. The world narrowed down to a single point.

She wasn't doing this for the gold. She was doing this to prove that the serum didn't make her a marksman. The work did. The discipline did.

She thought of the new lab she was building—not for human enhancement, but for a cure. Spinal Muscular Atrophy first. She would tear that disease apart, cell by cell. She would be ready.

Because Unity was out there.

The FBI had scoured the earth, but the Romanos had

vanished, taking Unity with them. Mia knew her sister was alive. She could feel it, a phantom limb sensation that tugged at her chest when the nights got quiet. They were hiding her, likely using her as leverage.

They thought they had won. They thought Mia Peers had retired to a life of celebrity and signing autographs.

Mia watched the crosshairs settle over the bullseye. The tremor stilled, just for a heartbeat.

I'm coming for you, Sis.

Mia squeezed the trigger.

The report cracked like a whip, echoing across the valley. She didn't need to look through the spotting scope to know where the bullet hit. She stood up, dusted off her knees, and sauntered toward Chris without waiting for the score.

The game wasn't over. It had just moved to a new board.

Epilogue

Mia

The Shenandoah wind snapped the flags atop the new facility, the sound like pistol cracks in the crisp autumn air.

Mia sat in a folding chair on the dais, smoothing the fabric of her dress. Her hands were sweating. The tremors were there, a subtle vibration in her fingers that no amount of therapy had fixed, but she clasped her hands together in her lap to hide it.

To her right, Chris squeezed her knee. He looked good in his new suit—better than he ever had in his regular courtroom attire. He leaned in, his breath warm against her ear.

"Breathe, Dr. Peers. You've faced down missiles. You can handle a ribbon cutting."

Mia forced a smile, the tension in her chest loosening.

It had been a whirlwind year. The wedding had been small—just them, the justice of the peace, and the mountains. The construction of the lab, however, had been a spectacle. She had burned through her bank accounts, and stacks of cash from near-endless donors, to get it done, bypassing government oversight with sheer financial brute force.

She glanced up at the glass-and-steel monolith rising behind them. Four floors. Forty-five of the world's best minds. And on the top floor, a penthouse apartment where she and Chris lived, because old habits died hard. She still liked a fortress.

In the front row, Chuck from the homeless shelter waved. He wore a new jacket, his face beaming. Behind him, Brian Carter sat with his arms crossed. He was the head of R&D now, though he still scanned the perimeter like he expected a black SUV to crash through the gate.

Mia stood up.

The applause rolled over her, a physical wave. She walked to the podium, the wood smooth under her shaking hands.

"Thank you," she said. The microphone whined slightly, then settled. "Standing here today... it's the only finish line I ever really wanted to cross."

The crowd cheered. Cameras flashed in a blinding strobe.

"We built this place on a promise," Mia continued, her voice strengthening. "To eradicate the diseases that steal our families. Cancer. Parkinson's. Spinal Muscular Atrophy."

She paused, letting the weight of the last one hang in the air.

"We are open. And we are ready to work."

The applause thundered again. Mia stepped back, reaching for the giant pair of ceremonial scissors Chris held out.

Movement flickered in her periphery.

At the edge of the press pit, a young girl in a white gi slipped past the velvet rope. She moved with an eerie grace, ghosting toward the security detail. She handed an envelope to the lead guard, stared directly at Mia, and smiled.

Mia's heart hammered a warning against her ribs.

The girl seemed to have Mia's eyes. And Unity's chin. A secret triplet?

Before the guard could react, the girl turned and melted into the crowd, vanishing like smoke.

The guard frowned, staring at the envelope, then up at Mia.

"Bring it to me," Mia commanded, her voice cutting through the applause.

Chris stepped forward, his smile fading. "Mia? What is it?"

The guard handed the envelope over the railing. Mia snatched it. Her name was scrawled on the front in elegant, old-world cursive.

On the back: *The Angels won 37-36.*

A code. The baseball game from her near-death experience. The score of her life.

The world went gray at the edges. The sounds of the crowd—the clapping, the camera shutters—dulled to a roar of static. Mia tore the envelope open.

Dear Mia,

You killed my children. Sophia, Alessia, Gabriele. You think you have won because you buried the pawns, but you have forgotten the Queen.

Nowhere you go will be safe. Not this fortress. Not your husband's arms.

As for Unity... congratulations. You are as bright as Jeffrey designed you to be. Yes, my dear, I know the secret of your father's arrogance. But our scientists understood his mistake years ago. When he cloned you and programmed you to protect her, he didn't just copy the body. He unwittingly split the soul.

You are one person in two vessels.

If you want Unity to live, you must find her. But know this: your life has an expiration date. My calculations give you less than two years before the meltdown. We call it the Syndrome. That's what your serum was meant to fix. By the look of your shaking hands, you've failed. And if your half of Unity's soul dies, so does Unity.

Tick tock, little experiment.

— The Matriarch

The paper slipped from Mia's numb fingers, fluttering to the stage.

"Mia?" Chris was at her side, gripping her shoulders. "Mia, you're pale. What's wrong?"

Mia stared out at the sea of faces—smiling, oblivious people cheering for a future she might never see. She stared at the mountains in the distance, vast and empty.

She grabbed the microphone stand to keep from falling. She turned to Chris, her eyes wide with a horror that went deeper than bone.

"She's alive," Mia whispered, her voice trembling violently. "Unity is alive."

"That's good," Chris said, keeping his voice low, urgent. "We knew that. We'll find her."

"No, Chris. You don't understand." Mia stared at the letter on the ground. The clock had started. "We share a soul. And if I die... so does she."

Acknowledgments

I will forever start by thanking my wife, Michelle. You, you are my rock and soulmate. Thank you, babe.

My son, Connor Baldwin, for introducing me to *Save The Cat! Writes a Novel* by Jessica Brody.

My daughter, Sydney Baldwin, for her encouragement and support.

My son, Tyler Baldwin, for his technical expertise to market this novel.

About the Author

Paul Baldwin is a retired Airman living in Virginia who navigated a C-130 and rocked life as a public affairs officer from the Pentagon. As a second lieutenant, Paul stared at a heavy 1990s computer monitor attempting to craft a novel about adventures in the Air Force. After waiting more than twenty-five years, his writing dream finally took flight. When he's not authoring, editing, rewriting, and then crying (you get the picture), Paul contemplates exercising more and eating fewer Biscoff cookies topped with their oh-so-incredible cookie butter. Paul is a former owner of two 1981 DMC DeLoreans who treasures his wife and three adult children more than time machines.

By Paul Baldwin

Serum
Syndrome